Acknowledgments

To RHP, who laughed at all the right bits.

WATFORD UNDER WOOD
First of a series of novels by Lynn Phillips

Readers' Comments

'I just finished 'Watford' and was more than suitably impressed. Normally I don't care for 'detective novels' but this one was a jolly good read! (I couldn't resist this bit of English.) I am so impressed that you could put it all together and tie all the loose ends up in such a tidy manner at the end without getting obvious , silly or outlandish. We are looking forward to great things for you in your literary future.'

Bebe Zigman

'The Watford portrayed in her novel Watford under Wood is in many respects a familiar one, but with the sort of intrigue that would have local newspaper journalists salivating. There is murder, sex, corruption, cover-ups and more . . .'

Martin Booth, Watford Observer

'Greta Pusey is the plausible and determined young detective assigned to investigate this truly complex case. In Watford under Wood, Lynn Phillips has accurately captured many of the frailties that Police officers experience.

This an interesting "warts and all" tale.

Inspector Neil Collin,
Officer Commanding Ruislip Police Station,
London Borough of Hillingdon

'Readers who relish the combination of a gripping detective story with a wealth of recognisable geographic details have a new location to savour. To Morse's Oxford and Rebus's Edinburgh is now added - Greta Pusey's Watford.'

Northwood Residents Association Newsletter

'I just finished "Watford" and was more than suitably impressed. Normally I don't care for "detective novels" but this one was a "jolly good read". I am so impressed that you could put it all together and tie all the loose ends up in such a tidy manner at the end without getting obvious, silly or outlandish. We are looking forward to great things for you in your literary future. Let us know as soon as you receive your first invitation to Buckingham (Palace) or anything else that would excite envy in the hearts of lesser mortals.'

San Diego Book Club, California, USA

'I've just finished reading your book and was highly entertained. Many congratulations. When's the next one coming out?'
PS Is the Watford police station really in Shady Lane?'

London reader

'This is a great book, compelling and intriguing. Lynn Phillips has the ability to keep the reader hooked until the very end. An excellent read.'

Reader's review on Waterstone's/Amazon's website

Watford is a pleasant town, unjustly derided by some. But Lynn Phillips knows better. After a work history zigzagging through different countries and occupations, her final job before becoming a full-time writer was in an office a few hundred yards from Shady Lane Police Station - in Watford. With a background as diverse as a cowgirl in a farm in Suffolk, running a laundry on a kibbutz, and for many years as the International Advertising Manager for Outspan, she now keeps her hand in by working part-time for the Hillingdon Police. She has had a number of prize-winning short stories published, and *Moon over Watford* is the second of her Watford series of novels to appear in print. The prize-winning *Watford under Wood* was the first.

Chapter 1

'Don't come in, Inspector,' I said, 'it's a right mess in here, blood everywhere.'

'What have we got then, Sergeant?' he asked.

We were being formal with each other because of all the uniforms and forensic bods milling around. Detective Inspector Michaelson and I were usually much less formal than that. It was always 'Greta' and 'Derek' with us, except when he was off me – then I was 'Pusey'.

Also, it was my first try at being in action with the Scene of Crime Officer, and Derek was kind of testing me out in this new situation, to see if I could handle it. I was thrilled with myself, still pleased at having been made up to detective sergeant after passing the exam first go, and this was another step up in my brilliant career. After only three weeks' induction, SOCO was allowing me to be present at an actual scene of crime! And being sent on this special course showed that Superintendent Moon had more confidence in me than I sometimes thought.

'No doubt of it, Guv,' I said, 'it's murder alright. And quite a messy one–'

'–any sign of a weapon?'

'I should say so! The victim's head's been bashed in – looks as if it was done with that heavy table lamp. And they've cut off his cock and stuffed it in his mouth.'

There was a moment's silence. Then my friend and colleague, Detective Sergeant Alfie Partridge, spoke up with his usual wisdom. 'Omerta,' he said.

'Do what?' Derek sounded as if he couldn't believe his ears.

'The Mafia,' Alfie rumbled through his beard, positive as always. 'That's what they do when somebody breaks the rule of silence. They call it omerta, and they cut his dick off–'

'–well, thank you, Sergeant Partridge,' Derek said, 'for your valuable and scientific analysis. I'm sure Mr Moon will be glad to hear of your contribution. Omerta!' he added bitterly.

I managed not to laugh. Derek and Alfie often crossed swords in this way. Alfie was one of the old school, heavy, reliable, not quick-thinking. Derek was much younger, fast-stream, brilliant, handsome, and I loved him to bits. I'd been pursuing him ever since we first met, but for some reason he didn't seem to want to get involved with me. I couldn't believe it was only because I was a good few inches taller than him. Surely such a clever man wouldn't be put off by a small problem like that? After all, lots of other men found me attractive enough.

Anyway, at the moment I had to concentrate on this murder. My instructing officer wouldn't think much of me if I took my eye off the ball now. I couldn't agree with Alfie's theory, but I was determined not to ignore any possibilities. I might put it forward myself at the right moment.

Although, come to think of it, the impression I'd got from Hollywood films about the Mafia was that if someone broke their rule of silence, they cut his tongue off. But then what would they cut his cock off for? I put that puzzle out of my mind, and went on taking directions from my team leader. MY TEAM! That sounded good, but I wouldn't let it go to my head.

The doc had already been and made his unnecessary pronouncement that the victim was dead, the photographers had done their bit, and we were waiting for the body boys to take the corpse to the morgue. I had to put the penis into an evidence bag, because with all those people tramping about, it kept falling out of his mouth, and I didn't want anyone to tread on it. I wasn't sure why. Just my natural squeamishness, I suppose.

I came out of the flat into the corridor, where Derek and Alfie were still hanging about like spare guests at a funeral, Alfie towering over Derek and occasionally making useless comments.

Eventually, Derek asked, 'Do we have an identity for the victim?'

I had to give the unhelpful answer, 'Yes and no. We know the name of the occupant of this flat. What we don't know is whether this is him – or, I mean this *was* him. But if not, who could it be? There's nothing on him to give a clue, he's just got money in his wallet, no identification.'

'Well, who called it in?'

'One of the two ladies upstairs. There's only two other flats occupied. The one who phoned us is a Mrs Dunkerley. Just a sec, here's my notes. But I expect you'll be wanting to talk to her yourself. And the other one is a Mrs Winkelhorne.'

'OK then, Sergeant Partridge,' (Derek obviously wanted to keep up the formality, who knew why.) 'You speak to Mrs Winkelhorne and I'll take Mrs Dunkerley.'

That got them out of the way for a bit while we SOCOs searched and dusted and hoovered and tip-toed round the wood chippings where the door had been busted open, and didn't leave an inch of the place unchecked.

After a while Alfie came lumbering down the stairs again, muttering to himself.

'What's up?' I asked him.

'That Mrs Winkelhorne, what a pain in the neck. First she tells me how handsome I am and what a pleasure to see such a fine figure of a man, and went on about my lovely beard, offering me a cup of tea and all that.'

'Well, that was nice. What was wrong with that?'

'She's a big heavy lady, about ninety years old, deaf as a post, and she wanted to tell me all about her husband. Well, you'd think when an old lady tells you she's lost her husband, you think he's dead. But it turned out he'd run off with the Jamaican tart from the newsagents down the road. Then she had to tell me what he said last time she saw him, and all this time I'm trying to get her back on about the murder. I couldn't tell if she couldn't hear me or she was just taking no notice.'

I could see he was well choked, so just to wind him up a bit more, I asked, 'Well, what did he say last time she saw him?'

Alfie gave me a sharp look. 'He said, "Goodbye Anna, I'm going out to buy a newspaper. I may be gone for quite a while." Turned out it was the truth. She says he's been gone more than three years now. And in case you want to know, Sergeant Scene of Crime Officer, no, she never heard a thing last night, didn't know why I was asking her, didn't know anything about us being all over the place, and the only thing she could tell me was that the occupant of this flat was a Mr Leonard Gilmore. Talk about wasting police time!' he finished in disgust.

Luckily, at this moment Derek rejoined us, all business-like.

'Method of entry, Sergeant?' he asked me.

'That's a genuine lulu,' I had to tell him. 'A real puzzle. The downstairs street door works on an entry-phone – you know, the caller speaks into a–'

'–yes, yes, we all know what an entry-phone is. What's the problem?' Derek interrupted. He seemed to have got very testy since he'd interviewed Mrs Dunkerley. I wondered what she'd said or not said that upset him, but I knew better than to ask him.

4

'Well,' I went on, 'maybe the victim knew his attacker and let him in downstairs with the entry release. But then, why was it necessary for the assailant to break this lock here on the flat door? Or if he didn't know him, how did the murderer get in the downstairs door without breaking that lock too?'

Alfie said helpfully, 'Mrs Winkelhorne didn't let anyone in last night. What about Mrs Dunkerley, Guv? Did you ask her?'

'It's Miss Dunkerley, and obviously she didn't let anyone in either. That was a particularly stupid question, Sergeant.'

There was a pause while we all reflected. I don't know what the others were thinking, but I was wondering what was biting Derek. This wasn't like him at all. Could his interview have been even more irritating than Alfie's?

'The weapon. Was it all done with the table lamp?' Derek asked my team leader.

Before she had a chance to make one of her usual noncommittal grunts, I chimed in for her.

'It certainly looks like it, it's in there, what's left of it,' I answered smartly. 'See, it's got a steel upright set into a heavy marble base, so it was probably used a bit like a hammer. Pretty sure the post-mortem will verify that.'

'And what about the knife, the one that was used to, ah, that he cut–'

'No need to tiptoe around it, Guv.' I thought it my turn to be a bit sharp. 'You mean what was used to cut off the victim's penis. Here it is,' and I held up an evidence bag with a knife in it. 'Come into the kitchen, and I'll show you where it probably came from.'

I showed them the knife block with the one empty space.

'So it seems as if the murderer didn't bring anything lethal with him, just picked up what was handy about the place,' I said. 'Maybe not premeditated, then. Anyway, then there's this.'

5

And I held up the other evidence bag. Derek winced and said, 'Mr Moon isn't going to like this.'

I shrugged. Coolly I said, 'Right. I don't suppose the victim did, either. This is it, what was cut off with that missing knife. I had to bag it, because it fell out of the victim's mouth, and some careless bod might have trod on it.'

'Crikey,' Alfie said, 'what a whopper! After what it's gone through, too. What must it have been like before, I wonder. Good thing you had a bag big enough!'

Ignoring these helpful remarks, Derek said, 'At least we can surmise that this mutilation was done after the murder, judging by the lack of blood in that area. Although of course we'll have to wait for the final word on that. What else has your lot got so far, Greta?'

Cheers! He was calling me Greta again, although the others were still around. Looked as if I was back in favour, and it was Alfie's turn in the doghouse.

'No whole fingerprints so far, only smudges. No identifying papers – no letters, passport, bank statements, credit cards, photographs. I think I told you there was only money in his wallet, but there's nothing in the flat either. Bit of a mystery man, our victim. Unless, of course, he's got nothing personal here because this isn't his real home. This could be a pied-à-terre.'

I was quite proud of myself for knowing that expression, but I could see Derek wasn't impressed.

'He could be a business man who travels up North a lot but needs easy access to London,' I blundered on. 'Watford's an ideal base for that. Or he could even be a politician.'

'I see,' Derek said in a voice heavy with sarcasm, 'yes, I see. That would account for no fingerprints or credit cards, wouldn't it? So, no personal papers, but are there any documents at all, of any description?'

'Yes,' I admitted, 'receipts for services, you know, gas, electricity, rent. And–'

'–rent? Who does he pay his rent to? That's worth following up.'

I thought, but didn't say, he could have asked his *Miss* Dunkerley about that. Perhaps he had. He was being a bit close altogether about his conversation with her. I couldn't think why. I'd had a few quick words with her when I'd arrived at the scene, and she'd seemed a very plain ordinary sort of person.

'Yes, but there's something even more interesting here,' I went on, and I showed him this cardboard box full of plastic oblongs. 'No fingerprints, again. We tried every single one of these plastic pieces. But don't you think they look like blanks for credit cards? What do you think, Guv?'

'There you are, there's your Mafia connection,' Alfie broke in, having been unusually silent for several minutes. 'Forged credit cards, Mafia, see?'

Good job for him there was an interruption at this moment. One of the others on my team came and told us something that we should all have noticed from the first minute. But we hadn't. What it was, the wood chips from where the door of the flat had been jemmied open were *on top* of the blood from the murder, instead of underneath. So the murderer didn't break the door open to get at the victim, since the door was broken open *after* the murder.

'Right, otherwise the blood would have been on top of the bits from the door,' Derek summarised.

I was blank. 'Does that mean that two different people made unlawful entry into this place last night? And can that mean that one, known to the victim, did the murder, and then the second one did the mutilation? In that case, how did the second one get into the downstairs door? And then have to jemmy open this door?'

Derek picked up the cardboard box with the plastic

oblongs in it, and dumped them out on to a table. Oh hell, I hadn't thought of that!

But before Derek could do another thing, Julie, my team leader, came storming up. This was a first, because she was usually a woman of a very few words.

'Inspector,' she said, all icy, 'are you aware that this is still a scene of crime? The very fact of your presence and that of Sergeant Partridge is enough to corrupt any evidence. And now you are handling possibly important items before we've had a chance to examine them for forensics. I have to ask you to leave the scene immediately. And as for you, Sergeant Pusey,' she went on, turning to me, 'this is the end of your training in this department. You've forgotten everything you learned about contamination of the scene of crime. I shall report that you are unsuitable material for this work.'

I was crushed. I'd thought I might have been doing well as a trainee SOCO, but it seemed as if I'd blown it on my first day in the field. And on such an unusual case, too. Oh well, it meant I'd still be on Derek's team, so that more than made up for it.

Meanwhile I could see Derek was not even slightly bothered by being told off by a Scene of Crime Officer, even though he knew it meant he'd get it in the neck eventually from the head of her department. Or worse.

Calmly he turned the box over, and read from the underside, 'Juan Garcia, 0208 582 3471.'

Chapter 2

Still amazed at how quickly we'd got the information from the phone number, Alfie and I made our way to the address in Hendon where we expected to find this Juan Garcia, whoever he was.

I rang the bell and would have waited for someone to come to the door, but Alfie had one of his impetuous moments and hammered on it at the same time. When it opened we were both surprised, but in different ways. Alfie has always been susceptible to a certain kind of woman, and this positively was that kind. She was glamorous in a barmaid kind of way, over made-up including false eyelashes, very curvaceous and wearing a dress which would have been tight even if it hadn't been two sizes too small.

'Does a Mister Joo-anne Garsher live here?' he wheezed, while I stood there like a lemon.

'Oo wants ter know?' she challenged in a dark-brown, sexy too-many-cigarettes and too-much-whisky kind of voice.

I could see this wouldn't do. Briskly I showed her my warrant card, introduced us both, and tried to improve on Alfie's pronunciation. Not that I knew exactly how to say anything in foreign, I just didn't think he had it right.

'Mr Garseer?' I offered, and she seemed to understand, because she let us in, saying his room was there at the top of the stairs, but she didn't know if he was in or not.

I trotted up the stairs, with Alfie stumbling behind me,

still breathing heavily from the impact of the tarty landlady, and of course when we went into the room she'd indicated, not a soul was there. We looked around – well, to be honest, we searched, although we knew we shouldn't without a warrant, but we couldn't find anything that meant anything to us.

'Come on,' Alfie said, opening the door, 'this is just a waste of time–'

There was a sort of a howl from the stairs below him, and Alfie started down, bellowing, 'Here, you! Stop! Come back here!' and other useless plod-type remarks that I guessed he'd been taught back in the prehistoric days when he was a rookie.

At the same time, sexpot landlady started up the stairs, going, 'Ow, Sarge, wotever is the matter,' and managing to collide with him. I'm sure he'd have been delighted at such a close encounter at any other time, but at that moment duty called. He shoved her out of the way and pounded on, by which time I'd overtaken him and was legging it out the front door and down the street after whoever it was we were after. It was a good guess that it was this Juan geezer, but at this point it could have been anyone who took fright at seeing Alfie suddenly coming out of a room where he had no business.

It was all happening at once, this little swarthy man running along, me after him, Alfie puffing behind, and out of the corner of my eye I seemed to see a motorbike idling slowly alongside us, keeping pace. But I didn't have time for that, because suddenly this little idiot stopped, turned round, produced a gun and fired at me! I didn't know if I'd been shot or not, but I fell down anyway. Dimly I heard Alfie let out a roar, then everything got confused.

Afterwards, Alfie told me all that happened was that as he launched himself into the air to tackle Garcia, a kid came round the corner on a bike, tripped Garcia over, and

Alfie landed smack on top of the lot – Garcia, the kid and the bike. Then Alfie called for help and back-up and ambulance and God-knows-what, and all this time, as it turned out, there was nothing wrong with me except that I'd fallen down and bruised my bum. And I certainly wasn't going to hospital for that. Garcia's shot went well wide, which should have given us a clue to what an incompetent little felon he was, because it could have been point-blank in my face. Must have been my lucky day.

Anyway, as we guessed, it really was Juan Garcia we'd been chasing, so we took him in. Of course, until he'd been so stupid with his gun, we had nothing against him – it was hardly against the law for a murdered man to have his phone number. But now we could charge him with assault with a deadly weapon, maybe even attempted murder, and that was plenty to hold him until we could maybe winkle something out of him about his connection with Mr Leonard Gilmore and his credit card blanks. The silly little bugger first pretended he didn't understand English, then started crying, then said he didn't want an interpreter or a lawyer. It was hardly the high spot of our day. Derek decided we should leave him to stew for a while.

Back in his office, Derek said to me, 'I thought you did well at your first day out with SOCO, Greta. I was proud of you. Pity they won't keep you on with your training. I'm sure you would have been an asset to the department. It would have been understandable if you'd felt a bit queasy, given the circumstances of the scene, but you held up like a trouper.'

I was a bit baffled – which often happened to me with Derek's vocabulary – but as usual I managed to wing it. Queasy I guessed meant sick, but 'like a trouper' could have meant anything. Well, I could tell he was praising me, so I settled for that and didn't bother with the details. I'd have liked him to say something on the lines of SOCO's loss being his gain, but a few kind words were better than none, I suppose.

'What I'd like you to do now,' he went on, 'is to go and have a talk with that Miss Dunkerley. She was very unforthcoming with me. She answered my questions straightforwardly enough, but maybe you can get more out of her. She said she saw Gilmore's door open on her way downstairs to work – she says she's a computer programmer – and peeped inside, saw the mayhem in there, and went straight back upstairs and called us. She says she hardly knew him, just passed the time of day, thought by his accent he was American, and that's about all.'

'American, eh,' said Alfie, darkly. He'd been strangely quiet until then, and I just hoped he wasn't going to start his nonsense about the Mafia again. Maybe he was, but Derek got in first.

'What I want you to do, Alfie, is go back to Hendon and interview Garcia's landlady, see what you can find out about him from her. How long he's lived there, how he found himself a room in Hendon of all places, you know, anything you can get.'

Alfie's eyes had started sparkling as soon as Hendon was mentioned. Without realising it, he'd straightened up, puffed out his chest, smoothed down his beard and moustache and generally started acting like someone half his age going out on a date. Derek didn't seem to notice, so I hid my grin and just gave Alfie a big wink.

And off we both went.

On the way back to see Miss Dunkerley, I got to thinking about the fleeting impression I'd had of her when I'd first arrived at Robin Hood House in Squash Court Road. She'd seemed a dull little person, no make-up, dowdy clothes (although I shouldn't talk, being no fashion plate myself), greying hair, quiet voice. Still, I'd do my best to get her talking about her dead neighbour downstairs. And maybe she might even have something interesting to say about the other neighbour, Mrs Winkelhorne across the hall, to add on to Alfie's anecdote about the lost husband.

Well, of course when I'd first seen this Miss Dunkerley, I'd been preoccupied with my duties as SOCO, so maybe I hadn't paid her enough attention. But this second time, I felt as if I was meeting a different person altogether. Not more interesting, just different. The first thing I noticed was that she was a blonde, not greying at all. Then I saw, looking more closely, that if she hadn't had such a red nose and red puffy eyes, she might have been quite pretty, and she was certainly a lot younger than I'd first thought.

'Come in, Sergeant,' she greeted me, 'how are you? Can I offer you a drink? I'm just having a little stiffener myself.'

And she waved at a glass on the table behind her, which at first I'd thought was full of water. But I soon realised it was mainly either gin or vodka, with not too much of a mixer. I refused her offer, even when she said it'd be no trouble to make me a coffee.

'Course I know I mustn't offer you this stuff,' she said, pausing to have a good slurp of whatever it was, 'while you're on duty. But p'raps you'd like to pop in some time when you're not working, and have a little drinky with me?'

I muttered something that could have meant anything. This was certainly not at all the Miss Dunkerley I thought I was going to see.

'I didn't want your inspector to get the wrong impression, you see, Greta,' she said, giggling, 'so I tried to make myself look older. Actually, I started putting some old woman's make-up on before he came to speak to me, but then I thought, that's silly, so I wiped it off again. I've got a box of that sort of stuff that I call my disguise box, just for fun you know...'

None of this made sense, but the real puzzle was how she knew my first name and why she thought she could use it. I hardly knew what to ask her first.

'What do you mean about the wrong impression, Miss Dunkerley?'

'Oh, please don't call me that, my name's Kate. There you are, you see, I told him it was Kitty, that makes me sound different, doesn't it. See, I didn't want him asking what a pretty young girl is doing living on her own in this expensive place, so then I told him I was a computer programmer because they probably get lots of money, don't they.'

She paused for breath, and I thought, I don't really have to ask her any questions, just sit here and let her ramble on.

'The fact is, I'm only twenty-four but I've got private means so I don't need to work and you might not believe it to look at me now, I know I look a bit of a wreck, but normally I'm quite a looker. But I've been crying a lot, you see.'

She suddenly went quiet, sipping at her drink, so I picked up from there.

'Were you fond of Mr Gilmore then, Kate?'

'Fond? No, what do you mean, I hardly knew him, it was just the shock of seeing all that blood and stuff down there. I expect you police are hardened to that sort of thing, but I've never seen anything like it and I'm still very upset.'

She gave an unconvincing sniffle, and I noticed that every now and then her eyes slid away from me and towards a rug covering a part of the polished floor. Maybe I'd seen her do that as soon as I'd arrived, but at first I thought I'd imagined it. What was there about that rug, I wondered.

'Seriously now, Kate, can you tell me anything at all

about Mr Gilmore or anything that you know about last night?'

She put her drink down and started plucking nervously at the arm of her chair. Again she glanced at the rug, then back at me.

'No, honestly, Greta, I just passed him on the stairs sometimes and we'd say hallo and something about the weather. Really I didn't know him at all. We all keep to ourselves in this little block, that's one of the things I like about it. Deaf old Mrs Winkelhorne lives just across the hall from here, but I hardly ever speak to her either. I think she's a widow. She and Mr Gilmore were already here when I moved in, and the other flat, on the same floor as Mr Gilmore's, has always been empty. Same as the shop on the ground floor. Always empty. No-one seems to want it.'

Her words were tumbling out faster and faster, until at the end she was positively babbling. Then she seemed to realise it, and shut up abruptly. Bit of a weirdo we had here, I thought.

'And last night?' I prompted. 'Did you hear anything unusual?'

She took a deep glug of her drink, put it down, and started picking at her chair again.

'No, er, well, you know this little block is very well-made, practically sound-proof, I'd say.'

I gave her a hard look and was quite surprised when it worked.

She went on, 'But I did hear something, I just didn't want to tell your inspector, in case he misunderstood. But you'll understand, won't you, Greta?'

There it was again: 'Greta'. Where did this come from? She'd have to be pretty sharp-eyed and quick to have read it off my warrant card, but there was no other way for her to know my first name. So she was brighter than she seemed, maybe.

'Of course I will,' I said in my most sympathetic voice. Hypocrite.

'Well, some time in the small hours, I don't know what time it was, I heard a really weird noise, like someone howling on the stairs outside here. So I looked out of my peephole in the door, and there was a little dark man running down the stairs away from me. I thought, well if he's a burglar he's not coming this way, so I didn't do anything. Then I heard the downstairs street door bang closed, and I thought I'd make sure he'd gone. Wasn't that brave of me? I went down as far as the floor below, and I saw Mr Gilmore's door open and all that, you know, what it was like, and I got very frightened and ran back here and locked myself in and stayed under the bedclothes for the rest of the night.'

'But then you hadn't just discovered the murder when you phoned us? Why didn't you phone us as soon as you saw what had happened?'

She gave a childish whimper.

'Oh Greta, please don't be cross with me,' she whined, her eyes once again sliding across to that rug. 'I was just so terrified, I left it until the morning because I hoped, I hoped, I don't know what I hoped. That maybe somebody else would deal with it. Or it didn't really happen at all, it was just a nightmare. But I did ring, didn't I? I did my duty in the end, didn't I?'

It was like talking to a child or a retard. Hopeless.

Giving her another of my special hard looks, I said, 'Well I hope you'll soon feel fit to come to Shady Lane Station and make a formal statement. Please make it as soon as you can.'

And I left. But not the building. Only her flat. I went down to the street level and slammed the door to make

16

her think I'd gone, then I went quietly back to the scene of the crime and started having a careful look at the ceiling. I knew I wasn't supposed to go back there, with the tapes still closing it off, but I had this idea. I thought the ceiling was the one place the team hadn't thought to check. Just as well, really, since I had no idea what I was looking for, except that it might be in the area that corresponded to the rug that Miss Kate Dunkerley couldn't keep from looking at. What might there be under that rug that drew her eyes like a magnet? Failing lifting the rug to see if there were any bloodstains on the polished wood floor underneath it, my next best plan was to examine the ceiling below. I couldn't see a thing special about it, even standing on a chair to get closer. Yes, there was something, like a sort of dark mark on the edge of the moulding round the light fitting. I got down and turned the light off, and then at last a bit of luck came my way.

Kate must have moved her precious rug, thinking I'd left the building, and a little shaft of light suddenly shone through where I'd thought there was a dark mark. It was a peephole that she used to see straight down from her flat into Gilmore's. This put an entirely different slant on the whole case. No wonder she'd seemed so nutty to me. It was because she had something important to hide and she was scared stiff we'd find it out.

I couldn't wait to get back to Shady Lane to tell Derek and ask him what he thought we should do next. Lucky for me he didn't think we needed to tell the SOCO about it. But I had a disappointment coming. Instead of telling me to bring her in, or saying we'd go together to question her further, he decided to pop round there on his own to see her again.

'And you two can have a go at this Juan Garcia,' he told me, 'as soon as Alfie gets back from Hendon. And no rough stuff, Greta, understand?'

17

Chapter 3

'You lead,' I told Alfie. 'I want a chance to look this fellow over before I say anything about him trying to shoot me.'

'Now then,' he said to Garcia, 'the first thing we want is to see your passport.'

'I don' have it with me,' he replied. 'I lef' it in my room.'

'That's not true,' Alfie said. 'Sergeant Pusey and I searched your room thoroughly. No passport.'

'Then why,' Garcia suddenly turned to me, 'why she have to chump on me, heh? I could have bin injure. I could have had broke all my bones. How you like she chump on chew, huh?'

'Who?' Alfie asked, innocently enough.

Garcia appealed to me again. 'What she mean, who? She chump on me then say who?' he exclaimed passionately, pointing a quivering finger at the baffled Alfie.

This was too much.

'Never mind that,' I snapped. 'I hope you realise, Mr Garcia, that you're in a very serious situation here. You fired a gun at two police officers: that's attempted murder–'

'–is not true,' the little bugger protested. 'Was not a real gun–'

'–looked real enough to me,' I interrupted. 'Obviously you don't understand the law in this country–'

'–no, for me is difficult. In my country, everybody is shoot at everybody else, is the policia or nobody–'

'Well,' Alfie broke in. 'I can tell you it's a very serious matter here if you fire at police officers… and anyway, you haven't told us yet, what is your country? And why haven't you got a passport? And how did you get into this country without one?'

Of course we'd taken the gun off him when we brought him in, and we'd seen right away it was only a starting pistol, but we weren't going to let on to Garcia about that.

'And you'd better tell us why you ran away when we came to question you,' I added.

Garcia blinked at us confusedly, but answered readily enough, 'Am ronning because I theenk thees are not true policias. Am theenking they are here to keel me–'

We were getting nowhere. It was a pity that Garcia's English was a muddle between 'he' and 'she', but that wasn't really important. Except maybe to Alfie, who was easily baffled.

After a short silence, Garcia clearly decided to improve his situation, so he went on, 'Am from Colombia. You know thees? Is famous country, I theenk. My boss, he is in Colombia. He send me with stones to Meester Geelmore. Meester Geelmore, he suppose to give me money. I take it to my boss's boss. Then I go home. But it all go wrong.'

'You mean,' Alfie said excitedly, 'your boss in Colombia has a boss here in England?'

'Sure,' said Garcia, pleased with Alfie's response.

Alfie gave Garcia a pen and writing pad.

'Write the address here.'

'I don' know thees.'

'Come on, you just said you were going to take the money. You must have the address.'

'No, thees I don' know. The number I suppose to phone, I call him up when I get those money, he tell me where to meet.'

'So write down the phone number.'

'I can no do thees. I had in my mind the number, but I forget it when you chump on me. How chew like–'

'–OK, OK,' I broke in, 'we'll give you time to remember that number. But you'd better think of it, or you'll find yourself in worse trouble. But first, tell us how you got into this country without a passport?'

'Is no true I have no passport. When I come first, I have to give it to Meester Geelmore to show he can truss me. He got it still.'

'Truss?' Alfie said. 'Why should Gilmore want to truss you?'

I gave him a look as hard as a kick, and he shut up. Then I plonked down on the table the shoe box that had led us to Garcia in the first place. The pieces of plastic were still in it.

'Now then,' I said, 'do you recognise these?'

His shoulders slumped, his eyes filled with tears, and he gave a deep sigh.

'Yais,' he said, snuffling, 'is belong Meester Geelmore. He want me to help with these cards when they are made to use.'

Now we were getting somewhere.

'What is your relationship to Mister Gilmore?'

'Is no relation, am doing some work is all.'

'When did you last see him?'

'Meester Geelmore, he phone and he tell me, come to my flat tree o'clock the morning. I say, "Fonny time to come." He say, "Never mine, come when I say." Tree o'clock I buzz the door in street, nutten happen, so I sleep the lock, is easy. I go up the stair to his door, the lock he won't sleep like the one in the street, so I use the jeemy and open.'

'Why? Why didn't you just go away again when you saw the door was locked and there was no answer when you buzzed and knocked?'

'He say to come, I come when he say,' Garcia explained simply but bafflingly. What could be the connection between these two men?

'So I jeemy open hees door, and I see heem there all in the bleed, and I shout "Aaargh!" like thees,' and he screamed convincingly before finishing, 'then I ron.'

'You ron?' Alfie joined in at this, again picking up the least important point. 'What do you mean, you ron?'

'Am ronning away very queek,' Garcia's voice was getting higher and squeakier as he was clearly remembering his terror. 'Wooden chew, if you see thees?'

This time there was a long silence. I didn't know what Alfie was thinking, but I was wondering which of all these promising leads to follow up. Garcia spoke in an off-hand way of having a jemmy with him. He said, or implied, he was prepared to help Gilmore in passing cloned credit cards. He also seemed to be confessing to smuggling some sort of precious stones from Colombia. And even if it wasn't a real gun, he'd seemed at the time to have had a serious pop at me. Finally, I thought I'd leave all these fascinating lines of enquiry for Derek to decide about. I was going to concentrate on the murder.

I switched off the tape, ignoring Alfie's raised eyebrows.

'Now,' I said, in my deepest voice, 'we'd better have a few truthful answers. Otherwise, I warn you, things could get a little rough–'

'–steady on, Sergeant Pusey,' said Alfie, 'we don't want any of that sort of threatening talk. Look here, Mr Garcia, I'm sure, if you'll give us some reasonable answers, we can work all this out without anybody getting hurt.'

'OK,' I barked, 'enough of this. We know, Mr Garcia, that you had a row with Len Gilmore and you killed him.'

'No, no! I tol' you already, I h'ain't keel nobody. I find heem already keel. You know thees.'

'But now we can prove you were in Gilmore's flat *before* he was killed.'

'How chew going to do that, huh? I tol' you–'

'–OK, Juan,' I broke in, 'how many pairs of shoes have you got?'

Both men looked at me in surprise, but Garcia answered readily enough.

'Back home in Bogotà, in my house, I got lots of chews, plenty chews. But I come here travel light, so I only breeng one pair. Them what I wear now.'

'Take off your right shoe. Put it here on the table. Now look at this. This is a photo I took in Mr Gilmore's flat, from *underneath* the blood. It's the footprint of a man's shoe. The design of the sole is quite clear, and if the pattern on your shoe sole matches it, then we've got you fair and square.'

'I don' know about squares,' Garcia muttered.

'Look at this, Sergeant Partridge,' I said excitedly. 'Look at this! A complete match–'

'Blimey!' Alfie said. 'If you say so–'

'Show me,' said Garcia, 'I can't see–'

'Look, Sergeant Partridge, clear as day,' I said. 'Exactly the same print! Right, you're done for now, Juan. I reckon that proves you murdered Gilmore, after all. Then you went back and jemmied open the door to make it look as if you found him already killed. And you know what we do with murderers in this country?'

'No, I don't know. What chew do? Shoot 'em? The electrical chair?'

'No, we hang them. With a rope,' I said gloatingly.

'Santa Maria! Leesen, leesen, maybe we do a deal here–'

'Sorry, Juan. We don't do deals in this country.'

'OK, OK, I tell you the true, maybe you believe me.'

'Try me. Maybe we'll believe you, maybe not.'

And then, blow me if he didn't tell us the same story as before all over again. I was disgusted. The little clown went on and on about how he'd rung the bell from the street and slipped the lock when there was no answer, then couldn't slip the lock on Gilmore's own front door, so he'd jemmied it open and found Gilmore lying there in a pool of blood. Boring.

'After that,' he went on, 'I am worry. I don' touch nothing. I seen plenty cop shows on the TV so I know not touching nothing. I don' see nobody, neither, except dead Geelmore, so I scream, loud, and I go away. And tha's the God's true, I swear on the Holy Virgin. You ask that woman, Kate, is leevin up the stair. She see me–'

While I was having a coughing fit to hide my excitement at this major bit of news, that Garcia apparently knew Kate Dunkerley, Alfie cut in with, '–well, OK then, Mr Garcia, I should think that puts you pretty well in the clear–'

'–in the clear, my arse!' I said, crudely. 'What might put you in the clear is just one thing. Come on then, tell us, where was Mr Gilmore's cock when you saw his dead body?'

Garcia's face was a study. Shock, horror, confusion flitted across his swarthy face like a Method actor trying out for a difficult part.

'Hees cock?' he repeated in a hoarse whisper. 'Why I should know thees? You mean, you mean it was not – not in the pants where should be such theeng belonging? Somebody stole from Meester Geelmore such a theeng?'

He'd gone a nasty colour, sort of greenish grey. I thought he was going to faint. Obviously Alfie thought so too, because he stood up as if to catch him as he fell. But Garcia didn't fall. He pulled himself together and answered my question.

'I never have see the cock of Meester Geelmore, dead or not dead, all the time I know heem,' he declared. 'Now I tol' you the whole true, now you got to let me go.'

'Bugger that for a lark,' I said. I could see that puzzled him, but it didn't matter. 'You're going nowhere, my lad. The only place you're going is back to the cells. Then maybe tomorrow we'll put you on trial for being an accessory to murder. And the day after, we'll hang you. With a wet rope.'

Garcia started to scream, 'Not to hang! Not to die! I swear–'

Alfie hustled him away, still yelling. When he got back, he said, 'Well, Greta, you certainly got him going – all that malarkey with hanging and wet ropes and photos of footprints. You piled it on a bit, didn't you? I must say, I couldn't see the photo looked anything like the sole of his shoe–'

'–come on, Alfie, get smart. Of course they didn't look alike, because that photo was one I took of a different case altogether. That was the break-in and burglary round in St John's Road, you remember.'

'Blimey, Greta, you took a few chances today. Suppose he twigged–'

'–no danger. How could he? That little shit knows bugger-all.'

'Your language has got very coarse lately, Greta. You never used to talk like that. You used to be such a lady.'

He's right, I'd better watch it, I thought. I never would have used that sort of language when my Gran was alive. And I'm sure Derek wouldn't like it, either. It must be something I'd picked up from Jim. Let's hope that's all I'd picked up from him.

Jim was my bit of rough. He was a long-distance lorry driver who spent nights with me when he was passing through Watford on his way, either from home to wherever, or back to his wife and kids somewhere up North. But I was getting pretty tired of him, and only this very morning I'd told him to find himself somewhere else to camp on his odd nights. And I wasn't very flattered when he'd pointed out that if he stayed in a B & B he'd have to pay.

'Is that all I am? Free lodging and breakfast!' I'd shouted

at him, and slammed out of the front door before he had chance to say whether that was what he'd meant or not. Knowing him, it would have taken him ten minutes to think of an answer, anyway. I hadn't taken up with him for his IQ in the first place. Just a bit of comfort and a little nooky now and again. But he was beginning to clutter up my nice little home as well as my life.

I wanted to concentrate on my career and my fancy for my handsome little boss, although I didn't always know which came first with me.

Chapter 4

'Look,' Derek said, 'this whole thing is going too fast. I never thought I'd say that about a case, but the fact is that we've amassed so much information that we're not making optimum use of it all.'

'Optimum, eh, Guv,' Alfie said admiringly. 'You've got a really good command of words.'

Derek ignored him, but I was thinking this was one of the great things about him. That he spoke so well, and the fact that he was sexy and handsome and I couldn't get him to see what a great couple we'd make, even if I was a good bit taller than him. Lying down it wouldn't matter anyway, would it. He had no idea how he'd changed my life, that before I met him and fell for him at first sight, I'd had it all planned out. How I was going to use men like Jim, the Long-Distance Lorry Driver, for convenience (the way some men still use women in this enlightened age), while I pursued my brilliant career to the very top of the police in England.

'Let's have a review of all we know,' Derek went on, not seeming to notice Alfie's approving look or my soppy one. 'You say Garcia admits to jemmying that door open, to being a courier in the precious stones business, to being willing to use bogus credit cards for the late Mr Gilmore. OK, obvious conclusion one: Gilmore was a crook.'

'One other thing,' I put in, 'he mentioned that Miss

Dunkerley from upstairs had seen him, and he referred to her by *her first name*.'

'Yes, well, she told you herself that she'd seen him,' Derek said.

'But not that they knew each other,' I insisted. Why was Derek avoiding the point I was making? 'What else did you get from her at your last interview?'

Derek looked uncomfortable.

'She, er, she's not at all the person I first took her for,' he said. 'What did you make of her yourself, Greta?'

Now was my chance to rub in how bright I'd been.

'Well, I think she's very devious, she knows a lot more than she's letting on, and she's trying to fool us by pretending to be older and plainer and more ordinary than she really is. But I think the most important thing about her is that spyhole in her floor. I don't think she's just a nosey parker. She's been watching Gilmore for a reason, and Garcia knowing her first name must mean they're all connected. Maybe she even actually saw the murder.'

'Or had more to do with it than seeing it,' Alfie suggested.

'Oh no,' Derek said. 'I can't see her as a murder suspect at all. As for her watching Gilmore, we have no evidence of that. We don't even know if that spyhole had anything to do with her. It might have been there before she moved in.'

What was the matter with the man? He was usually brighter and more suspicious of everybody near a murder scene than this. I was going to start arguing with him when Alfie saved me the trouble.

'Bit of a looker then, is she, Derek?' he leered. 'More fanciable than we thought, eh?'

'Don't be ridiculous,' Derek snapped. 'I just think we shouldn't jump to conclusions. As a matter of fact, she did admit to me that she actually knew Gilmore better than she'd first told us, but naturally thought if she pretended not to know him she would be left out of our investigations.'

I gasped. He didn't seem to realise the implications of what he was saying. But I didn't say a word.

He went on, 'She said it was the most amazing coincidence, when she moved into this flat, to find that Gilmore was in the flat below. Apparently she'd known him slightly when she lived in New York for a while. So they occasionally had dinner together, or went to the cinema. That sort of thing. Casual acquaintances. More interestingly, she said she knew he was in the emerald importing business and told her he had a lot of worries with the Department of Trade and the Customs and Excise people, who seemed to delight in making his business difficult. He had a lot of callers, she said, but if she was ever in his flat when someone came, she always left. When I mentioned not finding any documents there, she was amazed. She said he was usually so untidy she wondered how he found anything in all that jumble of papers.'

He paused for breath, and Alfie and I just sat. I don't know what Alfie was thinking, but my reaction was misery to discover my beloved wasn't as clever as I thought he was. This girl was taking him for a fool, and I was worried about how she was doing it.

There was quite a long silence. I suppose Derek was waiting for one of us to make some comment, but after a while he gave up and asked us what had transpired in our interview with Garcia after we'd switched the tape off. Transpired! Another of his posh words. But this time I wasn't so impressed.

'Nothing much,' I said, giving Alfie one of those 'keep your mouth shut' looks. 'I tried to trip him up about the mutilation of the body, but he clearly didn't know anything about it. I believed him, anyway. So in that case it must have happened, not just after the actual murder but also after he jemmied the door later on. It looks as if we had three lots of people on the scene that night.'

'Hm, maybe so,' Derek said, scribbling away. 'Doesn't seem likely, though, does it. Three separate lots of different people on the same murder scene at different times of the night. Now, Alfie, what about your interview with Garcia's landlady? Did you get anything out of that?'

Alfie's face was a study. I guessed that he might have got something out of it that had nothing to do with police work, and certainly nothing he'd want to report to Derek. He flipped open his notebook and cleared his throat. He'd gone a bit red, and I hoped Derek hadn't noticed.

'Mrs Susan Slipworthy of 142 Dickens Road, Hendon NW4, runs a guest house. She says Juan Garcia had stayed there on previous occasions, was a quiet lodger, never caused any trouble. She's known him on and off over a period of two to three years. She seems a respectable sort of person as far as I could tell.'

'But Alfie!' I exclaimed. 'Didn't you ask her if she knew Kate Dunkerley or Leonard Gilmore? Did you ask if Garcia had any visitors at all whenever he lodged with her? Does she own the house, and if not, who does? Has she got a husband, and if so, where is he?'

'Come along, Greta, don't pick on Alfie,' Derek ticked me off. 'These questions are farfetched and irrelevant. And anyway, Alfie is an experienced sergeant, and it ill behoves you to tell him how to do his job.'

Right then. That told me where I was. Behoves, eh.

'Superintendent Moon wants to know,' Derek went on, 'how the little boy is getting on.'

'Little boy? What little boy?' Alfie and I said together.

'The one at the bottom of the pile when you detained Garcia,' Derek reminded us. 'You must remember that your report mentioned this child coming round the corner

30

on a bicycle and tripping Garcia up, whereupon you, Alfie, jumped on them both. Mr Moon is anxious to know if the boy was badly hurt, and how he's progressing. After all, it's our responsibility if he's been injured.'

That was just like Mr Moon. Here we had a complicated and baffling murder case, with ramifications we were just beginning to uncover, and he picked up on this detail we'd all forgotten. I should learn from this, I thought, if I ever want to be a superintendent myself.

The phone went, and a really wet expression came on Derek's face as he listened. While I was trying to work out the possible cause, it changed and he frowned.

'Are you sure?' he said. 'Wouldn't you rather – no, OK then, I'll send her. Goodbye for now,' he said in a soppy voice.

And in a different voice he said to me, 'Just pop round and see what's up with Kate Dunkerley, would you Greta. She's asked for you to come and see her as soon as you can. Apparently nobody else will do.'

'What the hell!' I said. 'Who does she think she is, sending for me like a pizza delivery? Why can't she come here if she wants to see me so specially?'

'Now, Greta, don't be difficult. She's had a frightening experience, and she's nervous about going out at the moment. It's not far and it needn't take you long. Perhaps she needs to talk to another woman. Meantime, Alfie, perhaps you'd see what you can find out about that little boy you jumped on and let me have a report for Mr Moon asap. Off you both go then.'

And we were dismissed like a couple of rookies, both of us scowling.

'Never mind, girl,' Alfie said, trying to cheer me up. 'I'll see you in the canteen later and treat you to a nice cake for your tea.'

I hate when he calls me 'girl', it's so sexist. I know he

doesn't mean anything by it, and it's the way he talks to every female, including his wife Betty who's nearly twice my age and probably can't even remember being a girl. That's what you get when you work with an older colleague, I suppose.

When I got to Kate Dunkerley she was in a blue funk. Jittery and twitchy but looking a lot better than when I'd last seen her. Come to think of it, each time I saw her she'd improved, and now I saw she was quite a dolly-bird. I ground my teeth thinking that was the reason for Derek's soppiness.

'Oh Greta, I don't know what to do,' she began. 'It's about my neighbour, Mrs Winkelhorne. She called me in to her flat and started asking me all sorts of personal questions, and then all of a sudden I saw that she was a man!'

I didn't say anything, but I must have made some sort of disbelieving noise, or else it was written all over my face that I thought she was several eggs short of a dozen, because she went on.

'I don't blame you for not believing me, after all she's lived next door to me since I moved in, but you see I never really looked at her properly before. We've never had a proper talk, just passing each other and saying "Good morning" now and again–'

I couldn't resist. 'Oh yes, just like you told us was the case with you and Leonard Gilmore. Except now we hear that you actually did know him a little better than that. Tell me, what brought you to this mind-blowing discovery that deaf old Mrs Winkelhorne is not Mrs Winkelhorne at all?'

She didn't notice the sarcasm, just answered as if I'd asked a sensible question, 'It was when she laughed, you see. This is why I wanted to talk to you about it and not a man, because men don't understand these things, about women's bodies. But you will. Just think about seeing a fat old lady laugh. Everything goes up and down, doesn't it? But when she laughed at me because she thought she'd scared me, *her bosom stayed in the same place* and everything else went up and down. See?'

I was grateful that her doorbell went at this moment, just when I couldn't think of a thing to say. But she jumped a foot in the air and went dead white.

'Who could that be?' she whispered. 'Nobody can get in downstairs unless I push the entry-button. Sssh, don't say anything, I'll look through the eyehole in the door, and if it's him again we can pretend not to be here.'

It took me a few seconds to work out who she meant by 'him'. It wasn't until she'd crept up to the door and was looking through the peephole that I realised she'd been talking about Mrs Winkelhorne. So whether or not she really believed this inoffensive old bird was a man, it seemed she'd made up her mind to convince me. Anyway, whatever it was she saw, she decided it was OK to open the door.

There stood a complete stranger of a type that I personally always found, to put it politely, really icky. He was tall, well built and handsome in that unreal Hollywood way, complete with deep tan, blue eyes, black wavy hair, thick black eyelashes and flashing toothpaste advertisement smile. Yuck.

I could see at a glance that Kate Dunkerley's taste in men was nothing like mine. She stood there like a hypnotised rabbit, blushing (as far as I could see) from head to foot, fluttering her eyelashes and then going so pale I thought she was going to faint.

'Hallo,' she said in a tiny voice, 'what can I do for you?'

Clearly she meant she'd be glad to do anything he wanted. But it seemed his mind wasn't going her way.

'Good afternoon,' he said in a polite but definitely

American voice. 'I thought I'd better introduce myself. I'm Simon Winkelhorne–'

'not, not her missing husband,' I interrupted, hardly able to speak for laughing.

He glanced over at me with the same lack of interest he'd shown Kate, giving that false kind of ha-ha-ha meaningless laugh and flashing those teeth. Bet they were false too.

'No, no, I'm your neighbour's son. She called me and told me about the terrible murder of your other neighbour, and I thought she might need me with her. She seems very upset.'

'Won't you come in and have a cup of coffee,' Kate offered, 'and we can tell you all we know so far. This is Detective Sergeant Pusey of the Watford CID.'

He nodded politely towards me, flashed 'the smile' again at Kate, and said, 'Thank you. Very neighbourly of you, but I'll get back to Mother now.'

So much for Kate Dunkerley's latest tall tale.

Simon Winkelhorne didn't think his mother was a man.

Chapter 5

'Your team did a great job, Greta,' Derek said. 'Look at this forensics report.'

And he chucked a great wodgy file over to me.

'What?' Alfie said. 'Anything outstanding, is there?'

'Oh yes,' I said, leafing through and speed-reading as fast as I could. 'What about this bit about the female hairs they picked up? From at least four different women! And – wow! – this is great! They found a toe-print in the blood. How did I miss that? Oh, I see, it was sort of a partial. And that's a woman too. Well, Derek, I reckon we'd better have little Miss Kate Dunkerley in for a few more questions, don't you?'

I was surprised not to get a quick nod. He seemed a bit undecided, not like his usual self at all. But his solution came right on cue. A call from the front desk that a Miss Dunkerley was there asking for him.

'I'll go,' I said, and nipped fast out of the room before he had a chance to draw breath to stop me.

When I got there she was a sight to behold. Tarted up to the nines in the tiniest micro-skirt and highest heels I'd ever seen, made up like a pop-star, and not looking the least bit like I'd seen her previously. I had to admit to myself she was a knockout, and I started racking my brains how to stop Derek seeing her looking so sexy. The strangest thing, though, was that I had to speak to her about five times before she heard me, she was so wrapped up with watching and listening to some other woman talking to the station reception officer. I couldn't work out a reason for her to be so fascinated by some Irish tart talking about a burglary, but when I finally got her attention she jumped a foot in the air and then looked disappointed at seeing me.

'Oh, hallo Greta,' she said (how was I going to stop her calling me that?) 'nice to see you, but I asked for Detective Inspector Michaelson.' She spoke in a tiny breathy kind of voice that went with the dainty doll-like appearance.

'He's busy at present,' I lied. 'You'll have to make do with talking to me again. Come into this interview room, and tell me how I can help you.'

Close to, I could see now that each time I'd seen her before this, she'd been taking some trouble to hide her natural good looks, and now she'd decided to kind of come out from behind the sort of disguise of plainness she'd adopted. She really was like a little doll, just coming up past my shoulder, even with those terrific high heels. But I wasn't going to let her see my surprise.

'You don't look exactly amazed to see me,' she said. 'Don't you think I look different today? This is my real self.'

Then, without waiting for an answer or even a nod, she suddenly said, 'Who was that woman at the reception desk just now?'

Puzzled, I said, 'I don't know, just someone talking about a burglary, I think. Why, do you know her?'

'Oh no, no, of course not,' Kate said in a panicky kind of way. 'No, how could I know her, I don't know anyone in Watford now that Len Gilmore's dead.'

And bugger me if she didn't burst into tears. I just didn't know how to cope with this woman. I couldn't make head or tail of her. I decided to try some unsympathetic rough stuff.

'So have you changed your mind about Mrs Winkelhorne being a man?' I barked. 'Now that we've both met her son?'

She mopped her eyes. Annoying that this time they didn't go red, her makeup didn't run, her nose didn't go red – she still looked a picture.

'That's one of the things I wanted to talk to the inspector about. I don't know what to think now. And anyway, maybe whether she's a man or a woman, it's probably got nothing to do with the murder.'

'So exactly why *are* you here?'

I felt a complete idiot when she answered with a look of angelic innocence, 'Well, you did ask me to come in to make a formal statement, didn't you. And I thought before I did that, I could just have a quick talk with the inspector to apologise about not being completely frank with him at first, you know, about knowing Len Gilmore slightly in New York, and all that.'

I gave up trying to get somewhere with her. I was tempted to ask her about Garcia knowing her first name, but thought I'd better leave Derek to handle that question.

'OK,' I said, 'I'll see if Inspector Michaelson is free to see you now.'

Of course he was. He nearly fell over his own feet in his eagerness to see her again. I couldn't hide it from myself any more. He was well smitten. Then she let the cat out of the bag in a big way. More of a tiger out of a suitcase.

Before Derek had a chance to say more than a big hallo, she began with, 'I've been thinking about your problems, Inspector. You know, when you mentioned to me at dinner last night that you were looking for a place to live?'

He went bright red. Whether it was because of what she'd given away or that I was glaring at him fit to kill, I couldn't tell. But not only had he shown his preference for dainty little blondes, he'd also committed a serious offence. And he knew it, too.

'Er, erm, Miss Dunkerley, I thought that was in confidence between us–' he started, but she was ploughing on.

'Well, I had a brilliant inspiration. There's an empty flat in Robin Hood House, you know, our little block. Why don't you rent that, at least until you decide what you want to do next?'

And he hadn't even told me he was looking for a place. He shuddered.

'I couldn't live in a flat where someone's been battered to death. And anyway, it has to be kept sealed up until we've completed our investigations.'

I gave a meaningful cough. She gave a big sigh.

'No, not that one,' she said in a voice like someone explaining to an idiot. 'You remember, there's another flat, on the same floor as where Len Gilmore was, that's been empty for ages. I expect you'll want to talk to the agent about Len. You could enquire about the other flat at the same time. And I'd feel a lot safer if there was a man living on the premises, after all that's happened.'

So she wasn't going to try again to pull that rubbish about Mrs Winkelhorne being a man. But she was going on with her spiel.

'Specially if those murderers were burglars as well–'

My chance had come.

'–*those* murderers?' I interrupted. 'What makes you think there was more than one?'

This time it was her turn to go red, and mine to let out a big sigh. Derek looked all in bits. After a silence while I could tell she was trying to think of an answer and Derek was trying to think of anything except how much he fancied her, I decided to keep the interview in my own hands.

'Juan Garcia, a little crook at present detained in one of our cells, claims to know you personally,' I shot at her. 'He says you saw him on the stairs after he'd discovered Gilmore's body, and he referred to you by your first name.'

I pretended to consult my notes.

'Ah yes,' I went on, 'here it is. "Ask that woman, Kate, she saw me when I screamed after I saw Mr Gilmore in all the blood." May we have your comments on that, please, Miss Dunkerley?'

Derek had pulled himself together by this time and decided that he was the boss after all. So instead of waiting for her answer, he butted in with a question of his own.

'And what can you tell us about the spyhole in your floor which enabled you to watch Mr Gilmore's activities?' he asked, trying not to sound as soppy as he had before. 'Perhaps there's a connection between that and your referring to more than one murderer?'

But she turned to me, all innocence again, and stammered, 'What-what was that name again, Greta?'

I was fed up with her act, and Derek's silliness, and her cheek in keeping on calling me Greta.

'Oh come on, Kate, don't start that wide-eyed business again,' I snapped. 'Don't you know by now it doesn't work with me. He knows your name and where you live and your connection with Gilmore, and he's given you as a witness that he didn't do the murder.'

It was clear she couldn't think of a word to say. Or maybe nothing that wouldn't make matters worse for her. She sniffled and scratched and walked up and down a bit. Then she sat down and looked at me dumbly. I didn't know if there was something in that look that melted me a bit, or I was just following my instincts. But whichever it was, I opened up a bit. Derek was still silent, so it looked as if I was taking over anyway.

'We found Garcia's name in Gilmore's flat, and when we tried to talk to him, he took a pot shot at me. So we're holding him on assault on a police officer with a deadly weapon. He seemed to think we'd arrested him for murder. His English isn't great. Anyway, he panicked and told us all about what happened that night. And he said if we didn't believe him, you'd tell us it was true, because you saw him break in after the murder. Anything to say now, Kate?'

'Yes, OK,' she muttered, 'it's true. I didn't want to tell you about him because I knew he had nothing to do with the murder, and I thought it wouldn't matter that he'd been there. I suppose you could have him for breaking and entering, now that I've told you, but does it make any difference?'

'Oh yes, certainly it does. We want to hang on to him until we find out his connection with Gilmore. And what business they were running together, and how much you know about it, and a whole lot more about you and Gilmore. And it'll be easier coming from you, because it takes hours to have an interview with him with his rotten English. That's our side. But also, you'll be in a better situation with us yourself if you co-operate with us.'

Derek suddenly came to life. About time, I thought.

'And you may as well tell us about that spyhole, too,' he said.

Then there was a long boring silence. Now that Derek looked as if he was going to take over again, I thought I'd keep shtum. And as for little Miss Kate, either she was trying to make up some new story or she'd gone into a trance. So we all waited for one of the others to say something.

Finally Derek switched on the tape machine with the recording of his own interview with Garcia. It took place after ours, but Derek's voice came first, so it seemed as if this was all we had from Garcia so far. My boss was not so daft, then. My recent opinion of him went up a notch from zero.

We heard him ask Garcia, 'Why did you have to visit Mr Gilmore? You say you had to go to his flat at whatever time he said, but you haven't told us yet what business you had with him that was so important. You probably came to England on a visitor's visa, as a tourist. And now you say you had to do whatever Mr Gilmore said. You'd better tell us a lot more, my lad.'

Sounds of loud sobs from Garcia.

'My boss, he send me to take stones to Meester Geelmore. And he say to wait and Meester Geelmore give me stuff to bring back. So Meester Geelmore, he say to me while I wait, I help heem with the cards. And he say, "You do what I tell, or the worse it be for you." So I do.'

'Stones? What stones? What do you mean?'

Then there was a torrent of Spanish, sobs and snorts from Garcia, but nothing that made any sense. Derek switched off the machine.

'Well, Kate?' he asked in his real inspector's voice, not the soppy one. This was excellent, but he was still calling her Kate, which was not so good. 'What stones?'

It must have been the wrong question, because she suddenly looked relieved.

'Oh, that! Is that all you want to know? I already told Sergeant Pusey that Len Gilmore was in the emerald business. Well, you must know that emeralds are one of Colombia's three main exports,' she rattled off like a tour guide. 'Colombia is the greatest producer of emeralds in the world. So I suppose this fellow Garcia was delivering a consignment to Len, and waiting for the payment to take back to his boss, whoever he was.'

'Come on, Kate, don't be stupid,' Derek said quite coldly. I hugged myself. He was going off her rapidly. 'All this pretence is getting you nowhere. You know as well as we do that if this had been a straight-forward business transaction, even if the delivery of precious stones had needed a personal courier, the payment would have been dealt with electronically through banks. The courier wouldn't have had to hang around to take actual cash back home with him, and there would absolutely have been no need for a meeting in the small hours of the morning. Nor could he have been bullied into handling forged credit cards. And he certainly wouldn't have known how to slip a lock. Not to speak of carrying a jemmy and knowing how to use it.'

I knew I shouldn't butt in while he was in full flow, but I couldn't resist.

'–and he knows you,' I added.

I think Derek and I were equally surprised at what Kate Dunkerley said next. Whatever we expected, this wasn't it.

'Len always said to me,' she said in a small sad voice, 'and he told me to remember it. "Shit happens, kid," he used to say, "but when it does, you don't have to stand up and take it full in the face. Lie down, give in, let it go over your head." He was right. I'll tell you everything I know. But I don't think it's going to help. And you'll understand why I've been so silly.'

Chapter 6

By now Derek was all business-like and no messing. If he still had a soft spot for this little dolly, he was hiding it brilliantly.

'This will be an official statement, Miss Dunkerley,' he said, switching on the tape and making the usual introductory declaration into it. 'Now then, please tell us what you know about Mr Leonard Gilmore of Robin Hood House, Squash Court Lane, Watford, his business affairs and your relationship with him.'

I could see her hands trembling. She took a few deep breaths. It was clear she was plucking up courage, but whether to tell the truth or not, who knew? Maybe she was taking the time to make up more stories. But what she'd said already about Len Gilmore advising her certainly sounded authentic.

'He was my lover,' she said. 'He brought me over from New York after I had a bit of trouble there. I really loved him, honestly I did. It wasn't just an arrangement. But you know what your other sergeant said about his wang being a whopper – well, I didn't want to share it with half the tarts in England.'

I gave a sharp intake of breath, but Derek flapped his hand at me not to interrupt. I was wondering if she realised how much she'd told us already. Was that a slip of the tongue, or did she know she was admitting to watching and listening to us at the spyhole in her floor that I'd discovered? How else would she know how Alfie Partridge described the detached portion of the deceased?

43

And her language wasn't too choice, either. Still, she was going on, in a small dead little voice.

'He was always bringing them home with him when he told me he had a business evening, and he thought I didn't know. So that night I told him I was going to the pictures on my own, and I sneaked back to spy on what I thought was going to be another one of his little bits of extra. And it was, it was one I'd seen before, but this time she came with two big thugs, and she just stood there while they bashed my poor Len to death. I panicked. I ran up and down with my hands clamped over my mouth, scared the three of them down there would hear me having hysterics. What could I do? I couldn't save him. But at least I could save myself. Then they left.'

She broke down. This time her tears were real, not those pretty little put-on sobs she used to get sympathy or win time. She was really upset, either at what she'd seen or the fact that she'd lost her meal ticket. I'm tough. I pride myself on it. I didn't soften towards her. Not at all. But even I wasn't prepared for what she said next.

'I was in a terrible state. I was terrified and heart-broken at first. But after a while I started to get angry. And it was Len I was angry with. If he hadn't been so keen on getting more and more nooky wherever he could find it, none of this need have happened. I got more and more furious with him. So I went down and hacked it off.'

Derek went white. I had no idea what colour I was. I think we were both in a state of shock.

'Hacked what off?' Derek whispered.

I could see he didn't want to believe it.

'His shlong, his tool, his penis – the cause of all our troubles!' Kate shouted hysterically, then collapsed sobbing as if she'd never stop.

'Get her something, Greta, a cup of tea or something,' Derek said in a broken voice.

But I wasn't about to miss anything. This was riveting stuff. I stuck my head out of the door, grabbed a passing plod and told him to bring three cups.

Derek signed off the tape machine and we all sat quietly for a while. After a bit, Kate wiped her eyes, gave a great shuddering sigh and started to sip her tea.

Quite kindly I asked if she wanted to go on with her statement.

'Might as well,' she answered listlessly. All the life seemed to have gone out of her. She didn't look nearly as tasty now as she had when she'd come trotting in, full of herself and asking for Derek so cockily.

Derek turned the tape recorder on again and made the resuming statement, and we both looked at Kate, waiting for her to go on. If she'd been telling the truth so far – and I couldn't believe even she would have made up such a story – she could hardly have anything worse to say. As a matter of fact, for some shameful reason I'd started to see the funny side of the whole thing, specially because of Alfie's opinion about the mutilation being to do with the Mafia. I could hardly wait to tell him how wrong he was about who'd actually done it. We were good mates, but there was always that bit of edge between us about scoring off each other.

Finally Kate must have made a decision, whether to come clean or not, who could tell. But she didn't seem to care whether whatever she told us was farfetched or not. She just got on with it. I was beginning to wonder if she was all there or maybe a bit wobbly in the top storey.

'I really want to help you find who killed Len,' she claimed. 'Believe it or not, I really loved him.'

I smirked a bit, and Derek looked sick. We didn't say anything, though, because we didn't want to interrupt her and spoil her thought process, if that's what it was.

'That girl who was at the desk, Greta, when I came in,

you know, the one talking about a burglary. Did you notice that she's Irish? Well, anyway, she was the one, the tart that Len was having it off with lately. And she was the one who came in with those two thugs. I can identify her, alright, if I see her again, no mistake. All you've got to do is bring her in.'

This was a bit thick, even for this little storyteller. Derek still seemed dumbstruck, so I took it up. I longed to ask her a whole pack of questions, like for example why she and her lover had separate flats, and how did it come into her head to cut his thing off even if she was furious with him for getting himself killed, and more about his 'business'. But I stuck to the main question.

'Tell us exactly what you saw through your spyhole when the girl came into Len's flat with the two thugs,' I suggested.

She answered readily enough, which showed either that it was the truth or she was prepared with her story.

'He buzzed her up, that Irish girl, I suppose he'd been expecting her, and he opened his front door and those two heavies pushed in behind her. I couldn't hear what they all said because they spoke so quietly, but whatever it was, Len brought out a gun. The girl stepped back and the men sort of rushed Len, and one got hold of his gun arm and the other one picked up the lamp and started – you know, you know what they did. But the first one seemed to try to stop it and it looked as if they were all in a panic and they rushed out.'

'And the gun? What happened to that?'

'Oh, the gun. Oh yes, I'd forgotten that.' She shut her eyes for a moment, as if she was picturing the scene. Then she said, 'The girl picked it up. I've already told you what happened after that.'

'Yes, but you've told us so many different things,' said Derek, suddenly coming to life. 'Perhaps you'd like to tell us now what happened to your lover's personal and business papers? As you probably know from watching us, they were all missing from his flat.'

'I have no idea.'

'And of course you don't know who wiped all the fingerprints, either?'

'Well, of course I wiped the knife I used,' she admitted.

Derek shuddered. I couldn't help it, I gave a bit of a snort. Of course it was shocking and disgusting, and I could see it was upsetting for a man to hear, but it had its funny side too. Mafia, eh, Alfie!

'But I don't know any more, I can't tell you anything else, surely I've helped you enough? Will I be charged with a crime?' she asked, back into using her little girl's voice. 'Like mutilating a dead body, or something?'

'Obstructing the police in the course of their investigations, interfering with evidence at the scene of a crime, withholding vital information, just for starters,' Derek snapped, looking stone-faced. 'And there are many more questions we have to ask you.'

She gave one of those big sort of sobbing sighs that she was so good at.

What she said next was the last thing we would have expected at this point. She was full of surprises, I had to admit.

'This certainly isn't my lucky week,' she muttered, 'nor Len's.'

*

Alfie came thundering in just as I was about to escort dear little Miss Kate Dunkerley to a nice comfy cell pending further enquiries, as we say.

'Quick Guv,' he panted, 'something else has happened at Robin Hood House. It's the old lady, Missis Wotsit, she's fallen out the window, her son's with her, PC Brown's just called it in, he's in a flap.'

He and Derek dashed out, Derek shouting at me over his shoulder to put Kate in a safe place then follow them. I knew what he meant about a safe place, although I wasn't sure if he wanted her charged or not, so I just put her in a holding cell and told the custody sarge to hang on till we got back.

When we got there, the poor young PC who'd been on duty outside the little block of flats was standing there, white-faced and overwrought.

'I don't understand,' he said. 'How could he have got an ambulance so quickly? He was kneeling beside his mother and using his mobile while I called in what happened, and suddenly there was what looked like a private ambulance and they'd all gone before I could do a thing to stop them.'

He stood there looking baffled. We all looked at the pavement. There was a wig and a puddle of blood and what looked like some spit and something else like what I'd seen around Gilmore's head at the scene of that crime.

We stood there too, looking at the ground, then at each other, like the proverbial group of dumb monkeys. What struck me most was the wig. Was it possible that Kate had told the truth about Mrs Winkelhorne, and she was a man after all? Of all her tall stories, that seemed the most pointless, but maybe – no, that was silly. After all, some women did wear wigs, that didn't mean they were really men in disguise. While I was turning all this over in my mind, Derek had been busy on his mobile.

'Brown, you stay here,' he barked at the poor young plod, who was in a right state. 'Don't leave the spot for anything, understand. Forensics will be along soon. Greta, you stay with Brown and liaise with SOCO. Alfie, you come with me.'

And he strode off, all masterful, back to being the man I admired. Even if he had forgotten that I wasn't SOCO's favourite person just then.

*

By the time I got back to Shady Lane, it was quite late, but I didn't care. This case was hot and getting hotter, and I couldn't bear to leave it, even to go home to get some sleep. Also, there was a risk that if Jim the Long-Distance Lorry Driver was there, I wouldn't get much sleep anyway.

'All the NHS hospitals in the area have been checked,' Derek told me, 'and most of the private ones, and not one admission matches up to what happened to Mrs Winkelhorne. She, or her body if she's dead, seems to have disappeared.'

'Frankly I don't believe it was an accident,' I offered. 'I think that young feller, who *claims* to be her son, had that so-called private ambulance waiting round the corner while he chucked the old girl out of the window. But even if that's right, are we investigating two separate crimes or one big complicated one? What could be the connection between Mrs Winkelhorne and Len Gilmore?'

Alfie came bursting in while we were pondering.

'Guv! Simon Winkelhorne came back to the scene! When we went to arrest him on suspicion of attempted murder of his mother, he claimed his name's not Simon Winkelhorne, it's Simon Goldfeather. He showed identification proving he works at the US Embassy, so we couldn't charge him anyway. Diplomatic immunity, see. But he says he knows a whole lot more about Gilmore, and the old lady wasn't his mother, she wasn't even a woman! The wig, see, the wig was the clue.'

And he flopped into a chair, panting and red in the face. Derek got snappish all over again.

'What the devil are you wittering on about, man. You're not making any sense. Slow down and tell us properly, will you. Mrs Winkelhorne wasn't a woman? What do you mean, the wig was the clue? This fellow's name is Goldfeather? I don't believe any of this. And where exactly is this so-called American Embassy man now? More to the point, where is Mrs Winkelhorne, man or woman, alive or dead?'

A bit subdued now, Alfie said, 'I don't know where the victim is, Guv. But Goldfeather wouldn't come here to the station with me. He says he'll meet you at Robin Hood House and talk to you there.'

'Oh, not the Embassy then? Strange. Anyway, Alfie, you come with me to talk to him, and Greta, you stay here and have an informal chat with Kate Dunkerley. Make it seem like just a casual, unofficial conversation away from the men and not taped, OK? See what else you can get out of her. She must know a whole lot more than she's given us so far. Say anything you like that might soften her up – try one of your tricks to get her to blurt something out by mistake. She might be inclined to let something drop to you by accident.'

'Just a minute, Guv,' Alfie said. 'There's something I want to tell you about coincidences.'

'Well, come on then, you can tell me on the way.'

'No, seriously, Greta ought to hear this too. It's what I heard as I came in – Kate Dunkerley saying by coincidence she saw this Irish girl here, right on the spot in this very Station, who she said was involved in the murder of Len Gilmore.'

'Oh yes, what about it?'

'Well, I read this in the paper the other day. In Australia, it was, Sydney, or it might have been Melbourne.'

'Get on with it, man, never mind where it was. What are you talking about? What's this got to do with Kate Dunkerley?'

'This feller was walking down the street and on the other side he saw his long-lost twin who he hadn't seen for twenty years. So he rushed across the road and got knocked down by a–'

'–oh, for goodness sake, who cares what he was knocked down by – it could have been a kangaroo for all I care!'

'No, it wasn't a kangaroo,' Alfie said, quite seriously. 'But it wasn't fatal.'

'Anyway,' I said, bored with the whole thing, 'so there was a happy reunion after he recovered from the accident.'

'No, it turned out the twin he thought he'd seen was his own reflection in a shop window,' Alfie wound up triumphantly.

There was a short silence, then Derek said with overdone politeness, 'Would you mind telling us what this has to do with anything, Sergeant?'

'Kate Dunkerley seeing the girl here who was involved in that murder is too much of a coincidence. There's no such thing as a coincidence. They don't exist, see?' Alfie explained.

Another silence, full of deep breathing.

Then, with marvellous self-control, Derek said, 'Let's go, Sergeant,' and they left.

Chapter 7

Kate literally rushed at me when I went into her holding cell.

'What's happening, Greta? Am I under arrest? Why am I being kept in this room? Am I going to be charged with obstructing the police in their enquiries, or something?'

I was glad to see that she was in quite a panic. A cell could do that – it could destroy all your pre-planning. You walked in knowing what you were going to say, the line you were going to take with the police, and in the interview room you were OK. Maybe it was a bit unnerving, but not terrible. The thing was, it was just a room – a table, chairs, electrical sockets, a tape recorder, a tin ashtray nobody was allowed to use. The walls were institution yellow and the strip lighting burred continuously. Was it the noise that got to people?

There was probably a simpler truth. The interview room was in a police station, and if you were there, you were going to be interviewed by the police. And when it came right down to it, everyone had something to hide, some more than others. So that had some effect on her for a start. And now being in a cell was worse. Much worse. A fixed bunk, a basic loo, a door. That was it.

This meant she'd be more likely to co-operate. I thought the best way to begin would be to challenge some of her most obvious lies.

'Now calm down, Kate,' I said. 'You're not under arrest, you know very well you haven't been charged with anything. You're just helping the police with their enquiries, right? You can see there's no other witness in here, I'm not taping our conversation, I'm not even taking any notes. So you can tell me for a start, just between ourselves, why did you give us that cock-and-bull story about seeing the Irish girl *here*, at the station. The very same girl who brought those two men into Len's flat who you say killed him?'

Kate's reaction amazed me. She burst into hysterical laughter. I had to smack her a bit to calm her down. Then I got her a cup of tea. Then I let her repair her makeup. Then I asked her the same question again. This time she was calmer.

'I'm sorry,' she said. 'That was a bit silly, but there was no need to give me such a whack. Was that a sample of police brutality?' she giggled. 'But when I tell you the joke, you'll probably laugh too. Out of all the things I've told you that might not have been the real twenty-four carat truth, you've picked the one absolutely genuinely authentic fact. I know it's unbelievable, I could hardly credit it myself, but it's the God's honest truth. She *was* the girl who brought the two men into Len's flat, and I *did* see her right here, at the front desk, talking to the duty officer about a burglary. And all you have to do is get her name and address from your own records, and bring her in. I'll identify her for you alright. Then maybe you'll get her to tell you about those two thugs, too. I'm telling you, Greta, you've got the whole case at your fingertips, if you'll only believe me.'

'Yes, but why should I believe you? Suppose you just saw some woman at the desk here and made up a whole story about her involvement in Len's murder. And we bring her in on suspicion of being an accessory to a non-accidental death, and it turns out you've lied to us again. I'm going to look a right Charley, aren't I? She'll deny it

54

anyway, won't she, whether it's true or not? It would be just you against her. Why should I take your word for it? What evidence have I got, other than what you tell me, when we all know you've told us one lie after another ever since we set eyes on you?'

There was a long silence. I could see Kate going paler under her makeup. And the little wheels going round in her head.

Finally, she said, 'I think I'm going to need a solicitor, don't you?'

I didn't answer. Just let it lie there, to give her more time to think. Then she surprised me again. There was no end to the shocks this girl dished out.

'Have you ever heard of the dress and knitwear designer, Curleigh?' she asked me. Of course I had. There couldn't be a woman in the world who hadn't heard of this man who was as famous for his Third World charity work as for the fabulous clothes he produced.

'Well, I suppose you'll think it's another of my lies if I tell you he's my brother,' she went on.

This time it was my turn to get hysterical. She just didn't know where to draw the line. Talk about over the top.

'Oh, come on, Kate, don't be so ridiculous,' I choked out finally. 'Even you must see how far-fetched that is. Apart from anything else, how can a white girl have a black brother? And anyway, everybody knows his whole history from when he was abandoned as a baby. It's had enough publicity over the years. For goodness sake, girl, what do you think is the point of making up these stories? Don't you know the difference between truth and lies? At least try to think of something a bit more believable, if you must spin a yarn.'

She started to protest, 'No, honestly, Greta, if you'll just listen –' but I shouted her down. Any bit of sympathy I'd had for her had gone out of the window. She was not only a hopeless liar, she was a complete fool as well. Maybe even a bit unbalanced. Nobody in their right mind would go on spinning one yarn after another the way she did. I was beginning to think she had actually killed Len Gilmore herself. Although how such a frail-looking little creature could have got a six-foot bruiser to stand still while she hammered him to death was still a mystery. And even if we could figure that out, why should she have cut his wang off afterwards and stuck it in his mouth?

Unless she was *completely* demented. Not just a little, but an absolute psycho. Certifiable. That was a whole new thought.

*

Later, in Derek's office, he and Alfie Partridge and I were pooling information and talking it all over again. Both the men agreed with me that her story of being related to Curleigh should be ignored.

'Well, Guv,' Alfie said, 'she's admitted to doing the Bobbitty on him, so why don't we just charge her and hold her on that, for the time being?'

'A Bobbitty?' asked Derek.

'Yes, you know, years ago, that American woman who cut her husband's cock off and threw it in the bushes and they found it and sewed it on again for him. Too late to do that for poor old Len Gilmore, though,' Alfie added thoughtfully.

Alfie is such a clown sometimes, I can't help laughing.

'Oh Alfie,' I hiccupped, 'their name wasn't Bobbitty. He was John Wayne Bobbitt.'

'That was after she'd given him a trim,' he grinned. 'She cut his Bobbitty down to Bobbitt, geddit?'

'Never mind all these stupid jokes,' said Derek irritably.

'Where are we going with this case? It seems to me it just gets more and more complicated and we haven't got a clue. Well, if the Americans are interested, at least that tells us Len Gilmore was known to the police over there, for what good that does us. And this American Embassy feller, Simon Goldfeather – what is he, some sort of Red Indian, Big Chief Goldfeather? – I think his job at the Embassy is a cover-up. He's probably CIA or FBI or one of those. I'm always suspicious of these Embassy security men, anyway.'

'So do you think he's been after Len Gilmore all along?' I asked. 'But then what was his connection with Mrs Winkelhorne, or whoever she was, or he was, or…' My voice trailed away as I saw all over again how muddled the whole thing was. I made a different start.

'Did this Goldfeather chap tell you any more about Mrs Winkelhorne, Guv? About where she – or he – is now, for example?'

Derek shook his head dismally.

'He says Winkelhorne's a man who was hired to watch Len Gilmore and Kate Dunkerley. But he doesn't know who Winkelhorne was working for. Whoever they were, they owned the building, so they put Winkelhorne in place first, and then somehow manoeuvred Gilmore into taking those two empty flats. One each for himself and Kate Dunkerley. How could they do that? That alone is far-fetched enough. Then this Goldfeather expects me to believe that while he was getting all this out of him, Winkelhorne suddenly fell out of the window by accident, and he doesn't know where the so-called private ambulance took him! I like the bit about getting all this out of him – I wonder what his methods are for extracting this kind of information.'

'Did he tell you Winkelhorne's real name, or who he was working for?'

'No, he said that was all he knew.'

'Well, Guv,' said Alfie helpfully, 'maybe that's all true.'

'If you believe that load of crap, Alfie Partridge,' said Derek, 'you're a lot more gullible than I thought you were.'

And he looked up at Alfie's massive bulk with his usual mixture of scorn and envy.

It must be hell to feel so manly and look like an under-nourished schoolboy. But I can't help it, I love him whatever he looks like. And he *is* only a few inches shorter than I am in my flatties.

What could I do to make him see me as a woman, a sexual object even, and not just a sergeant a bit brighter and more presentable than Alfie Partridge?

*

That evening, my head was buzzing so much I thought I needed to get out into the air. Since I'd got a car, I'd given up using my bike or roller blades as transport, but now I took out the old blades and set off for a turn around the pedestrian precincts of Watford on them.

I'm not one of those heroines you read about in crime fiction, where they're forever going for five-mile runs before going to the gym at crack of dawn, then starting their day's work. OK, I got my Black Belt in karate, but not for love of exercise, more because I thought I might need it. It seems to me all this physical stuff is just to show how macho some of these women are supposed to be. And some of them are more like that Duracell Bunny in the advertisements, competing with all the normal bunnies, than a real honest-to-God flesh and blood woman like me. Myself, I'd rather have a good bunk-up (for exercise), a long sleep (to recover), and then a nice fresh croissant and a cup of tea brought to me in bed not too early the following morning. Dream on.

Because I love my home town of Watford, having a roller

blade around its quiet streets in the small hours is very settling for me. I don't know why people look down their noses at it – what's wrong with council estates, motorways and little old workmen's cottages, anyway? There's nowhere else I'd rather live, and they can keep their Thames-side high-rises and their Manhattan skyscrapers.

So I rollered about it for a while, feeling better all the time.

It cleared my head, but I didn't end up with any new ideas. Just the same old ones: insoluble case, unrequited love, career ambition on hold.

Back to bed then. A good sleep might help. Or not.

Chapter 8

Next day – new day, new thoughts. Derek sent me to talk to the woman Kate had accused of being involved in Gilmore's murder. She really had reported a burglary, and so the Crime Desk had all the details. She'd given her name as Christine Smith, which must have been the truth, as she wanted to make an insurance claim, and needed a crime number for the purpose.

She had that gorgeous colouring they call black Irish, with hair that seemed to have blue high-lights, it was so black, and a complexion of cream and roses, and eyes of an unbelievable shade of turquoise. Made me feel like a giant mouse. Me with my brown hair and brown eyes and legs like tree-trunks – why do I always have to come up against women like her and little doll-like blonde blue-eyed Kate Dunkerley?

'Ah, Sergeant, darling, isn't it kind of you to call on me yourself, now!' was her response when I introduced myself. 'And all I'm wanting is to make it official with the insurance so I can get the place made decent again.'

And she showed me her sitting room, which certainly looked as if it had been turned over by a professional. No two ways about that. But why? And did it have anything to do with our murder? And if it did, surely she wouldn't be stupid enough to call in the police and try to claim on her insurance? Who could tell. Each person I'd met in this case seemed nuttier than the one before.

'Well, do you think, now, I could at least tidy the place up a bit, now that you and the constable and the other sergeant have all had such a good look at it? And could you be giving me the certificate or the number or whatever it is I'm needing to show the insurance that it all really happened?'

It sounded as if she'd twigged we were making more of a dog's dinner of it than would be normal for a run-of-the-mill break-in. I got on the blower to the station, gave her the case number and told her she could clear up the evidence whenever she liked. I noticed that she hadn't asked the usual questions that most Joe Public would put, like whether we weren't going to take fingerprints and all that stuff that they got from watching the telly.

'There is something else I'd like to talk to you about, Miss Smith, if you wouldn't mind,' I said uneasily. I felt really silly about this, but I was determined to give Kate her chance. 'We have somebody in custody,' I used my most sergeant-like voice, 'who has made an accusation against you.'

'What, that I did my own burglary, is it?' she laughed.

'No, nothing to do with that, it's about an entirely different case. I have to ask you, Miss Smith, whether you are acquainted with a man named Leonard Gilmore, who lives in–'

I didn't have to finish. Whatever denials she was going to make, her face had given her away. As I watched, first it went bright red, then every scrap of colour disappeared, and she suddenly seemed to change from a good-looking young woman to a middle-aged person with a terminal illness.

In my time in the police, I'd seen some guilty looks, but I'd never seen anything quite as dramatic as this. When you see something like that in a film, you think it's just clever effects. You don't expect it to happen in real life. Even her breathing changed, and she seemed to be gasping like a landed fish. I helped her to a chair and got her a glass of water. Although she looked like a bit of an emergency and I should have been concentrating on her, I still noticed that her kitchen looked completely undisturbed. And that was strange, because all break-in pro's know that people often hide their jewellery in the freezer or a mock tin of tomato soup, so what did this mean? Only one room ransacked? Odd.

I noted to myself to look at the rest of the place when she'd recovered a little. Then I stood and watched her until she seemed to have got over the worst of the shock.

'Well, Miss Smith,' I said after a while, 'seems as if you have something to tell me about Mr Gilmore and what you know about him.'

I could see she was trying to get her brain into gear, but it was a losing battle. This explained her boldness in reporting the burglary. She had been so confident there was nothing to connect her with the murder, it didn't require nerve to go to the police. Just foolishness. And also certainty of our stupidity. I've noticed that brainless people often expect other people to be thick, too.

I knew she was going to cough up the truth. I could see it on its way. All I had to do was wait. But it was a surprise when it came.

'I was there, d'you see, when he died,' she offered simply. ''Twas a horrible shock, Sergeant dear, so it was, and I don't think I'll ever lose the sight of it from my mind. One minute there he was, his usual randy self, and – oh, 'twas terrible, seeing the poor man in that condition!'

'What condition was that, Miss Smith?'

'Why, you know, you must have seen him, with his poor dear head all bashed in like that! And all from a misunderstanding, too.'

I almost laughed. A man had his head smashed in

because of a *misunderstanding*? Come on, Miss Smith, I thought, you can do better than that. But I didn't let on what I was thinking.

Gently I said, 'Tell me all about it. From the beginning.'

She seemed glad to be getting it off her chest. It was as if she couldn't talk fast enough to offload the burden.

'Well, it was a strange thing from the beginning. Can you believe I was paid to pick him up one day when he was out shopping, and to have a bit of a flirt with him and so on. And I thought at first it wasn't quite a nice job, a bit like being a tart, you know, being paid to go to bed with a strange man, but he was so nice and such fun and attractive and *very* sexy, and I've always liked Americans anyway, so–'

'–whoa, just a minute, please. What do you mean, you were paid to pick him up and so on? Who paid you, and why? And how far were you supposed to go? And for how long?'

'Ah, well now, Sergeant, isn't that the mystery of it, for d'you see, I never did know who hired me, it being so anonymous and all. But I got all my instructions and the money and all delivered to me personally by a courier. And so it went on. And it was like being paid for having fun. For except that we never went out anywhere in public together, but always had our good times in his own home, I think I might have done it without the money. And he giving me the nice presents from time to time, too,' she added, wiping away a tear.

Which might have meant either that she'd got fond of him or she was regretting the loss of the nice little earner she'd been on to. But I didn't care which it was. Talk about the plot thickening! There was a long silence while I digested what I'd heard so far. Did I believe it? I couldn't decide yet. But since it was the most unlikely story I'd heard so far in an interesting career, probably not. Even a professional tart would hesitate to take instructions like that from an anonymous employer.

'Then came the courier with new directions,' she picked up the story in a mournful voice. 'Two men were coming to call for me to go with me to Len's flat, but I wasn't to let him know about them until we got into his own front door. I don't know who they were. They called for me in a big black car at my very door.'

'What did they say?' I asked.

'Not a word,' she said. 'I tried to pass the time of day with them on the journey, but never a word did they speak to me. Or to Len, I think, neither. He looked at them, then at me, then at them again, and suddenly he had a gun in his hand. He was saying something to me, I don't know what, and I tried to speak to him. Then the while he was looking at me, somehow one of them got behind him and bashed his head in, and I was crying and begging them all to stop – oh, Sergeant, dear, it was horrible!'

And this time it was obvious that her tears were genuine. Well, naturally, seeing somebody done in like that must be a terrible thing, and even more so if you were all prepared for an evening of fun and games with the victim. And I could see that talking about it made her re-live the sight.

Good thing she hadn't seen him after Kate had added her own bit of mayhem to the scene. Talk about the icing on the cake. I still didn't understand why Kate had contributed that little trimming, but that didn't matter. At the moment, anyway.

Well, I went on questioning Christine Smith, which turned out to be her real name, but I couldn't get her to budge from her story. Some of it might have been true, but the part about being hired to pick up Len Gilmore just stuck in my throat.

The only other information I got was about how she

earned her living. She was one of those girls who live on a mixture of bits of acting and modelling work (she actually showed me her Equity card) and hostessing and demonstrating household gimmicks at home exhibitions and all those different odd jobs that called for no particular talent except looking beautiful and being amiable. Most of this was through an agency, but of course it also involved putting her name and address about a fair bit. So she said that she wasn't surprised that her so-called anonymous employer picked her out for the job on Len Gilmore. She was mildly curious as to who he might be, and why he was willing to pay her to have an affair with a strange man. But as long as the money was good and the work so agreeable, she wasn't about to rock the boat by trying to find out any more. That was her story, anyway.

'But you must have thought it pretty amazing,' I pressed her, but she just shrugged, and didn't answer. Tall tales? I wondered. But no law against it.

Of course there was no point in asking her why she hadn't reported witnessing a murder. She was obviously terrified that the two men would come after her. That part was easy to believe. They had still been there when she had run out of the building. She didn't wait for them to give her a lift home. She just ran until she saw a taxi. She swore she wouldn't recognise them if she saw them again. Fear had clean wiped any recollection of their faces out of her mind, she claimed.

'And the gun? What happened to the gun?'

'What gun?'

'You said when Len Gilmore saw the two men you'd brought in with you, suddenly he had a gun in his hand.'

'So I did then. I don't know what happened to it, I just ran.'

Kate had said she saw the girl pick up the gun. It was a toss-up which of them to believe.

But of course, when I asked Christine if she'd ever heard the name Kate Dunkerley, or if she knew who else lived in that little block of flats, I drew a blank.

I really don't know why I asked her if she'd heard of Curleigh. Naturally she had. Who hadn't? But what did that have to do with any of our brain-draining mystery? Nothing. I must be going round the bend myself, I thought.

Willingly enough she showed me round the rest of her flat. Neat, tidy, quite undisturbed. I asked her if she didn't think it odd that only one room showed signs of being turned over, and even more curious that not much had actually been taken. She said she hadn't thought of that. I asked her again whether the burglary story was genuine, and she became quite indignant.

'Would I have to do with the police otherwise?' she demanded. 'Saving your presence, Sergeant, you're not everybody's favourite people, you know.'

It didn't add to our popularity when I told her she could be charged with being an accessory to murder. But then I pacified her by saying at the moment I just proposed taking her back to the station with me to give a sworn statement about the murder. Did she need a solicitor, she asked me. Not half, I replied.

I didn't tell her I suspected the break-in was probably a put-on just to scare her. Let her think what she liked about that.

Chapter 9

Like I've said, my idea of a good start to the day is being brought breakfast in bed by some tasty feller and then maybe indulging in a little horizontal exercise with the bringer. Followed by a little snooze, a warm shower, and then I'm ready to start the day, without any of that unnecessary fanatical running and stuff.

Of course, all that's just a dream, and very far from what I'd been getting with Jim, my lorry driver and part-time bed-sharer. To call him a lover would be a bit over the top.

Anyway, I'd told him to push off, and the only regret he'd seemed to show was at losing the occasional free accommodation in Watford, being a convenient stopping place on his way to and from his home somewhere up North. He'd said as much when he'd pointed out he'd have to pay for a B & B if I chucked him.

So imagine how my jaw dropped when I got home that night and saw him on my doorstep holding A BUNCH OF FLOWERS! As far as I knew, until then Jim didn't know of the existence of anything as useless as flowers. And anyway, he still had the key, so what was he hanging around on the doorstep for? I hustled him inside, giving him a piece of my mind for showing my neighbours even more cause for gossip than they already had. Some of them had mentioned to me once or twice that things weren't the same as when I'd lived here with my Gran, and I didn't want any more of those snide remarks. I snatched the flowers out of his hand, trying not to laugh at the sight of him looking nothing like his usual rough self.

'Anyway, I thought I told you to bugger off,' I finally shouted. I could see he was trying to make up to me so as not to lose the convenience of his Watford B & B & B (bed, breakfast and bunk-up). 'Why don't you just give me back my key and shove off?'

Then the most amazing thing happened. As I put out my hand for the key, he knelt down in front of me, took my hand and kissed it! Before I could yell another word at him, he blurted out a whole long speech about how he really loved me and wanted to leave his wife and kids and marry me! Oh God. What a horrible shock.

While I was trying to adjust to this new side of Jim's character, that I'd never even guessed at, I was kind of shaking my head and pushing him away and generally giving off negative vibes. But I hadn't said a word. I'm hardly ever dumbstruck, but this was one of those times. He got the message, though.

'No please, Greta darling, don't say no,' he babbled on. 'I didn't realise I loved you until you told me to go. You know you love me really, it's just that you got fed up with playing second fiddle to Annie.'

Second fiddle! Annie! I hadn't even bothered to find out his wife's name. Never gave her a thought until that minute. And I certainly couldn't see myself playing second fiddle to someone with a name like that. I finally recovered the power of speech.

'No, Jim, stop it, get up off the floor, please,' I started. 'I don't love you, I didn't know your wife was called Annie, I don't care, I don't love you, will you PLEASE STOP KISSING MY ANKLES!' I realised I was screeching at him, and managed to lower my voice a bit. 'Jim, I told you to go because I'm fed up with you, YOU ARE A BORE,' I explained. 'Now please give me my key and go.'

Then he tried a bit of cave man kissing and stuff, but I

demonstrated how I'd got my Black Belt, so he quietly gave me my key and hobbled out.

And I'd been looking forward to a peaceful evening, trying to sort out my thoughts about Kate Dunkerley and her tall tales.

Instead of that, I fell to daydreaming about how different the scene that evening would have been if it had been the delectable Derek at my feet instead of past-his-sell-by-date Jim.

But anyway, even that was probably better than brooding over this frustratingly baffling case. I've always tried to practice the neat trick of shutting off my feelings in connection with my work, but I nearly lost it with Kate.

For those of us who work in the so-called 'helping' professions – doctors, nurses, social workers, police, fire-fighters – emotional disconnection is the only way to function in the face of death, misery and attempts at manipulation. I thought I'd developed this habit of detachment, but there was something touching and pathetic about Kate... Mental health enthusiasts try to tell us that our psychological well-being is best served by staying in touch with our feelings, but that can't be the case with the icky, unwelcome ones. I'd got all this from a book Derek had recommended I ought to read. Copied big chunks out of it, too (as above). Studying it didn't seem to do much for me, though.

The more I thought about Kate, the more uneasy I became. So the answer was to switch off and dream on about what I'd like to be doing with Derek. I put on some romantic music and relaxed.

When the phone rang, I thought I'd let the answering machine deal with it, because it was bound to be the new, soppy, nerdy Jim, having another try at winning my heart. Was I glad I changed my mind! It was Derek, asking me if I'd meet him for a drink. Would I, hell!

'No, I'd rather not go out again tonight,' I cooed at him sweetly. 'I've just opened a lovely bottle of Merlot. Why don't you come over here and share it with me?'

I held my breath. What I was suggesting was against all his principles. Meeting in a pub for a noggin, OK. But visiting a junior officer alone in her home? I think it was my knowing his favourite tipple that did it. Whoosh, he said yes!

I rushed around like a lunatic, changing into sexy satin lounging pyjamas, opening the bottle of Merlot and swigging a glass right off. I put out tempting nibbles in little dishes. By the time he rang the bell, I was just checking that my make-up was about right for a casual evening in – and I hadn't done half the things I'd thought of in a flash when he agreed to come. Even then, after all that tearing around, when I glanced in the mirror I saw I was still managing to look cool when I opened the door.

'Greta, I don't like to pry,' he started before he was properly inside the place. Pry! Do! I thought. What could be better, I thought. He's taking an interest at last, I cheered silently.

But he went on disappointingly, 'There seems to be a rather loutish-looking fellow hanging around, gazing at your front door. Do you know anything about him? Do you need protection?'

I reassured him that it was just Jim, an acquaintance who had tried to get fresh and who I'd had to throw out. I mentioned my Black Belt, and Derek was impressed.

'Hidden depths, eh,' he murmured as I handed him a glass of wine.

'I like to think so,' I answered, trying to look sexy and provocative and interesting.

He didn't seem to notice. There was a short silence. The music throbbed away, sexy and dreamy and romantic. He didn't seem to notice that, either.

There was nothing else for it, so I said, 'I'm glad you wanted to discuss the case away from the shop. We can talk about aspects of it that I'm uncomfortable discussing in front of Alfie.' No response, so I went on, 'I'm really baffled and confused about Kate Dunkerley. We know she's a liar and, even if she's not bent herself, she's certainly spent a lot of her life with that fraternity. And yet, when she tells me stuff about herself, I feel so – I don't know – I suppose I mean *involved.*'

Tersely, Derek answered, 'It's easy. Just don't believe anything she says unless it can be proved.'

'But why should she tell me that whopper about Curleigh, for example? What's that got to do with the murder of Len Gilmore?'

'What do you know about liars?'

What a silly question, I thought.

'As much as any police officer,' I answered. 'What do you mean?'

'Liars – truly dedicated ones – lie because they can, because they're good at it. They lie for the pure pleasure, because they love getting away with it. That's what Kate is like – if she can tell you some lie – even if it means nothing, even if the truth is easier, even if there's nothing to be gained – she can't resist.'

'You mean . . . she's a *pathological* liar?'

'I'm not sure what that means, exactly. What I'm saying is that she enjoys lying. She can't help herself.'

'I'm not sure I can believe that,' I said. 'I happen to think I'm a pretty good judge – as good as the next cop, anyway.'

Derek held his empty glass out towards me. As I filled it again for him, he said wearily, 'Please yourself. Would you mind turning that music off? I'm not keen on that pop stuff. I really only like good music. Anyway, I didn't come to talk shop.'

My heart gave such a loud bang that I nearly spilled the wine straight into his lap. Was he interested in me after all? Was my luck in at last?

The answer to both was no.

'I've got personal problems, Greta, and I've got no-one to talk to about them. Outside of work, I like to think we're friends. Am I right about that? Do we have a real friendship?'

While he was making this little speech, I was nodding away like a ventriloquist's dummy, with a similar wooden smile on my frozen face.

'Of course, Derek, I'm glad that's how you see me,' I told him insincerely. 'How can I help? Have some crisps. Have you had anything to eat this evening? Would you like an omelet? Is there any other music you'd like to listen to?'

He shook his head. Obviously, it wasn't this sort of comfort he was wanting, and incidentally it also wasn't the sort I was busting to give him. What then?

Oh, the dreariness. He started burbling away about this bloody woman he'd been living with, Erica the high-powered City whiz-kid, with her lovely home in Highgate, and how it was all falling apart and he didn't know what to do, etc. etc. Well, it didn't make me fancy him any less, but it certainly didn't add to my opinion of his brainpower. But I perked up and started to take an interest when it became clear that his real problem wasn't sex or emotion. He had all that sorted. What he wanted was my advice about the practical issue of where he should live. If I didn't know better by this time, I'd have hoped he might have been hinting about moving in with me! More likely he was just taking Kate's suggestion seriously about renting the empty flat in Robin Hood House. Turned out that was a good guess.

'And by the way, Greta, have you got any opera amongst your CDs?'

I admitted I hadn't, but he didn't seem too disappointed, just nodded and went on with his sad tale. All this time, he'd been slurping away at the wine in an absent-minded way, and I'd been not too obviously pouring refills for him. I needn't have bothered to be sneaky about it, though, because he was so taken up with his troubles he didn't even notice when I opened another bottle with a loud pop.

'You see, Greta, before we found out so much more about the Gilmore case, Kate Dunkerley mentioned that one of the flats in their little block had been empty ever since they'd lived there, and she shuggested I might rent that. But I've got a feeling that Mr Moon might take an ant-antag–' he stumbled, and started again. 'Might not like me to do that, in view of all the complashuns about the case, with the Winkelhorne, and so on. What's your pinion, Greta?'

In the meantime, during his droning on about his aborted sex life, he had quaffed most of the first bottle and nearly all of the second one I'd opened. I noticed he had trouble with one or two words. Probably he wasn't used to more than a glass or two. Or maybe he was just very tired. Also I was pretty sure that normally he wouldn't have dreamed of asking me, a mere sergeant, my opinion of what Mr Moon would think.

Now his eyelids were drooping and his speech was getting less and less clear. I wasn't at all sure how I felt about this. I'd only had a glass and a half myself. Did I really want us to have an all-guys-together friendship based on getting pissed together? Especially as we seemed to have such different taste in music. I mean, what did we actually have in common?

'Well, Derek,' I found I was shouting a bit to get his attention, 'the main question is, how urgent is all this? I mean, have you got to get out this week, tonight, tomorrow, when?'

Too late.

He was fast asleep.

Chapter 10

Next morning, I could see Derek was nervous and on edge. Although I'd made up my mind not to say anything about the previous night, I couldn't help asking, 'You OK, Guv? I think you're looking a bit peaky.'

I was hoping he might say something about our evening together, but nothing like that. It was as if he'd managed to forget it.

He bared his teeth at me. It could have been a grin. Or a snarl. But he didn't say anything, so I thought I might as well go and have another entertaining chat with Kate Dunkerley. Against my better judgement, I was beginning to have a soft spot for that girl. Goodness knows why. I should have seen her at best as a pain in the neck or at worst a murder suspect. But maybe it was because I thought she was a bit barmy, and also I was beginning to think she didn't look so much like competition in the Derek department any more. Anyway, whatever the reason, she seemed to be getting to me.

On my way to her cell, I was thinking about this Goldfeather geezer. Because the name sounded like someone from a Bond movie, it was difficult to believe it was real. But then, didn't that mean that it must be, because why would anybody make up such a fictional-sounding name? What with one confusion and another, I was actually humming the theme from 'Goldfinger' when the duty sarge let me into Kate's cell. I was either light-hearted or light-headed by that time.

'Oh Greta, I'm so glad to see you,' Kate said. 'If I don't

talk to someone, I'll go mad. I've got to tell you everything from the beginning.'

'About the murder?'

'No, about my life.'

That was all I needed just then, to sit and listen to a pack of lies about some tart's life.

She'd changed again. The sharply dressed sexy cookie had gone, in the same way as the drab middle-aged woman I had first met had dissolved into someone else. She had transformed herself into a wide-eyed, soft trembling little girl. It was some trick this woman could perform. I'd love to know how she did it. Sure, make-up and hair made a difference. But this was something she did *from inside* to somehow make herself appear to be another character. And this time she was just a kid.

After only a couple of minutes with her, I was having trouble remembering what she'd looked like before, and what she'd done, and what I'd thought of her. I'm a tough police sergeant, I kept reminding myself, and I'm talking to a criminal, and probably even a half-mad one. But it didn't quite work. I could feel myself softening towards her, against all my better judgement.

And it all happened while we were exchanging those first few words, even though I'd been thinking to myself that I was going to hear a version of a high-class whore's life story.

'I've kept all this to myself too long, Greta. I've got to tell someone. Will you let me tell you? Please. You're the first kind person I've met for such a long time–'

I wasn't too completely melted to interrupt, '–I thought you said Len Gilmore was kind to you?'

'Oh yes, but he wasn't the sort of person who understood these things. I can tell you all about what happened when I was little,' she said, looking unbelievably frail and vulnerable. 'Maybe we had the same sort of mother…'

Even while a part of my mind was going, 'How the hell does she *do* that?' I still felt an urge to pat her cheek and give her a lollipop.

I heard myself saying in a really soppy voice, 'What happened to you when you were little, Kate?'

Her mother had been on the game (no surprises there) and of course she didn't know who had been the fathers of her two children, Duncan and Kate. She didn't care much for either of the children. So from Kate's first recollection of life, it had been Duncan – she called him Dunkie – who had fed her, cared for her, protected her. He was only seven years older than she was, but he was better than two parents to her. They slept together and he kept her warm, and if she woke up in the night, frightened at noises coming from the next room, where their mother was, Dunkie was always there to soothe her back to sleep.

He taught her to read when she was three, and writing and sums at four. When she was nearly five, and looking forward to going to school, their mother got a new boyfriend, Bobby. Dunkie knew him from school, although he wasn't there very much and was a bit older than Dunkie, anyway.

'I didn't know about toyboys then, but I s'pose that's what he was. He must have been about seventeen or eighteen, I think. Bobby liked me a lot,' Kate said in this new little-girl voice of hers, 'and when Dunkie was at school sometimes, Bobby'd take me into bed with him and Mummy and we'd have games together. Well of course I know a lot more about those games now, but I was only a little kid then, and I didn't know there was anything wrong. Anyway, Mummy wouldn't hurt me, and Bobby seemed alright because he was the same colour as Dunkie.'

I'd been listening quietly until then, but I couldn't stand much more of this. I had to interrupt.

'What do you mean? What colour? What colour was

79

your mother? What *is* all this about colour?'

Kate blushed. Another trick in her bag of games. How do you blush to order? Wish I could do that, I jotted down in a separate part of my head, although still taken up with her story. Also, I was beginning to get an idea of where we were going with this. The detective in me wasn't completely off on holiday.

'Mummy was white and blonde, like me, and I suppose my father was too,' Kate said, 'but Dunkie's dad must have been black, and he and Bobby were both a sort of dark brownish colour. Anyway, one night in bed I started playing one of Bobby's games with Dunkie. And he shoved me away and said what did I think I was doing, so I told him it was just a game I'd learned from Bobby when I'd been in bed with him and Mummy. Dunkie let out a sort of a roar and jumped out of bed and rushed into the kitchen where Mummy and Bobby were laughing and talking. So I pulled the covers over my head and stayed where I was for a long time, because I could hear them all shouting and screaming. Then it went quiet and I waited for ages for Dunkie to come back to bed. But he didn't so I went to look for him. Mummy was on the floor with a lot of blood coming out and Bobby was on the floor asleep and Dunkie was putting Mummy's sharp scissors in Bobby's hand. He looked round at me and told me in a funny voice that I hadn't seen anything and I was to go back to bed and wait. After a long time a lot of strangers came and took me away and I never saw Dunkie again. Then I got fostered.'

'Is Kate Dunkerley your real name?' I asked weakly. I was exhausted from just listening to this terrible story. If it was true, it explained a lot. If it wasn't, she should have taken up writing fiction instead of... whatever it was that she really did.

'Yes, my mother's name was Catherine Dunkerley, but she just called me Kate. It's not short for anything. She wasn't very clever about names – well, I suppose she wasn't clever about anything – so she called my brother Duncan Dunkerley.'

She was quiet for a bit, then she added, 'And I suppose he just took the end of it, Kerley, and called himself Curleigh. I told you he was my brother, didn't I?'

It was too much. She couldn't really expect me to believe that. I might have swallowed the rest, but not that.

'And when exactly did you come to the conclusion that Curleigh was your brother? If you thought you had a rich and famous brother, why didn't you contact him?' I asked.

She looked at the ceiling, the walls, anywhere to avoid my eye.

'Well, see, I did tell Len *some* of what happened when I was little,' she finally admitted. 'I told him on the boat when we were on our way from New York, and I asked him to help me find my brother. And he said I should leave it with him, and he'd find out about him for me. Then after a while he told me that Dunkie had become the famous Curleigh. I could hardly believe it. I knew Dunkie was clever, but for him to have become such a celebrity was just marvellous. But Len said he didn't think I should try to get in touch with Dunkie, because if he'd wanted to find me, he could have done it easily himself, any time he liked. So I had to believe him when he said most likely Dunkie didn't want to know me any more,' she finished with one of her believable sobs.

I had a million more questions I wanted to ask her. About who fostered her and what they were like. About whether, when she was a child, she had ever told anyone about Bobby and his games. What happened to her mother and Bobby and Dunkie? And most of all, why did she believe what Len Gilmore had told her, about why her brother had never found her again, if he had been so devoted to her. It was a moving story – if true – but it had too many loopholes. It was sort of open-ended. Like, fill in your own missing bits. I was not going to be sidetracked by this intriguing puzzle. It had nothing to do with our case.

Instead of taking up her sad tale, I asked her, in my most sergeant-like voice, 'Tell me again about the night Len was killed.'

I knew it was brutal and abrupt. But it's my job. I'm not her big sister, or even her friend. Her tragic life was not my business. I'm police, and I had a case to solve. Her wide violet eyes were wet and reproachful, but she answered me readily enough.

'Seeing what those two men did to Len was horrible, sickening. But somehow it all turned around in my head, and I got angry. Why should I have got angry with him? That's how I should have been feeling towards those two brutes, and that girl. But I wanted to say to him, "Look what you've gone and got yourself into now, Len Gilmore, you cock-led fool!" I always knew he'd get himself into some sort of trouble because of how he was about women, but I never dreamed it would be something that bad.'

She had gone pale and her voice and manner had returned to the real grown-up Kate Dunkerley. The little girl, telling about Mummy and Dunkie and Bobby, had disappeared. I was fascinated. She was really re-living what had happened to Len Gilmore, and telling it more fully than she had in any statements so far. I was almost afraid to breathe in case I stopped her recollection of the murder. She went on, but her voice was getting dreamy, almost as if she was hypnotised.

'I paced up and down for a while, sobbing and swearing and trembling,' she said, in this strange sing-song voice. 'I was afraid at first, but after a while I got more and more furious with him for getting himself in such a mess. In the end I ran down to his flat and I stood and shouted at his poor bashed-up face. But that didn't make me feel any different. So I went into the kitchen and got the knife and, and-'

For the first time, she faltered. Then she went on '-and you know what I did then. What you don't know is that afterwards I went back upstairs and I was so sick, I thought I'd never stop. And I cried and I was sick, and I went through the whole thing over and over. In the end I had to take some Valium before I could phone you in the morning. Then I don't know why I did all that acting a part and telling lies and everything. I think I must have gone a bit crazy.'

She cried a little then. Not like someone putting on an act. Didn't make a performance. No loud boohoo-ing. Just quietly sobbed, in a tired kind of way, then blew her nose and mopped her face. But she kept her eyes down, as if she couldn't look at me any more.

I couldn't help it. It was against all my training, my self-discipline, my toughness. I went and put my arms round her. For some reason, I was more touched by this than by her sad tale of her early years. Maybe because I believed what she had just told me about her reaction to Len's death, but I couldn't quite swallow the story of her childhood. Anyway, neither of us made a big production out of it. I just gave her a little hug, and walked out of the room. Tell the truth, I was near tears myself. Poor little bugger, I was thinking. What a life. No wonder she seems a bit barmy. Specially if the early bit is true.

So it was quite a shock when I went into the Incident Room with the others, and we heard some more about her from Derek. It seems that, although all the different States of America are legally autonomous, there is a centralised bureau in Washington called the National Crime Information Center. And from that, our new American friend, the so-called Simon Goldfeather, had obtained a great deal of stuff about Kate Dunkerley and Len Gilmore, which he had kindly passed on to us.

Of course, Goldfeather and Derek were most interested in what Gilmore had been up to. But what knocked me back was about Kate. She had been living in a luxury Manhattan apartment as the 'guest' of a character called Jack Roc, who was well known to the New York police and to the FBI. But just when they were pretty sure they had built up a good enough case to arrest him, Kate had called the police to tell them she'd found him murdered – shot to pieces with more bullet-holes than a colander. They suspected she was implicated in some way. Not necessarily as the actual murderer, but maybe she'd helped to set it up. It was clearly a professional job. No surprise to hear they couldn't find any evidence against her, so she was never accused of anything.

But she was in danger from Roc's family, who would surely have taken revenge against her if they thought she was involved in his murder.

At this crucial point in her life, an acquaintance of Roc's, called Len Gilmore, took her under his wing, and shortly after that, they'd left together for England. After a while, Goldfeather had followed.

'I've talked it all over with Mr Moon,' Derek added, 'and he's given me the benefit of his opinion. What he thinks is, for acquaintance you can read business associate. Whatever this fellow Roc was into, it's pretty certain that Mr Leonard Gilmore was involved in at least some of the same. And our little Kate Dunkerley must know a lot more about it all than she's told us so far. So we've got to keep pressing her.'

Blimey, I thought, what would Mr Moon say if he'd seen me giving the highly suspicious Kate Dunkerley a sisterly hug a few minutes ago!

Chapter 11

When my phone rang at five the next morning, my first blurred thought was that it was that bloody Jim again, pestering me for some more B & B & B. When I heard Derek's voice, I perked up a bit, until I started to take in what he was saying.

An emergency? Duty sergeant had phoned him *and* *Superintendent Moon?* Mr Moon was livid and wanted us all there immediately!?! Oh God. What could have happened now. With a passing thought about those glowing fictional women detectives enjoying their long healthy runs at this insane hour every morning, I dragged myself reluctantly out of my nice warm bed and got going.

Somehow Derek had managed to find time to have a shave – for all I knew, he got up regularly at five every morning – so he was his usual immaculate self. I tried not to dwell on what Derek's intimate habits might be. Alfie, of course, never shaved, but his beard was neatly trimmed. His wife saw to that.

But our Superintendent Moon was not only unshaven and wearing an old tracksuit, he was such a dark puce colour from rage, I thought he'd have a stroke any minute. When I got there, Derek and Alfie were sitting side by side like naughty schoolboys, the Duty Sergeant was lurking by the door, and Mr Moon was thumping up and down his office with steam coming out of his arse.

'Hanged himself! Bloody hanged himself!' he bawled. 'Can anyone tell me how you lock a man into a police cell without either his belt or his shoe laces, and he bloody manages to hang himself!'

It wasn't really a question, but the Duty Sergeant answered anyway. Theoretically, it was all his fault, so he was already in the shit. Derek and Alfie both looked as if they'd decided they'd never speak again. Jaws clamped shut, and everybody avoiding everybody else's eye.

'He done it with his shirt, sir–'

'With his shirt? With his shirt!!' Suddenly all the fire seemed to go out of Mr Moon, his colour started to go back to normal, and he lowered himself heavily into his chair. Then he muttered quietly, broodingly, to himself, 'With his shirt, eh. Yes, I see. With his shirt.'

There was a silence. I wondered if it was really Garcia they were talking about, or some completely different prisoner who had nothing to do with our murder case. So far nobody had told me anything, and I didn't like to ask. I thought I'd just wait quietly for something to come out. After all, I had all day.

Finally, Mr Moon spoke again. All his anger seemed to have evaporated.

'Alright, Sergeant, I'm listening. Explain to me how this man, Garcia, managed to hang himself with his shirt,' he muttered hoarsely.

So it *was* Garcia. Did the Superintendent know about the way Alfie and I had interviewed him? It was obvious to me that we'd gone too far and frightened the poor little bugger into more desperate action than the situation called for. That was the trouble with foreigners, they just didn't understand our ways. Or our sense of humour.

The Duty Sergeant cleared his throat and gabbled off his report so fast that it sounded like one long word. He didn't glance at his notebook, so he obviously had it all off by heart.

'The man Garcia took off his shirt and climbed on to the edge of his lavatory pan. Then he managed somehow to tie one sleeve to the bars of the cell window. Then he tied the end of the other sleeve round his neck, and jumped off the lavatory pan. Unfortunately, the seams of the shirt gave way, and he fell into the lavatory and broke his ankle–'

'What! You mean he didn't hang himself!' Mr Moon exclaimed in relief. Obviously this was the first time he'd heard the complete story. He looked as if he was going to get up and kiss the Sarge. You wouldn't believe a man could be so delighted to hear that someone had broken his ankle.

I could see Derek and Alfie relaxing a little too. We were all thanking our lucky stars that Garcia was still alive, whatever bit of him was broken.

'Soon as we heard the noise,' the Sarge continued doggedly, 'we went in and found the prisoner in an injured condition. He was then transported immediate to A & E at Watford General, where the ankle was X-rayed and set in plaster. As the prisoner was in a highly emotional state, it was decided to keep him there under observation for twenty-four hours.'

'Who's there with him now?'

'Well, in view of his inability to walk, I deemed it unnecessary to post a guard–'

'Oh, you did so deem it, did you?' yelled Mr Moon, suddenly returning to full shout. 'Do me a favour, Sergeant, don't do any more deeming while you're working in my station, right? Go on, clear off, I don't want to hear any more from you.'

He picked up his phone as the relieved Duty Sergeant scuttled off. By the time he put the phone down again, I was wishing I'd been able to scarper too. Judging from their expressions, Derek and Alfie had the same sort of feelings. Superintendent Moon's face and neck had gone that dangerous dark colour again.

'Discharged himself,' he muttered hoarsely. 'On crutches.' Actually, it was more of a groan. 'Probably a key witness,' he went on. 'I suppose you've still got that woman, the victim's lover?'

'Yes, sir,' said Derek smartly, 'and I'm sure she is more crucial to the case than Garcia. I think he's just a glorified messenger boy, and I'm convinced he wasn't involved with the murder, whatever other skulduggery he was up to–'

Alfie suddenly came to life.

'Skulduggery!' he burst out. 'That's a real smashing word, Guv! Skul...dug...ger...'

His voice faded away as he saw how we were all glaring at him.

Derek didn't exactly snarl at him, but he sort of spoke through his teeth in a very gritty voice. 'Sergeant Partridge, will you please go to the lodgings in Hendon where you first found Garcia, and see if he's returned there, or if not, what else his landlady can tell you about him. And Sergeant, do I need to tell you, if he *is* there, please bring him back here, crutches or no crutches. Is that clear, Sergeant? Right, will you do that now?'

Standing as if to go, but not actually leaving the room, Alfie made some mumbling reply, of which the only word I could make out was 'breakfast'.

'No, Sergeant,' said Mr Moon wearily, 'none of us have had breakfast this morning. But Detective Inspector Michaelson is asking you to go now, not after breakfast. So I suggest you do that, NOW!'

Alfie left without another word or even one of his appealing looks at me. I was still scared what was going to happen to me if it came out how I'd treated Garcia, the lies and threats I'd used on him.

And if Derek and Mr Moon didn't know about it now, when we got Garcia back, would he tell why he got in such a state that he tried to do himself in? Was I in deep shit, or what?

All that happened was that Mr Moon said we could go.

It was hard to tell where we stood with him. In the three years since he'd come to run our cop-shop, we'd never had a case as baffling and complicated as this, so he was a bit of an unknown quantity for us all. It was different for Derek. He'd joined us at Watford at the same time as Mr Moon. So he hadn't known our old Superintendent, who hardly took any notice of anything that was going on, and just let us get on with things in our own way while he ran his own separate interests. But that was a different story.

All we knew about Mr Moon was that he was a little fat fellow with a reputation for being fair but irritable. And that he'd replaced our old Super after copping him for running a scam of his own. Well, we'd seen some of his temper this morning, and pretty scary it had been, too. I still wasn't sure if I was in for some heavy disciplinary stuff or what.

To add to my worries, just as we were leaving his office, Mr Moon called Derek back. I hung around outside the door until Derek came out with no expression.

He and I went off to the Incident Room for the day's briefing, and then on to the canteen for breakfast. That was a bit of compensation for a rotten start to the day. Having breakfast with Derek was as intimate as I expected us to get – this week, anyway. We were definitely getting closer, what with him telling me about his personal life, asking my advice, falling asleep on my couch, and now, having breakfast together.

'What did Mr Moon call you back for, Guv? Was he still in a temper?'

'Nothing for you to be concerned about, Greta. He wanted to know whether anyone had checked up on that little boy.'

'What little boy? Oh, that one. Mr Moon seems to worry about him a lot. He asked about him before, didn't he.'

'Yes, he has to worry about police liability as well as a

heavy case-load and all the cock-ups, without big sixteen-stone sergeants jumping on kids.'

Derek sounded quite fed up, as if he was the one with the burden, and not Mr Moon.

'I know,' I said, trying to sound sympathetic. 'So did you tell him that Alfie had been to see the kid and his parents after he'd been discharged from the hospital? He was only a bit bruised and shocked. So would you be if Alfie had chucked himself on you. Some people would say just the sight of Alfie is enough of a shock, without him landing on top of you.'

That lightened the mood a bit. Derek actually laughed, and said that should teach the kid not to cycle on the pavement, at least not going round corners at high speed.

I took the opportunity to ask him if he'd decided what to do about moving.

This time he laughed in a different kind of way. At least, I thought it was a laugh. A bit more of a painful grunt.

'I'd made up my mind to broach the subject with Mr Moon this very day. I thought I'd ask him outright if there was any reason why I shouldn't rent a flat in that little block where the murder took place. I'd got it all worked out, how I could put it to him that it might even help the case if I was living on the spot. Then all this happened, this farce with Garcia and the shirt, and of course he's in no mood to be approached about anything. I've never seen the old boy so furious. Lucky for me he'd calmed down by the time he asked about the kid. He likes children, you know. He's got five of his own.'

Then his expression changed. I could see he'd just had another thought.

'Why do you think Garcia felt so desperate?' he went on. 'Do you think he thought he was in more trouble than he was? Or – Greta – you didn't – did you put the frighteners on him? What did you say to the poor little devil? You didn't threaten him, did you?'

'Well, er, I did sort of hint to him that he wasn't quite in the clear about the murder.' I paused. 'And I might have somehow led him to believe that we still have the death penalty. He certainly seemed quite nervous at the end of the interview.'

'Where's the tape?'

I thought now wasn't the time to remind him he'd told us that we need not tape the interview.

'Well, we didn't exactly tape it...'

'Notes?'

'Er, no.'

'Oh, Greta, what am I going to do with you!' he exclaimed.

I thought: I know what I'd like you to do with me.

You look even more sexy when you're worried.

Chapter 12

Alfie said, 'Here, Greta, my Betty's been on at me again. She's been telling me for weeks now to bring you back with me for a spot of supper and a chat.'

'Oh that's nice, Alfie. Why didn't you say before?'

I was fond of Betty, a motherly type and a fabulous cook, who was the nearest I had to family since my Gran had died. She'd told me lots of times not to wait for an invitation. But I didn't like to just barge in, and anyway she had her hands full, what with their twins Neil and Carole, a strange couple of kids, and Alfie sometimes acting like an overgrown teenager himself. Also Carole had a dog, Freda, and Neil had a cat called Muriel, and they were both getting on a bit, so Betty had to look after them too.

'Come this evening then, you know Betty doesn't need warning, there's always plenty of grub. Plateful of one of her pies'll do you the world of good.'

On the way to his place, Alfie said to me, 'I was looking at myself in the full-length mirror after my bath this morning, and I was thinking, I'm still a fine figure of a man. No pot belly or bulges, just a few silver hairs in my beard. And I've still got the full head of ginger hair same as I had when I joined the Army as a boy all those years ago. Not even faded.'

Keeping a straight face, I said, 'Yes, Alfie, it's true, you're pretty good for a man of – what is it, forty-five? But what's this all about?'

I had an idea what it was about, but decided to wait to hear it from him. Seemingly I was wrong anyway.

'Well,' Alfie rumbled, crashing his gears as usual (how did a man get to his age and still be such a rotten driver?), 'see, this morning my Betty said to me that my trousers had got a bit tight round the waist-band. Well, maybe I've got a bit thicker in that part, specially when I don't remember to hold it in. But she says she thinks she'd better stop making so many pies. And her the best pastry-maker in the country, too. I mean, that's a rotten thing to say to a man you've been married to for twenty-seven years, isn't it, girl?'

I was so relieved that he wasn't harping on about his physical attractions because of anything to do with a certain sexpot landlady in Hendon, that I was ready to feed his vanity as much as he'd like.

'What! You certainly don't look old enough to have been married that long, Alfie. You seem like the perfect couple to me.'

'Yerss, we knew each other all our lives even before we'd been sweethearts, grew up together, really. Everyone said we were too young to get married when I first joined the army, but we've proved them wrong. Twenty-seven years, eh! That's like a miracle these days, with people not sticking together for as many months, and most of them not bothering to get married at all.'

Good thing he didn't know anything about my sex life, I thought. But we'd arrived by then, so after his usual hair-raising few attempts to get the car into the garage, we went in to Betty's warm welcome. But it didn't turn out a very happy evening, what with one thing and another. It started with Betty telling me that Carole had moved out, but was kindly visiting that evening. She sounded as bitter as such a sweet-natured woman could. I soon realised why. There was a bad atmosphere in what had been a warm, comfortable, happy home.

Carole didn't even look up when we went in. That was

unusual for a start. She and I usually got on quite well together.

Neil said, 'Oh hallo, Greta,' and while the wheezy old dog and the bad-tempered cat were both giving me a good eyeballing (we've never really been friends), he shouted at his father, 'Dad! What's that you're wearing?'

Admittedly Alfie's idea of smart dressing is not everybody's, but most of us tactfully don't mention that he never seemed to get the hang of civvies since he came out of uniform. Alfie didn't take to Neil's criticism.

'You think you know it all, don't you, my boy!' he bellowed at his son. 'Just because you're a middle-grade admin officer in the Min of Ag and Fish, you think you're the last word on fashion.'

'Dad, I've told you, it's not called the Min of Ag and Fish any more.'

They went on this way for a while, but Carole still didn't look up. Betty beckoned to me from the kitchen, and I was glad to join her. She gave me a hug.

'Can I give you a hand?' I asked, knowing that she never let me lift a finger. She plomped me down at the kitchen table and put a cup of tea in front of me.

'This'll keep you going till supper's ready,' she said. 'It'll be another half hour. And you don't want to listen to them two going on at each other as usual. Did you notice our Carole? I can't get a word out of her. I don't know what's the matter. Anyway, tell me all your news – no shop, mind, I don't want to know about no murders and that. I always tell Alfie, "leave that behind when you come home." '

I shook my head. 'No news, Betty. Not the sort you want to hear.'

We both knew she thought I ought to get married, and couldn't understand why I didn't have packs of boyfriends clamouring for my favours. Naturally, I wouldn't let on to her about Jim the Long-Distance Lorry Driver. That would only upset her. But I suddenly got the urge to tell her a bit about myself. Then maybe she'd understand why I wasn't as keen on love and marriage as she thought I should be. Perhaps listening to Kate Dunkerley's story of her early years made me want to talk about my own, for once.

'See, Betty,' I suddenly burst out, 'I never knew my mother. She was only fourteen when she had me, and she died in the street two years later. Drug overdose. She didn't know who my father was, so no chance for me to know either. My Gran brought me up.'

I don't know why I'd expected disapproval from Betty, of all people. She was so kind and understanding.

All she said was, 'You poor kid. No wonder you're always trying to be one of the lads. I know you lost your Gran a few years ago, you told me about her. But you never told me about your Granpa.'

I was already regretting opening my big mouth, even to Betty. I knew I didn't need to ask her not to tell Alfie, that wasn't the trouble. I just didn't want to talk about my history at all.

So I was a bit short. I just said, 'He was a Sergeant at Shady Lane. Died of heart attack on duty before I was born. Gran said it was a mercy he never saw what happened to his daughter.'

Already regretting getting into this, I changed the subject with, 'Is supper ready yet? Shall I start taking the plates in?'

We all set to with hearty appetites, except Carole, who was still sitting with her head down, not paying attention to anyone, pushing her food around her plate. Freda and Muriel were sitting close to her, looking at her hopefully, but she didn't even seem to notice them, which was unusual.

'What's up with you then, girl?' Alfie asked Carole. 'You done us a favour coming to see us, but there's not much point you visiting your old mum and dad if you're going to sit there like a dummy. And you haven't even said hallo to Greta yet.'

Betty was making shushing noises at him, but of course he took no notice, but just went on, as if he couldn't see he was making things worse.

'You could at least give me a hallo, even if you can't spare a smile,' he tried, but still got no answer.

'You want me to tell them then, Caro?' Neil asked.

'I wish you wouldn't call her that,' Alfie growled. 'How much trouble could it be to add the L on the end of her name? But you two have always made your own rules, that's the trouble. It's even worse when she calls you Nelly.'

I kept quiet, but I hoped Betty didn't know what a Nelly was.

'You two are a mystery to me,' Alfie bored on. 'How can two big healthy people like me and your mother have got ourselves a couple of weedy skinny kids like you? I'd have thought our children would be more like Greta here, a fine sturdy figure of a girl, like an athlete, she is. Lovely long legs. I dunno. It makes you wonder.'

By this time I was sorry I'd taken up Betty's standing invitation, however much I appreciated her warm welcome and lovely food. Anyway, Carole shook her head at her brother, sighed, and said, 'I'll talk for myself this time, thank you.'

'Well!' Alfie said. 'She spoke! Here, if you're not going to eat your pie and mash, pass it over. I can always find room for a bit more of your mother's cooking.'

This led to another argument through Neil criticising Alfie's waistline, and suggesting it would be better to give Carole's leavings to Freda and Muriel. Alfie, nettled at this reference to a touchy subject, said that if he was as skinny as Neil, he'd either shoot himself or try to build up a bit of muscle. One or the other. Wouldn't hurt him to go down the gym some time, he said. He appealed to me, but I refused to join in.

'Course it's a waste of breath telling you anything,' Alfie wound up.

By the time they'd finished going on at each other, Betty had gone into the kitchen to get the pudding, and Carole had followed her.

So whatever Carole's news was, we could all tell it was bad, because whatever she said made Betty drop the pudding with a loud sploshy crash. She was upset, and Alfie was too, though he didn't even know what the trouble was. All he knew was that he'd lost his favourite pudding, chocolate sponge.

Still, it made the evening probably one of the happiest Freda and Muriel had had in their whole lives. Obviously chocolate sponge was a popular choice for them too, as they licked it all up from the floor. I hoped it wasn't going to make them both sick, to add to Betty's troubles, whatever they were.

Carole and Neil left together right after that. Just called out, 'We're off now!' and marched out. I stood up to go, keen to get away from whatever domestic trouble was taking place, but Betty asked me so sincerely to stay a while that I couldn't refuse.

'Come on, girl, cough it up, it can't be that bad,' Alfie said. 'Tell us what Carole told you in the kitchen that made you drop the pudding. You can talk in front of Greta, she's practically one of the family anyway.'

Betty shook her head, sighed, mopped her eyes and looked at me for support. I'd have given it gladly if only I knew what was going on.

'Don't tell me she's pregnant,' Alfie pressed on. 'We don't even know if she's got a boyfriend. Since she moved herself off to Camden Town, we hardly ever see her–'

'Pregnant!' Betty said. 'I wish she was! No chance there! She's gone and turned into a lesbeen!'

Alfie's jaw dropped.

'A lesbian! Go on! Since when? Maybe it's just some idea she's got through mixing with that Camden Town crowd. Or has she gone and got herself a girlfriend? If she's got someone, p'raps it'll give Neil some ideas. I can't make that boy out at all, he doesn't even seem to like girls – or even boys. You can't help wondering what sort of children we've got ourselves.'

He laughed, but I could see his heart wasn't in it. And Betty seemed seriously upset. I tried to think of something to say that might make her feel a little better, though I knew that to someone like her it must seem like the end of the world to have a lesbian daughter. But Alfie wouldn't give up or shut up.

'There's worse things, girl,' he argued. 'She could have gone on the game, or taken drugs, or been a lap dancer.'

'It's not funny, Alfie, you might show a bit of feeling about a serious thing like this. Anyone would think you don't care if your daughter's one of them nor if your son was one of them gays as well.'

'Well, I'd rather he was one of them than one of nothing...'

I really couldn't stand any more of this. I gave Betty a big hug and a kiss and thanked her for the lovely supper and for being such a good, kind, understanding friend. I hoped that this might give her the hint to be a bit more broad-minded about her own daughter. But I didn't think so.

Next morning, it was as plain as his big fat nose that Alfie wasn't feeling on top of the world. He mumbled a bit to me about Betty thinking they had a tragedy on their hands, and that she wouldn't even let him give her a kiss and a cuddle to make her feel better.

'She's usually fond of it as a rule, and I said to her, "there's no sense in fretting if it's going to put you off normal married life." But she didn't want to know, so what with one thing and another, I didn't get my full night's shut-eye, and I feel really done in.'

I muttered something sympathetic, but luckily there was no time for more, because Alfie was called on to give an account of his visit to Hendon. This cheered him up a bit. He likes being centre stage.

'I'm pleased to report that I found Garcia back at his old lodgings and he came back here with me, no trouble. Mind you, I couldn't help wondering what kind of crooks had employed someone so lacking in brainpower as that little feller. You'd think that in the whole of South America they could have found a runner with a bit more in the top storey.'

'How do you mean, Alfie?' Fred Archer called out.

'Werl, just for example, he keeps going back to that place in Hendon like a homing pigeon, so it's always dead easy to find him every time he shoots off. But while I had him in hand, as you might say, I took the opportunity to tell him there was no danger of us hanging him, so there's no need for him to try to save us the trouble. He looked as if he understood, but I dunno, you can never tell with these foreign types.'

'OK, Alfie, let's leave that,' Derek said, a bit sharpish. I soon found out what was up with him.

'A body's been found in the canal down in Rickmansworth,' he went on. 'Of course, strictly speaking that's none of our business, but we'd notified them of our search for the missing Mrs Winkelhorne. I've already been there and identified the body, and it turns out that it was our missing person. However, he **was** a man, and not a *Mrs* Winkelhorne at all.'

'Just a minute, Guv,' Alfie interrupted. 'Far as I remember, you never met Mrs Winkelhorne. So how do you know the body in the canal is anything to do with our case at all?'

'It was clear enough.' Derek was at his most Inspectorish. 'But of course we'll get a more formal identification.'

I thought it was time to separate these two sparring partners.

'So is this another murder, then, Guv?' I asked. 'Do you think Mr Moon will want to call in the Yard now?'

Derek transferred his glassy look from Alfie to me.

'We haven't heard the cause of death from Path yet. But whatever they tell us, I doubt if Mr Moon will want to call for help from the Yard. He's very keen on us dealing with this case ourselves. And we need to sort out the truth about who this character really was and what he was doing passing himself off as an elderly widow. He had you fooled, didn't he?' he added to Alfie, who I had to give a kick to get him to hold his tongue this time.

Betty had told me that she'd been advising Alfie lately to keep quiet more often, specially since he'd been complaining to her that his little Inspector had been getting a bit sarky with him.

'Anyway, Greta,' Derek went on, 'I want you to get that Irish girl's formal statement, and then take her to the safe place in Hemel Hempstead today. She'll probably kick up a fuss, but you'll have to convince her it's for her own safety. Tell her the alternative is being charged with being an accessory to murder. It's fairly certain that her apparent burglary was a warning to keep her mouth shut, so it's up to us to protect her. You'd have thought it might have dawned on her there was probably a connection between her seeing those two heavies bashing Len Gilmore's head in, and her having a break-in the next day, with only one room turned over, and just her video taken.'

'What about Kate Dunkerley?' I asked in a loud voice to cover up Alfie's muttering about silly women.

'Well,' Derek said, 'the good news is that Mr Moon has reviewed the case, and he can see we're undermanned, so he's assigned DCs Fred Archer and Kevin Burton here to join our team. I've decided to let Kate go, and have them follow her, to see where that gets us. If it doesn't help, I'll see if I can get a warrant to search her flat.'

Let Kate go! Alfie gave whistle and I let out a sort of 'Ow'. Then we looked at each other and at Fred and Kevin. It was true we could do with more troops to help us out, and very likely Fred and Kev were better than nobody. And at least nothing more had been said about Garcia's suicide attempt. I couldn't guess what Mr Moon might have said in private to Derek about that. And I didn't want to.

All I could hope was that I wasn't in any trouble about it and any possible connection with our unrecorded interview with him. What if Mr Moon found out about me lying to Garcia and threatening him with the death penalty? Then I'd be in the warm and nasty, no mistake.

Chapter 13

I was well choked with myself. And it didn't help that Derek was being kind about it, either. If I was any kind of detective I should have made sure of Christine Smith without having to be told. And now she'd disappeared, and it was my fault. At least a key witness, if not an accessory, and I'd let her get away.

Alfie gave me a consoling pat on the arm.

'Don't blame yourself, girl,' he said.

Derek and I both glared at him. I could see he was puzzled. Knowing Alfie, he probably just thought he was being helpful and friendly. Derek and I shrugged at each other, and for a moment I felt warm and comforted. Then Derek did one of his turnabouts. He started sighing and pacing up and down, so I should have guessed what was coming.

Sure enough, he started, 'We've got the whole Force on the look-out for her. Pity you didn't find out where she came from in Ireland. We might have checked up if she'd gone back home to her family. Well, at least you got her statement about her connection with Gilmore, for what it's worth. And her version of the murder. I suppose you might as well go and take Kate Dunkerley to the morgue to verify my identification of the man known as Mrs Winkelhorne. And see if she'll let slip whether she knew all along that he was a man, and whatever else you can find out from her about him.'

By this time I didn't dare tell him what Kate had said to me about this Winkelhorne character. I just gave him a very subdued, 'OK, Guv.'

Of course, Alfie couldn't let anything alone. He chimed in with, 'P'raps it'd be better if I went to the morgue, seeing I was the one who interviewed the so-called Mrs Winkelhorne while she was alive.'

I started, 'I wouldn't mind–' but Derek came in sharpish with a reminder to Alfie that he hadn't noticed anything suspicious about this person when he'd interviewed him, as if that had anything to do with identifying the body.

'Kate lived next door to that person for three years. If her identification isn't good enough, yours won't help,' he said. 'Anyway, I've got a bit of old-fashioned sleuthing for you to do, Alfie. I want to know everything you can dig up about Kate Dunkerley, from the day she was born right up to when she phoned us about Len Gilmore's murder. Never mind what Goldfeather told us about everything that happened when she was in America. We need a lot more than that. Somehow or other I'm sure she's the key to the whole thing...'

Trust Alfie.

Eagerly he said, 'You mean you think she's the mastermind? Like manipulating all these men? She could have murdered that other American man, too, that Jack Roc she lived with in New York.'

'No, nothing like that,' Derek said wearily. 'But it can't do any harm to find out her life story, and if the yarn she spun Greta had any truth in it at all.'

The rest of the day was dreary, with Alfie glued to the phone and me banging out reports and trying not to look at Derek like a kicked puppy. Still, it ended on an up-note, with Alfie proving that when it came to it, he could do his stuff. Before we parted for the day, he read us his notes.

'I bet the big shock for you both,' this was Alfie at his most self-important, 'is going to be that a lot of what Kate Dunkerley told Greta was true. There, you didn't expect that, did you.'

'Get on with it, man,' Derek barked. 'Never mind the introductory speech. Just tell us what you've got.'

Unruffled, Alfie went on, 'Well, it was in Birmingham. A Catherine Dunkerley *was* stabbed to death by her young schoolboy lover, Robert Fraser, who was then hit over the head with a chair by her eleven-year-old son, Duncan. Fraser died a few days later without regaining consciousness. Duncan was put into a hostel for unmanageable children, and the other child, four-year-old Kate, was fostered by a couple who were already fostering two other children of about her age. I couldn't get any information about the father or fathers of the two children, so there's no support for Kate's story that her brother was black. Anyway, two years later he absconded from the youth detention where he was, and that was the last heard of him. Don't suppose there was much of a search for him anyway.'

Alfie cleared his throat, looked to make sure we were listening, and said, 'Not much about our Kate, though. She stayed with her foster parents, a Mr and Mrs Brown, up to the age of fifteen, then she disappeared too. She came back to them three years later, asking them to help her get a passport. That's all.'

'I don't suppose you found out anything about our famous young knitwear and dress designer, did you?' I asked, not knowing why I should bother with such a question.

'Oh yes, the famous Curleigh,' Derek added. 'What about him and his connection with our Kate that she claims?'

'Couldn't find anything about that,' Alfie said. 'Mind you, I couldn't find any corroboration of the story we've all heard about him having been found as a baby and becoming a Barnardo's Boy. Barnardo's've got no records of him at all.'

'What! All that publicity about it and they've never told the Press it wasn't true?'

'No, well, they said they didn't want to spoil his reputation, and they didn't mind taking some of the credit for his success – showed them up in a good light, didn't it. Anyway, he's not the first boy with a dodgy background who invented himself a romantic history after he made good, is he.'

And Alfie sat back looking well pleased with himself. But not for long.

'Well, that's all very well as far as it goes,' our very own whiz-kid said, 'but there's much more, isn't there? Have you interviewed Kate's foster parents? Have you found out whether Catherine Dunkerley had any family – parents, brothers, sisters? You can't get enough just by talking on the phone. I think you'd better hop on a train and go up to Birmingham and see this Mr and Mrs Brown and go to the Social Services office and have a longer talk with whoever you spoke to on the phone. Dig deeper, man.'

Dejected but unsquashed, Alfie said, 'OK, I'll go first thing in the morning–'

'What's wrong with now?'

'But, Betty, my supper, why now–' Alfie started bleating, but Derek, still being the hard man, just said, 'Greta will fix you some accommodation and ask the locals to meet you and help you with transport. Off you go.'

'I'll just nip home and get my pyjamas,' Alfie said. 'It doesn't take long to get to Birmingham, I'll still get there in time for a good night's sleep and an early start in the morning.'

And he marched out. I expected him to do something out of character like slamming the door, but being Alfie, all he did was leave it open instead.

I turned to Derek, not trying to hide my temper.

'What's the matter with you, Derek? Why are you behaving like some petty dictator all of a sudden? You're always telling me to give Alfie some respect because of his age and experience, and then you treat him like some little pimply trainee!'

He would have been in his rights to bob me down, but he just gave a big sigh, flopped down in his chair and gave me a doggy kind of look.

'You're right, I've been all over the place lately. It's not just this case, my personal life is a mess as well, and I can't seem to find the right opportunity to ask Mr Moon about taking one of those flats in Robin Hood House. What do you think, should I phone Alfie and tell him not to go until the morning?'

Of course, like the great softy that I am, right away I melted and stopped wanting to give him a demonstration of my skills in karate. There were some other skills I'd rather have shown him when he looked at me like that. But he was going on.

'Do you think I'm losing my grip, Greta? I know you'll tell me the truth, I can rely on you.'

'No, course you're not. And I don't think you should change your orders to Alfie. It won't do him any harm to go tonight. I'll get some train times and ask him which he's getting, then I'll phone the local nick and ask them to fix him up with transport and accommodation. But what I suggest, Derek,' and now *I* tried to sound firm and bossy, 'is that you go right away and have a talk with Mr Moon. It's late enough that he won't be too busy, but you know he'll probably still be at his desk. Go on, do it now!'

I was a bit surprised that without another word he did as I said. Hm, I thought, maybe that's what he needs, not someone adoring but a tough bird to order him about. Could that have been the attraction with that Erica who he was about to leave?

After I'd made my calls I hung about waiting for him to come down and tell me what happened with the Super. It was a long time, but he finally appeared, looking a bit the worse for wear.

'What?' I asked him as he slumped back in his chair, shaking his head in a baffled kind of way.

'An amazing man,' he finally muttered, more to himself than me, which I thought was a bit rotten considering I'd been waiting all this time to hear the verdict. After a while, he added, 'I hate whisky, even if it is his best single malt.'

'Derek!'

'Oh, what, oh yes, Greta, thoughtful of you to wait. Well, Mr Moon was very considerate and understanding and told me a lot about his personal life and kept pressing this loathsome drink on me. I had to take it, didn't I, after all, it was very generous and he is my superior officer. But I wish he wouldn't... Oh, yes, he thought it was a good idea for me to ask the agents about renting that empty flat at Robin Hood House. But he doesn't think we're making much progress with the Gilmore case. Tell you what, Greta,' he said, brightening up a bit, 'how about you coming with me to pick up my things when I go back to Highgate? Bit of help with the gear, moral support, all that. Would you mind?'

As a matter of fact, I minded quite a lot. But that might be a way of getting closer to Derek, and also I'd see what I was up against with this Erica person. I had seen her once before, but only from a distance. And I'd rather be Derek's best friend and helper than just his favourite sergeant.

'OK,' I said, 'I'm free this evening. Why don't we go now?'

'But I haven't got the flat yet. Well, I suppose I could stay in a hotel for a couple of nights. Yes, you're right, let's not put it off. Let's go now. But you'd better drive. That damned whisky is making my head buzz.'

That's what happens when a wine-drinker takes to strong spirits. Derek had trouble staying alert enough to give me directions to Highgate. But every now and again he'd jerk himself awake and tell me a bit about himself and Erica. I suppose I should have been flattered that he wanted to confide in me, but it depressed me to think that he didn't even realise that my own feelings might be messed up in all this.

'You don't think perhaps it's a bit late to show up to collect your gear?'

'No, we'd agreed I'd move out of the penthouse as soon as I could find a place,' he mumbled. 'In happier times, in the first romantic flush of our affair, she'd have been waiting up for me with soothing words and sympathetic enquiries about my latest case. But we've been long past that for some time,' he sighed.

Well, I saw when we arrived that one thing hadn't changed. She *was* still up. But not waiting up for Derek. The place was absolutely vibrating with the sort of hard metal music I knew Derek hated. I wondered if the neighbours complained, or if they were among the crowd heaving about the place, shouting, laughing, drinking, dancing and probably inhaling prohibited substances. How could Derek have been so foolish as to think it had been a good idea to give up his own home and move in with this woman? Even if they'd been in the grip of mad passion and thought it would last forever, it only took half a glance to see how unsuited they were.

'Come on,' Derek said grimly. We went in to this penthouse like a film set, and Derek pushed his way through the crowd to what he told me was the spare bedroom where he'd been sleeping. There were four undressed people on the bed, rolling and writhing about. It was hard to make out exactly what they were doing, but I didn't really want to know any details, and I thought Derek didn't either.

'Excuse me,' he said. Then, as one of them rose up from the scuffle, he added, 'Oh! Erica!'

Even in that shambolic state she was gorgeous. It was disheartening to see that her perfect little face and body were like a mini-model's and even in its messy state her hair looked as if she'd just spent a fortune on it. She probably had. But she was a right cow, and that made me feel better.

'Derek!' she yelled. 'What are you doing here? I thought you'd moved out days ago.'

'No, well,' Derek started, but she interrupted with, 'Never mind, darling, you can go now. Come on, I'll help you pack. I see you've brought a friend with you to lend a hand.'

She started emptying cupboards and drawers, throwing things on top of the other three people on the bed. In the end, in spite of drunken attempts by some of her friends to rally round, we finally got all Derek's things packed, with what wouldn't go into his own cases going into her set of Vuitton luggage. We all staggered out to the car, and Derek and all his belongings – probably with some of Erica's too – were bundled in, and they all noisily waved us good-bye, still with no clothes on. She didn't offer Derek so much as a farewell kiss or a friendly parting word.

She just called out, 'Don't forget to bring my cases back, darling!' before going back to her party and presumably (hopefully) disappearing from his life. Apparently she had no regrets, and I hoped Derek didn't, either. I couldn't tell whether he was slumped in his seat because of exhaustion or grief, so having no idea where to go, I just drove aimlessly in the general direction of Watford. I was still half hoping he'd ask if I could put him up for the night, but I knew really there wasn't much chance of that.

After a while, he muttered, more to himself than me, 'It wasn't only physical. She admired me for the work I did, my commitment to serving the public and what she thought was my erudition. She's very clever, so young to be a sharp City whiz-kid, earning fabulous amounts, looking so smart and beautiful and being so cool and laid-back.'

By this time I was grinding my teeth, but he didn't notice, just droned on, 'Now I know sex and mutual admiration aren't enough. She's a party animal, Erica, she loves noise and booze and thumping music and great mobs of people.'

No kidding, doesn't feel the cold either, I thought, but still kept shtum. Just let him go on to himself, as if I wasn't there and the car was driving itself.

'I'm quiet, reflective, I like pleasant wine, good music, especially opera. I'm more the occasional tête-à-tête type.'

I couldn't stand any more. I had to say something to remind him I was there too.

'Where would you like me to drive you now, Derek?' I tried to sound sympathetic and understanding, but I had to admit it came out a bit cool.

'Oh, er, I, er, let me think.'

He really had forgotten about me driving him about. He'd thought he was talking to himself, he was so whacked out he hardly knew where he was. It was my chance. I could take advantage of his disorientated state and just take him to my place and maybe even take a few liberties with him.

Dream on.

'How about the Watford Fulton?' I said. 'It's not exactly luxury, but it's clean and not too dear. You must get your head down, otherwise you'll fall in a heap.'

'OK,' he said, still without so much as a 'Thanks for your help, Greta.'

And so ended another romantic evening in the love life of Detective Sergeant Greta Pusey and her darling boss, the brilliant but quiet and reflective DI Derek Michaelson.

Chapter 14

Next morning I decided to forget personal matters. Kate hadn't left her flat since Fred and Kevin had been watching, but she'd phoned to ask us to come to a meeting there. So just now all I wanted was to concentrate on our case. I had a feeling this meeting was going to be crucial. I made up my mind that nothing personal should be allowed to distract us from being our most alert. I was puzzled about Kate's obvious terror. Perhaps we could find out the reason for it. I didn't think she was putting it on – she was in a genuine funk. I pointed this out to Derek.

'Well, she saw her lover being bashed to death,' he said. 'Wasn't that enough to make her permanently terrified?'

'She wasn't too scared to go and hack his willie off afterwards,' I reminded him. 'She wasn't in that state when we first met her. I think something else is getting to her. Something that's happened since then. And we have to find out what it is.'

'To protect her? So you're coming around to my opinion, then.'

'Maybe. But it's more important to know what – or who – we need to protect her from.'

I gave a big sigh. I knew Derek didn't approve of my attitude to Kate these days. Of course he'd forgotten that he rather fancied her when he first set eyes on her. No, it was me being soppy ever since I'd heard the sad story of her early life. Now he thought I was far too sympathetic towards her. He didn't have to remind me that Kate was at least connected with villains, if not an active one herself.

And maybe she should be treated accordingly, regardless of her rotten childhood. I was usually too good at my job to need telling not to get emotionally involved, but Derek seemed to think I was choosing this time to go soft on him.

In a way, I could see that Kate was a bad lot herself, and not just unluckily involved with crime and criminals. And anyway, at the very least she was a bit dotty, or at worst maybe she was a psycho. In any case, possibly dangerous. But in another way, a victim herself.

'There is a little complication I ought to tell you about,' I said. 'When we were having one of our all-girls-together chats, she confided to me that she fancied Goldfeather something rotten. Of course, that was when she thought he was Simon Winkelhorne. I don't know if that makes any difference–'

I looked at him hard. Not much reaction. Then a little lecture.

'I'm not sure of your purpose in telling me this. It's more gossip than fact, and you don't usually go in for tittle-tattle. You're much more one of the chaps, as a rule. A certain amount of chat is permissible, but this isn't really appropriate. What could Kate being attracted by that American have to do with our case? Especially as she didn't meet him until after Gilmore's death.'

I knew better than to answer when he was being pompous. I shut up.

When we got to the building, a workman was busy at the street door, installing a video entry-phone where the previous squawk-box had been. That was one safety measure that might have saved Len Gilmore's life if he'd had the sense to have it installed when he moved in to the place. Strange that a man like that should have been so careless of his safety, considering his 'business' connections. But then, according to Kate, he'd had a procession of strange women in his home, too, regardless of danger – of any sort.

Upstairs, Kate's front door was opened by a man I'd never seen before. But I felt as if I'd known him for years. What you might call a familiar type. If you'd asked Central Casting in Hollywood for an actor to play a smooth, rich, expensive, top-class lawyer, this was the man they would have sent you. It was like a stupid joke. He had one of those faces which put you on the alert, it was so clever-looking, and far too handsome. His expensive tan was just the right shade to show off his sharp pale grey eyes, which exactly matched his elegant Armani suit. I told him who we were and we showed him our ID.

'And you are?' Derek asked him, even though the answer was ridiculously obvious.

'Charles North, of Abel, Levi and North, solicitors, here representing Miss Dunkerley's interests,' he said, in a voice as smooth and superior as his face, his beautifully styled iron-grey hair, his matching grey silk tie. I was sure he was wearing pure silk underwear and socks, too, and probably his sheets at home were hand-laundered silk and changed every day. He positively oozed privilege and smug self-assurance, and I could see Derek trying not to hate him. I had no problem with that – I just let it happen.

'And just how long,' Derek snapped, 'have you been Miss Dunkerley's solicitor? I wonder why she thinks she needs someone of your, er, calibre to speak for her?'

He knew very well what Derek meant by calibre. How many hundreds of pounds per hour did he cost, and how could Kate afford him?

'I'm afraid I'm not at liberty to answer questions of that nature, Inspector. Suffice it to say that Miss Dunkerley will feel more comfortable at this meeting while I am present. She tells me that this man, Simon Goldfeather, at whose request we are all here, first introduced himself to her as Simon Winkelhorne, son of the occupant of the other flat on this floor. At the time, that person was believed to have been an elderly widow. Now we know otherwise.

You will understand we regard the man Goldfeather with a certain amount of misgiving, not to speak of suspicion. Hence my presence.'

All this told us nothing. While talking, he had led the way into the sitting room, where Kate was standing by the window with her back to us. She turned towards us, and I was shocked at the change in her appearance. She looked tired, frail and almost ill. But then, how many times had she managed to look different – the dowdy, middle-aged, clerical type I thought she was at first, the tart who'd come to see Derek at the nick to flutter her eyelashes at him, the pathetic little girl who'd told me about her tragic childhood...

I thought of what I'd read about multiple personalities. No, that wasn't the answer, because hers were deliberate changes. One thing was sure – we shouldn't believe anything she told us in the future unless it could be verified. I looked at Derek for a reaction, but he was po-faced.

'Shall I make us all a cup of tea, Kate?' I asked. 'You look a bit tired.'

But I didn't put any warmth in the offer, no sympathy in the way I looked at Kate. It was just a way of passing the time. I hoped this satisfied Derek that I wasn't going to be fooled by any act that Kate might put on.

The doorbell went before she could answer. North came back again, this time with Goldfeather. I was watching Kate, and saw her face and neck flood with colour again. I couldn't see what she found so attractive in him, myself. But then again, maybe it wasn't attraction. How about guilt? Maybe they'd known each other before?

Well, I'd decided that I'd come to this meeting to listen, so I certainly wasn't going to start asking questions until I heard what Goldfeather had to say. But there was something else to think about: was it a coincidence that North had arrived on the scene exactly when Goldfeather had asked for this meeting? Had Kate sent for him? Did she know more about Goldfeather than we should have expected?

There were no social formalities. I didn't repeat my offer to make tea. Kate didn't ask if anyone wanted a drink. Nobody offered anybody a cigarette. North and Goldfeather had obviously introduced themselves at the door, and we all sat down on the nearest chair and waited.

Goldfeather began.

'I guess you've all deduced by now that I'm not just head of security at the US Embassy in London. I'm CIA, and I work closely with the FBI back home. Before we get to my reason for requesting this meeting, I'll clarify the background. I came to this country primarily to interview Len Gilmore. Unfortunately, as you know, it was too late. But we knew that Winkelhorne was an American private detective living in the same apartment block. How he fitted into our investigations was a separate question we wanted answered. It was my intention to persuade Winkelhorne to come with me to a quiet place where we could talk confidentially. I had a vehicle on standby around the corner for the purpose. Unexpectedly he attacked me and sadly while I was defending myself he accidentally met his death. Certainly I didn't intend throwing him out the window. He flung himself at me, I dodged, and – it just happened,' he shrugged.

At first it seemed that nobody was going to break the silence. It went on for some minutes. It was clear from everyone's expression that we were all doubtful about his account of Winkelhorne's 'fall'. Weak was hardly the word for it. It posed more questions than it answered.

Surprisingly Kate was the first to speak.

'Len and I came to England on the QE2,' she said. All the life seemed to have gone from her face, and she spoke in a flat, dull voice. 'On the journey, he got friendly with a blonde who said she was an estate agent in England. Len always got friendly with blondes. And brunettes and redheads. Anyway, when he told her we were looking for a couple of apartments near to each other, she said she knew just the thing. As soon as we landed, she took us to see them, here, of course. And Len thought they were perfect, even if they were in Watford, not London. He'd never even heard of Watford before, but when I told him it was the edge of the world, he said that was good. Ideal. He thought it was specially marvellous that only one of the other flats was occupied, and that was by an elderly foreign widow. As we thought at the time.'

Goldfeather nodded.

'Somebody knew his weakness for a pretty face,' he observed.

'He was a fool–' Kate started, but North interrupted.

'–please go on, Mr Goldfeather. I'm sure we're all tremendously interested in what else you have to tell us. No doubt the police will want to discuss the death of the private detective with you at some other time. But in the meantime, if you would care to tell us why we are all here...'

Goldfeather nodded. I saw that he was avoiding Derek's eye. Maybe we couldn't touch him for Winkelhorne's death, but probably Derek would still like to have a serious talk with him about how the body got into the canal at Rickmansworth, naked. Surely we could get somebody for that, even if he himself had diplomatic immunity? And all that thin stuff about taking Winkelhorne to a quiet place to talk – in a private ambulance! What was wrong with staying in his own quiet apartment? Anyway, for now we were letting him go on talking. Which he did.

'I guess you've all heard of Art Redondo,' he went on. 'He was a pretty famous investigative journalist in the U.S. Then he won the Pulitzer for his book on the street children of Rio. But even if you'd never heard of him on that account, once his kidnapping in Colombia hit the headlines, the whole world knew his name.'

Kate suddenly became animated.

'I remember that! I was still in New York then, and his girlfriend, Phoebe, was in the headlines and on TV all the time. She certainly made sure everybody knew about it. I expect all the publicity gave her career a boost, too,' she added with unnecessary bitterness.

Then she relapsed into her previous withdrawn pose, looking at her hands, as if to avoid seeing Goldfeather. I wondered again if she'd known him longer than they'd both told us.

'Well,' Goldfeather resumed his tale, which so far seemed to have nothing at all to do with us, 'finally the so-called bandits in Colombia released Redondo. Remember there was a helluva lot of public guesswork about why he was kidnapped and then why they let him go. Phoebe Lester always denied paying ransom. In fact, she kept on telling the Press they hadn't demanded any. So maybe no deals were done. Redondo never said what he was doing in Colombia. The government there said they made every effort to find the criminals and bring them to justice, but nothing came of that, either. So the whole thing just fizzled out, the media dropped the story, and that was the end of it. Nine-day wonder, right? OK. Forget it.'

'Rather pointless telling us about it, I'd say,' said North smoothly. 'What was your purpose in gathering us all together here today? Surely not to tell us this rather dull story which has no bearing on any crime committed in this country?'

Goldfeather was unruffled. Bit of a joke there, I thought. Feathers, ruffled. This just showed how little I was concentrating by this time. It was all, as North said, of no interest to any of us. Out of character, I let my mind wander. Was Derek going to rent the empty flat on the floor below, I was wondering, when I was brought back to the present with a sharp jerk.

'Here's the point, *old boy*,' Goldfeather said, in that way that only Americans can use the phrase 'old boy' to mock a certain type of Englishman, 'the point is that Art Redondo says he murdered Jack Roc.'

Now he had everybody's undivided attention.

'Jack Roc!' said North. 'You mean Miss Dunkerley's late friend, Jack Roc? Whom she found shot to death in his apartment in New York?'

'Right on, *old boy*. And we know that Len Gilmore did *not* kill him,' replied Goldfeather, looking directly at Kate for the first time. He saw, as we all did, that she had now gone so white that she was obviously about to faint. Before anyone could speak or move, she pitched forward out of her chair.

Then there was a bit of bustle and confusion while North and I looked after Kate, and Goldfeather and Derek just sat and looked at each other. So, I thought, perhaps Kate had been afraid all along that Len had killed her previous lover. Not for love of her, but to take over some of his activities. And the New York police had suspected that Kate herself had done it. I thought that showed bad judgement. Whatever illegal or immoral things Kate had done in her life, I was sure she couldn't do an actual murder. Maltreating a dead body, yes. The nerve for murder, no.

But we could all see from the way he just sat there, waiting, that Goldfeather had a lot more to tell us. I suppose, in his flash American way, he was the kind of handsome man that a girl like Kate might find irresistible. But sitting hunched like that, he looked to me more like a vulture. I couldn't fancy him at all, myself. Not my type, not like Derek.

Finally a revived Kate was sitting back in her chair, sipping a drink, and looking again at Goldfeather, the usual blush rising again, up her neck, and through to her hairline. He watched it, too, with a small nasty smug smile. When we were all settled again, he went on with his story.

'We all thought that when Redondo was kidnapped, he'd been researching the drug scene in Colombia, probably to get a new angle for another one of his exposés. Maybe to trace the international connections. The fact was, he was on quite another trail. He had discovered a trade in human organs for transplant. We knew that happened in the Far East, but this was on our own doorstep! He had tracked down a disbarred American surgeon working in a clinic in Médillin, who was offering the locals cash for healthy kidneys. He was on a sure thing there. The poorest peasants were glad to do the deal, once they understood they could live with only one kidney. Then Redondo learned something worse. Some were going to the clinic to sell a kidney and while they were under anaesthetic, *all* their vital organs were taken. Yes, hearts, lungs, kidneys and livers – the whole shebang. There was a crematorium real handy, next door to the clinic, where the remains were burned.

'Redondo says he was near to proving who in the States was on the receiving end of this filthy trade, when he was kidnapped. After his release he was in no condition to follow up his investigations. They'd taken one of his kidneys too. Reckon they thought that would keep him quiet for a while.'

Goldfeather was now looking steadily at Kate. As he spoke, the colour was slowly going out of her face again.

'Redondo gave himself up to the New York police last week,' he said, 'and confessed that he'd killed Jack Roc several years ago. He was raving. He said he'd learned enough to convince him that Roc was involved in this black market of human organs, but he couldn't get the evidence to persuade us to follow through. He said he felt justified in murdering Roc, because of what he'd suffered himself, and a man trading in human lives that way didn't deserve to live. Right now Redondo is undergoing rigorous psychiatric examination. He appears not to be in a real healthy mental condition. The New York police are not convinced by his confession. There is no forensic evidence to support it. However, none of that need concern us here today, folks.

'We do believe Redondo's story that this business of the illegal sale of human organs was one of Jack Roc's interests. We also think Len Gilmore took it over from Jack Roc, together with all his other activities. What can *you* tell us to help this investigation, Miss Dunkerley?'

She opened her mouth, but North forestalled her.

'My client doesn't have to answer any of your questions, Mister Goldfeather, but I would like to ask you some on her behalf. Why should we believe anything you have told us? And if we did, why should Miss Dunkerley be involved in any way? What is your authority to question her? Are you working with the police in this country? *Is* he, Inspector?' he asked, turning to Derek.

Sheet-white and trembling, Kate stood up.

'Please be quiet, Mr North,' she said. 'I don't have to be guided by you, I don't know what you're doing here, or who sent you. And I don't know if your advice is in my interests or somebody else's. I knew Len was a crook, of course I did,' she turned to Derek, turning her back on North and Goldfeather. 'But if I'd had any idea that he had anything to do with that horrible business, I'd never have had anything to do with him, or Jack Roc before him. I'll give you everything of his that I've got.'

What did she mean, everything? Papers, keys, passports? What else? Information? Who was she talking to when she said 'give *you* everything'? Who was she going to give it all to, us or Goldfeather?

Chapter 15

Before Kate could say another word, North murmured in his smarmy lawyer's way, 'Miss Dunkerley, I wonder if I could trouble you to show me the way to your bathroom?'

Of course, she had to do that, although I would have thought it was obvious where it was. There were only three doors in the room we were in. There was the one from the outside lobby, which led directly into the flat – the way we'd all come in. Another was the door to the kitchen, so the third one had to lead to the bedroom and the bathroom. We could all see he was trying to interrupt her, to get her on her own, try to persuade her not to say any more before getting his advice first. But there was nothing we could do about it.

As she led the way, I heard him mumble something to her, but couldn't catch a word. Give him the benefit of the doubt, maybe he was just saying something complimentary about her flat. But I thought not.

I had to admit, though, that from when I'd first seen it, I'd been green with envy about the place. Same number of rooms as I had, but they were all large and done up and furnished with no expense spared. Amazing to think it was built just the same as the flat below, where it looked so different. Gilmore's flat was no-frills, business-like. It put me in mind of those TV makeover programmes. His was the 'before', hers the 'after'.

I thought she'd come back straight away, but North must have got her chatting, because they were both missing for a while. A long while.

Bored, I started wandering around the room. First I pulled back the rug to show Derek the peephole in the floor that Kate had used to spy on Gilmore. That was how she'd seen him being killed. It didn't have a very big viewing range, but it must have been enough. Derek told me to make a note to ask Kate how she'd got it done without Gilmore knowing.

There was a bookcase, which seemed specially interesting. It was against the blank wall between the kitchen door and the way Kate and North had gone.

'Look, Guv,' I said,' this isn't a bookcase, they're dummy books!'

'Oh, yeah,' said Goldfeather, 'that looks like a Murphy bed. I didn't know you had them in this country. Look, just press that switch at the side there – see.'

And the whole bookcase lowered itself slowly to the floor, hinged at the bottom, and turned out to be a ready made-up bed. Derek and I were quite amazed. But Goldfeather was ahead of us, being a know-all as usual.

'Say, am I right in thinking you've never seen one of those before?' he asked. Seeing from our expressions that he'd guessed correctly, he went on, 'Listen, if they've had that installed, and she had that spyhole put in, seems to me they might have put in a few other tricky gadgets, am I right?'

In the same second Derek and I both got what he was getting at, and together the three of us made for the door that Kate and North had gone through, at least fifteen minutes earlier. We were in a tiny lobby, faced with three more doors, all identical, all closed. As if we'd planned it, each of us opened one.

The one Derek chose turned out to be a cupboard, full of suitcases. I guessed we'd have to go through all those some time. Perhaps one of them contained Gilmore's missing papers.

Goldfeather's door opened into the bathroom. Neither Kate nor her smoothie lawyer to be seen in there.

I opened the bedroom door. And what a bedroom! From the first time I'd seen it, I'd thought the sitting room was pretty swish. And the quick look I'd had of the bathroom looked lush enough for a film star, too. But the bedroom – I have to say magnificent was the only word for that. It was just breath-taking.

However, it contained no human beings. This was a puzzler. The only way out of the flat was through the living room and out of the front door. Where were North and Kate?

'Greta!' Derek barked. 'Quick, go back to the front door, and stay there. Nobody's to go in or out of that door, OK?'

I'm a good cop, but I'm human, too, and a woman, although I keep trying to forget that. I couldn't help giving one more lingering look round that stunning bedroom before loping back to the front door to stand guard. You couldn't blame me. My whole little flat would go into Kate's bedroom, and it would take more than a year's income to have a room fitted out like this. Not that it was exactly my taste. But still.

Floor to ceiling and wall to wall, one side was covered with mirrored door wardrobes. When you got into the room and shut the door, it was difficult to see where you'd come in, because the inside of that door matched in so perfectly with the wardrobe doors. Opposite, one corner had two windows at right angles, and in that corner was an absolute garden of flowers, with a dressing table in amongst them so cleverly that it looked as if it grew there with the flowers. Further along the wall was a bed piled high with cushions and furry animals. The fourth wall had a large window looking out onto the street, with a velvet-covered window-seat running along its length.

Goldfeather, being an American, and handsome in his

flashy way, had probably seen many a splendid bedroom in his time, but I could tell he was impressed by the way he muttered 'Wow!' to himself several times. Even Derek must have been able to tell that it cost a packet.

But neither Kate nor her lawyer was there.

Goldfeather and Derek looked out of all three windows. The two with all the flowers were difficult to get at, but they could see that Kate and North couldn't have left the place that way. The one facing the street had a fancy balcony, but it was one of those narrow ones for decorative purposes only that no one could stand on. And anyway, those two couldn't have climbed out and down the face of the building to get away. Why should they? North had no reason to run away, and nobody had even suggested that Kate might be accused of any crime. Not in this meeting, anyway.

Walking together out of the bedroom, Derek and Goldfeather met North in the small lobby, coming out of the bathroom.

'Were you looking for me?' he asked innocently. 'Sorry if I was a long time – you know how it is. Sometimes a call of nature takes a little longer than one expects...'

'You weren't in there just now when we looked for you,' Derek said, and I could hear Goldfeather behind him, grunting some sort of agreement.

'My dear man,' said North, sounding amused and smug at the same time, 'where on earth do you think I was? After all, this place is hardly a mansion.'

'And where is your client?' Derek snapped.

'Isn't she with you?'

The three of them came back into the sitting room. I was still standing by the front door, earwigging for all I was worth. Derek looked enquiringly at me. I shrugged. Kate wasn't there.

She came into the sitting room from the little lobby.

126

'Sorry to have held things up,' she said in a cool and calm voice. 'I took the opportunity to sit down in my bedroom and have a little think.'

Goldfeather said, 'We were in there just now, and you weren't–'

Her reaction to him had changed completely. No more blushing. She was back in control.

'You're mistaken,' she said. 'I was sitting on the window seat when you both came in. But never mind that now. I want to ask you if you can prove any of the story you told us about Jack Roc and Art Redondo. And I'd also like to know if you can demonstrate that you are who you say you are. I suppose you've seen his credentials, Inspector?'

Things were moving too fast and too confusingly. Derek just nodded and let her go on.

'And I'd also like to ask you, Inspector, whether you accept this man's story about the death of my neighbour. I know it's not for me to tell you your job. But whether Winkelhorne was a man or a woman, it seems to me that you should be taking more interest in how he came to die, and less in the far-fetched tales that this man is telling us. Surely whatever happened to Art Redondo in Colombia is no concern of ours. And I suggest the murder of my, my,' she stumbled for a moment, and then her voice got strong again, 'the murder of my fiancé should be of more concern to you than his perfectly legitimate import and export business.'

This was a turn-around. Wherever she and North had been hiding, he'd used the time to good effect. Something had happened between them out of our sight that had stiffened her backbone. The white-faced shocked little Kate who was going to tell us everything about Gilmore had gone. We were back to square one. And even her way of speaking had changed. This was yet another transformation, best I'd seen so far.

127

'What did you mean when you said you'd *give* me everything of Gilmore's that you'd got?' Derek asked. 'Did you mean *give* material of a physical nature, or merely reveal information?'

'My client cannot say any more until she gets some answers to her own questions,' North interposed. 'I think her doubts and concerns are perfectly legitimate, and she does not have to believe anything that this man tells us,' he indicated Goldfeather, who was looking furious by this time.

Derek sighed. He knew what he had to do. He'd known all along, but probably he'd delayed because he thought that might get him some new information. No chance. All he'd got was more puzzles. He signalled to me to be ready.

'Simon Goldfeather,' he said, turning to him, 'I am arresting you on suspicion of implication in the murder of the person known as Mrs Winkelhorne–'

Before he could get on with the customary warning, the blighter came straight at him and knocked him flying with his shoulder. That's the trouble with American football – it teaches all their college boys to do that body charge, and if you're not built like the proverbial brick wall, it can make you airborne for quite a distance.

Of course, even while Derek was still off the ground, I went rushing at Goldfeather and showed that my karate lessons hadn't been wasted. He couldn't have known that I was a Black Belt, and he must have thought it would be a walkover, getting away from a smallish chap like Derek and a woman. He was flat on his back while Derek was still getting up. Before he had a chance to do more, I hauled him up, clapped the cuffs on him and dumped him face-down on the Murphy bed, which had been left open all this time. That was a lucky stroke. We needed one.

Not even breathing hard, I whipped out my mobile and called for assistance. Not that I needed it. Derek gave me an admiring look, and I felt warm all over.

And no showing off, either. It's not my way. I just said, 'You OK, Guv?' and got on with it.

During all this, Kate and her legal defender were standing paralysed. Clearly this was the last thing they'd expected, and I could see it was all too fast for them.

'Now, Miss Dunkerley,' Derek said in his most official manner, taking charge again, 'while we're waiting for the police transport to take Goldfeather to the station, perhaps you'd like to show me round your flat. I think you may have a few hiding places to show me. And that would include a concealed safe, I presume.'

North butted in again.

'I do think you must have misunderstood the geography of this establishment, Inspector. Evidently you believed that Miss Dunkerley and I were hiding, when she was merely showing me that there are two routes to her bathroom, one from the small lobby and the other from her bedroom. Perhaps you will permit me, Miss Dunkerley, to show the Inspector?'

Derek was usually a bit formal in the way he spoke, it was just his natural manner. But he couldn't match this feller North for pompousness. Every time he spoke it was like a politician making a speech. What a stuffed shirt. Derek wasn't in his league. But then he wasn't an expensive lawyer.

Even while Kate was murmuring her permission, North was leading us out of the room into the lobby with the three doors. He pranced into the bedroom, with us on his heels, and he closed the door behind us. Right away it was impossible to see which of the mirrored doors was the one we'd come through. He re-opened it, and then walked along, opening all the other doors on that wall. One after another, we saw clothes hanging from rails, shelves of sweaters and shoes and handbags, drawers which probably held underwear, all the stuff you'd expect. Enough to open a boutique of her own. Until he came to a door which opened on to a space.

'Now kindly step inside this empty area with me, Inspector,' North invited, and then opened another door on the other side of the space. And we were all in the bathroom, with an open door behind us which was yet another full-length mirror.

'Ingenious, isn't it?' this pain in the neck smirked. Right away Derek and I could see they'd used this little hidey-hole for their quick conference while we were in the sitting room, innocently showing each other the wonders of the Murphy bed.

What was most interesting was that it had to have been Kate's idea, because North couldn't have known about it previously. One minute she was all shattered and trembly, and the next she was sneaking off for a quick private word with him in a secret place. Or was it all just acting?

'Yes, I can see,' Derek snapped, 'everything about these premises appears to be most inventive. Would you happen to know, Mr North, whether it was Mr Gilmore or Miss Dunkerley who planned all these clever ideas? I'm sure none of it was already installed when they moved in to the place.'

Of course he had no idea. And while he was shaking his head, Derek went on, even more sharply.

'And, of course, the safe in which all Mr Gilmore's papers and effects were stored – that would have to be even more skilfully hidden, wouldn't it, Mr North? Perhaps you can show me where that is? Or shall I have to get a warrant to search the premises?'

'Oh come, Inspector, surely that won't be necessary. I'm sure Miss Dunkerley would be only too pleased to hand over any of Mr Gilmore's possessions which she was holding for him. You must have observed how keen my client is to co-operate with you in every way.'

'Frankly, Mr North, I have observed no such thing. Why don't we go and speak to Miss Dunkerley, and test the sincerity of her co-operation.'

And test which of them can speak in the most showing-off manner, too, I thought.

As we went back into the sitting room, the front door bell rang, and I looked through the security spyhole in the door.

'It's DCs Archer and Burton, Guv,' I said, 'and they've got some other geezer with them.'

Derek frowned at me. He probably didn't like me speaking in my normal way, when he was trying to compete with North on the long words front. Still, I thought karate was more valuable than the battle of the dictionaries.

'Who is the other person?' Derek asked.

'I don't know – oh yes, I do. It's that feller who was putting in the video entry-phone downstairs,' I said. 'I expect he wants to come and fix up the other end in here. Shall I let him in, Guv? Is it convenient? What about you, Kate? Is it OK for you?'

'No, tell him to come back another time,' Derek answered before Kate had a chance. 'Just let Archer and Burton in to take Agent Goldfeather back to the station, and we'll follow when we've finished our interview with Miss Dunkerley here.'

I opened the door and Fred Archer and Kevin Burton fell in on top of me. As the three of us lay sprawling on the floor, we were followed by the workman we'd seen down at the street entry door when we'd arrived.

But he wasn't a workman.

He'd given Fred and Kevin a hard shove in through the door, landing them on me and putting me out of action.

And he was now standing in the doorway, steadily pointing a large handgun at all of us.

'Hands up,' he said unnecessarily.

Chapter 16

What was even more painful than the disaster at Kate Dunkerley's flat was the interview with Superintendent Moon when we finally got back to the nick that evening. And it was much worse for Derek than it was for me.

'What did you expect me to do, Michaelson, put the damned folder in your hand? It was on your desk, for God's sake, man!'

Derek made the mistake of trying to answer him. He should have known better by this time.

'When you told me you had the confirmation of his status from the Embassy, sir–'

'But the details, man, the photograph! It was all in the folder! I took the precaution of putting it on your desk with my own hands! If you'd just taken the time to glance at it!'

He was going that nasty purple colour again. We all got worried when that happened. He looked as if he might pop off at any minute. But we knew by now the only thing to do was to sit tight and let him blow off steam until he wore himself out. And it looked as if he was definitely in the right. If Derek had found time to look at that folder, whatever it was, it turned out he'd have seen that we had the wrong Goldfeather. Or the man we thought was Goldfeather was someone else, and he'd got clean away. And made us all look like a bunch of idiots in front of Kate Dunkerley and Charles North, as well as those two clowns, DC Fred Archer and DC Kevin Burton.

And now, on top of being in dark brown trouble with Mr Moon, Derek was going to have to face an interview with the real Goldfeather. When he showed me the folder later on, I could see from the photograph that he was nothing like the bogus Goldfeather. He was a balding, middle-aged man so ordinary that he'd never get a second glance in the street. He certainly didn't have those film-star looks that made Kate Dunkerley blush every time she looked at him.

But maybe Kate's blushes had nothing to do with her fancying him, like I'd said before. Seemed to me it was more likely she already knew him. Unless he'd put on his accent as well as his identity, he was an American. So he could have been working with Jack Roc or Len Gilmore, or both. But then what was his connection with this Winkelhorne character, and why did *that* mystery man have to pretend to be some old woman?

While I was turning all this over, Derek must have been doing the same, because there'd been quite a long silence. Mr Moon broke it.

'Michaelson!' he barked. 'Am I talking to myself here, or what? Have you got the temerity to fall asleep while I'm reprimanding you? First you try to put the blame for this fiasco on to me, saying that I gave you confirmation of this man's status, then you calmly doze off while I'm trying to discuss the case with you? Do you like being a detective inspector, Michaelson? Because if not, we can always remedy the situation!'

Things were getting worse. I'd thought we'd reached rock bottom, but now I felt we were all sliding slowly further downhill.

Of course Mr Moon was bang to rights being so furious. And it did look as if it was all Derek's fault. He should have read the folder with the information from the US Embassy about Goldfeather long before we went to the meeting with him at Kate's flat. But it was no good him trying to explain.

He just said in a really humble voice, 'Sir, I can only apologise for this serious oversight. Of course you're quite right. If I hadn't overlooked the folder which you so thoughtfully placed on my desk...'

Mr Moon had gone that awful colour again. And he banged on his desk. I was really worried about him. And us. Would we all live through this interview?

'Michaelson!' he bellowed. 'Are you taking the piss? Do you like living dangerously, man? Or are you a complete idiot?'

It seemed as if Derek thought best not to try to answer. Maybe Mr Moon didn't really want him to. So there was another long silence, broken only by some heavy breathing on the other side of the desk. Meanwhile I tried to look invisible.

Finally, Mr Moon spoke again, in kind of a broken voice but more calmly. He said, 'Tell me again everything that's happened on this case, Michaelson. Leave nothing out. Don't be afraid. Confide in me. Let us try to face our problems together. Perhaps we can still salvage something before all our necks go on the block.'

So Derek gave him a recap of the whole case. Starting with the call from Kate Dunkerley that brought us to the body of Len Gilmore with his cock in his mouth, he finished with the gunman disguised as a workman bursting in and getting the bogus Goldfeather away from us, handcuffs and all. While he was talking, I saw a whole lot of different expressions occurring one after the other on Mr Moon's face. Poor Mr Moon. I did feel for him. Even more than for Derek or myself.

Amazement, disbelief, disgust, wonder, and sometimes even a little bit of a smile came on that podgy intelligent face. And that, by the way, was another thing. He'd put on a lot of weight in the three years he'd been our Super.

When Derek finished, there was another silence. Then Mr Moon sighed, and shook his head, but this time not in a disapproving way at all. His look had changed by this time. Now he was more sad than angry.

'My word, Derek,' he said. 'What a bugger. What a tough run you're having. I hadn't taken in all the ramifications until now. I've handled some difficult cases in my time myself, but this is a prizewinner. You'd better have a drop of this.'

And he brought out a Scotch bottle from his bottom drawer. I knew Derek didn't care for the stuff. He'd rather have a nice glass of Merlot. But it was such a relief that Mr Moon was softening – and calling him Derek again – that probably he'd have accepted a drink of washing-up water to keep him in this better mood.

'I have to admit,' the Super said, pouring out generous splashes of booze, 'in all my experience in the Force, I've never heard of such a complicated case. Now tell me, did you believe any of the false Goldfeather's story about this American journalist – what was his name? – and the black market in human organs? And if it wasn't true, why do you think he spun such a yarn?'

'Well, sir,' Derek said, sipping and probably trying not to shudder, 'of course it's very difficult to know what to think, but what got me going was that everybody's heard of this fellow Redondo and his kidnapping. It made world headlines for a while. As you say, what would be the purpose in telling a tall tale like that. And then again, we do know that this disgusting trade does go on in the Far East. But does that prove anything? Or was he just taking those well-known facts and weaving them into a story to frighten Kate Dunkerley?'

'Frighten her into what? Giving him information he was after?'

'I suppose so.'

'But we can't know what he's up to until we can get a clue about who he is. Give me your take on the whole thing, and let's bend our minds to what it might all be about.'

This was better. He was beginning to relax. And his colour was better, too.

'How I see it, sir, is that there are two separate lots of villains in this case. We have our Mister Big at the top of one lot, who employed Christine Smith and the man Winkelhorne to watch Len Gilmore and Kate Dunkerley. I think that Mister Big also sent Kate Dunkerley her expensive solicitor. Maybe, too, he was the one who sent those two thugs to frighten Gilmore about something or other, but I suspect there really was no intention to kill him. If there had been, they'd have brought their own weapons instead of just picking up a handy lamp. It seems the situation got out of hand when Gilmore unexpectedly produced a gun, and they panicked and over-reacted. That's all one set of people, so to speak. Then there's another lot, of which the bogus Goldfeather is one, who are much harder to guess about.'

His voice tailed off, just died away. I knew he didn't have a theory about the rest. Mr Moon listened, but there was no way to tell if he was impressed or not.

All he said was, 'Well, Derek, it's a good thing we've got this meeting at the Embassy with the real Goldfeather tomorrow morning. Perhaps we'll be able to sort something out with his help. We could do with a lot more information, seems to me. But now tell me,' he said, settling down cosily and pouring himself another generous small torrent of Scotch, 'you say DS Pusey had this fellow handcuffed and flat on his face when he resisted arrest? Does karate, does she?'

By this time I could see they'd both forgotten I was still

sitting there, I'd been trying so hard to be invisible. But if they were going to talk about me, it was time to remind them I was there. I cleared my throat and they both jumped and gave me a dirty look. Well, it wasn't my fault. Nobody had told me to go.

'Um, you don't need Sergeant Pusey to stay now, sir, do you?' Derek asked, in a really smarmy sort of way. There was no need for that. He didn't have to crawl. I was sure that wasn't the sort of thing Mr Moon wanted. Anyway, he just told me I could go, and I was glad to scarper as fast as I could. Whatever was coming next between the two of them, I didn't want to be there. If it was anything Derek thought I should know, he'd tell me later.

Finally he tottered back into his office, where I was still waiting, though I didn't know what I thought I might be waiting for.

'Oh Greta,' he said, slumping into his chair, 'I've always been an ambitious man, but now I'm beginning to have doubts. Not of my ability to climb the ladder and get promotion. But seeing the effect on Mr Moon of dealing with errors and idiots, I wonder if I want to go through such pain. The poor man is suffering. That business with Garcia's attempted suicide, for instance.'

I gave him a sharp look, but he wasn't having a go at me about my part in that. He was just droning on.

'When you look at the photograph on the wall behind him, celebrating the day he took over this Station, you can see how much he's aged in those three years. Some days recently he's looked like a man in terminal decline. What I ask myself is, is it Watford that's such a difficult posting, or is it the same for every Superintendent?'

I could see he didn't want an answer, so I gave him a question back.

'What was all that about a folder?'

'Well, as Mr Moon said, he'd put the folder about Goldfeather on my in-tray himself. Look, here it is. What we both didn't know was that another folder, labelled "Returning young offenders to detention" had been put squarely on top of it. For some reason, I assumed that the folders had been put there in order of importance, and had started to read the top one. I suppose it was foolish of me, but that's what happened.

'I ploughed my way through quite a lot of it, but felt myself going quietly hysterical by the time I'd got to, just a minute, I'll read you a bit.'

He rummaged in his in-tray, fished out a folder and started to read:

'The combined effect of the deeming provision in section 40(4)(a) and section 51(2) was that an order made under section 40 would be aggregated with any new sentence to create a single term. Having referred to R v Foran ([1996] 1 Cr App R (S) 149), R v Worthing Justices, Ex parte Varley (Note) ([1998] 1 WLR 819), R v Secretary of State for the Home Department, Ex parte Probyn ([1998] 1 WLR 809) and R v Lowe; R v Leask ([1999] 3 All ER 762), His Lordship said...'

By this time I was laughing and feeling a bit out of it myself, and I hadn't had the amount of whisky he'd probably drunk by then.

'OK, I get the idea, stop now,' I giggled. 'But it's part of the job to read this muck, isn't it?'

'Yes, but at the time, my feeling was that I really didn't need to cope with all this. And I thought the rest of the heap of files was the same kind of heavy stuff, so I decided to leave the whole boiling until I had more time to put my mind to it. Of course, I see now that was my big mistake. Or rather, one of several.'

I wanted to steer him away from that, so I asked what he'd answered when Mr Moon asked about my karate.

That was worthwhile, because he suddenly gave me a big beaming smile. What a handsome little bugger, I thought to myself. I'd rather have him than ten of that greasy pretending-to-be Goldfeather.

'Oh yes, I told him about your Black Belt, and what a great asset that is in a rough situation. In fact, I told him how much I appreciated having you on my team in any situation.'

I tried not to look too pleased with myself.

'And he said?'

Derek looked a bit uncomfortable.

'Well, er, he said he could see that, and that he thought you were a fine big sturdy girl. As a matter of fact, I thought he looked a bit lecherous when he said that. That's not like him, though. Probably I imagined it. Then he said, "Seems to me, Derek, I've seen her eyeing you in a certain way sometimes. Think she's attractive, do you?" I was very embarrassed, and didn't know what to answer. I mean, I thought I was beyond surprise, but the Old Man wanting to have a gossip about one of his sergeants left me speechless.'

I smirked. 'Maybe he's got a romantic side? So what did you say to that?'

'I said I think she's a damned attractive woman.'

'Oh Derek–' I started, all soppy, but he was going on.

'He smiled at me quite kindly. A far cry from the thundering purple-faced fury we'd faced at the beginning. But then I was even more amazed at his next remark.'

I was getting hot by this time. I couldn't wait for the next bit.

'He said, "Time you thought about settling down, young feller. Have you ever thought of that?" I couldn't think what to say, but by then I could see he was beginning to nod, and his eyes were not so much bloodshot as disappearing. He mumbled, "Tell me tomorrow, Derek, on the way to the US Embassy." So I left him to it.'

'That's it?'

'Yes, I think I'm in the clear with him now. Let's call it a day and go home, Greta.'

So there I was, up in the air again.

Chapter 17

It was a bit of an embarrassing time in the Incident Room next morning, trying not to look foolish telling about the escape of the bogus American Agent. Then Derek and Alfie and I went back to the office for a chat about Alfie's trip to Birmingham. He was full of it.

'It's a funny thing,' he started, 'when you watch one of them police things on the telly, they go to make a call on someone and that person's always at home. My experience, it's the opposite, specially if you want to catch them by surprise. Mind you, that wasn't exactly the case with this Brown couple. It wouldn't have mattered if they'd expected me or not.'

Derek was tapping on his desk by this time.

'Are you going to tell us anything or not, Alfie? Get on with it, man.'

'Well, that's what I'm telling you. They were out. So I went on to the Social Services. Not much joy there, either. There was nobody left who'd been working there when Catherine Dunkerley was killed. They all looked straight out of school themselves, so that wasn't surprising. Kids seem to run everything these days. Anyway, they showed me the same records they'd already read out to me on the phone. What good was that. Another wasted journey. Still, they did give me the name and address of the home the boy, Duncan, was sent to after the mother was murdered. It was on such a scruffy bit of paper, I couldn't hardly read it. But while I was still trying to make it out, this young bit of a girl said the place had been closed down five years ago.'

'Are you trying to tell me there was no point in my sending you to Birmingham, Alfie? Because if so, why not come straight out with it, instead of all this roundabout stuff?'

'No, I'm just filling you in on all the details, like you said. I thought the next bit was quite interesting. This girl didn't seem to want to tell me why the place was closed, umming and erring, like. But finally she admitted it was after one of those scandals about the chap in charge fiddling about with the kids. Disgusting, that is. Call themselves caring professionals, then they take advantage of defenceless little kids. I don't care what crimes those children might have committed, they don't deserve that. Anyway, maybe that's why they had no idea in that office how I could set about tracing Duncan Dunkerley's present whereabouts.'

'Right,' Derek said crisply. 'One dead end. Next?'

'Well, I really wanted to tell you about these Browns, who fostered Kate. I got them at home next try. He was a weaselly little man and she was like an anaemic prune. They both looked as if they'd never had a kind thought or a warm feeling in their lives. Just right for fostering poor little kids who'd had a bad start in life, I don't think.'

Alfie seemed to have come back from Birmingham carrying a lot of righteous anger on behalf of the two Dunkerley children. Later on he let slip what that was really about, but at the time I didn't connect it with his own family life. Meantime Derek was looking resigned. I could see he'd decided not to keep prompting Alfie, but let him tell it at his own pace.

'As for their house,' he went on, 'I've seen some miserable places in my time, but this was horrible. Best you could say, it was clean. But everything in it was dark. The walls were brown, the curtains were brown, the carpets – if you could call them that – were a sort of dirty fawn colour. They lived up to their name, the Browns did. No pictures, no ornaments, as for flowers! Don't make me laugh. They certainly didn't take up fostering for love of children, you could see that.'

He consulted his notes.

'Mrs Brown said, "That little Kate Dunkerley, she was a dark horse. Quiet as quiet, did as she was told, helped around the house, you'd think she was a little angel. Not like some we've had. Had to give some back to the Social. Uncontrollable. And language, you wouldn't believe. Not her though. Polite, worked hard at school, run errands for us." Mr Brown said, "That's why it was such a shock when she run off like that. Only fifteen. Not long come on with her – you know." '

Alfie suddenly slammed his notebook down and burst out, 'What a horrible way to talk! Our Carole ought to hear this. She doesn't know how lucky she is, having a lovely home and a mother like my Betty. And then to go and upset her like that...'

Seeing Derek looking blank, he pulled himself together and went back to his notes. I'd twigged by this time that it was about Betty being so upset at finding out that Carole was a lesbian. Talk about old-fashioned! So I suppose Alfie's home life had probably got a bit less comfortable since then. But of course Derek had no idea what was biting Alfie.

'I asked what Kate had looked like in those days, and Mrs Brown said she was very pale, pale hair, pale face, quiet voice, little for her age, you'd hardly know she was there. That was before she went off, she said. Mr Brown said, "Different story when she come back, though. She was all tarted up, very smart, and like, come out of her shell. We asked her straight out, gone on the game, have you, but she just said she'd got a good job what paid well, and she'd saved up and wanted to go abroad. So she'd got a copy of her birth certificate and the form and some photographs, and she wanted to apply for a passport. And that was the last we seen of her."

'So I asked them what they did when she ran away. Only fifteen, she was, you'd have thought they'd have been bothered. Oh no, they just told the Social and the Social told the police, but they said they had so many missing teenagers, they couldn't start searching the country for them all. I said she might have been murdered or abducted, or anything, if she was such a quiet well-behaved girl, they must have been worried at her just disappearing. "Oh well," they said, "she took her clothes and her photographs and a bit of money what she got from her paper-round and helping out the local hairdressers." And they had the cheek to be pleased with themselves that they'd let her keep her own money!'

I'd been quiet all this while, but I had to put my two penn'orth in by this time. There was such a change in Alfie's attitude.

'You seem to be feeling a bit sorry for our little Kate now, Alfie. Not how you felt before, was it?'

'No, well, I thought she was a slippery little madam. I couldn't see why you seemed to be getting a bit soft towards her. But when you think the poor little blighter lost her family, such as it was, when she was only four, and then she had the next eleven years with this rotten couple. No wonder she went to the bad. Pity I can't tell my Carole about her. At least Kate could plead a lousy start to life. But anyway, I picked up on the mention of photographs, so I asked if the Browns had ever seen them. Oh yes, old dog-eared photographs she took everywhere with her, even to school, but nosey old Ma Brown had managed to get a look at them alright. "Nothing interesting," she said, "a blonde woman, quite pretty, might have been her mother

146

what was murdered, with a little black boy, laughing together." I asked Mrs Brown, if that was Kate's mother, who did she think the little black boy was. She thought it would have been Kate's half-brother, the one that done in the boy what stabbed the mother. She said Kate never heard nothing from him the whole time she was with them, so they thought they wasn't close. Not a Christmas card, birthday card, nothing. She said Kate never saw what happened to her mother, herself. She was in bed asleep the whole time. The police and the Social couldn't get nothing out of her, and she never told the Browns nothing, neither. So all they knew was what was in the papers. I got all that. Here's all the photocopies.'

He plonked it all down on Derek's desk, looking pretty well fed up.

'What do you think, then, Derek? Wasted journey, or what?'

Derek looked at him thoughtfully.

'Are you sure that's all you want to tell us? I've got a feeling there's something else.'

Alfie looked a bit shifty.

'Werl, there was this, like, incident on the train coming back. Not what you sent me to Birmingham for–'

'Go on, then, Alfie,' said Derek, looking resigned. 'You may as well tell us everything you've got on your mind. Even if it turns out to be nothing to do with our case, carry on.'

He didn't need any more encouragement. He plunged straight in with his story. Derek had been right. There was something he wanted to get off his chest. So we had to sit through it, even if we had a thousand more important things to do.

'See, I met this very interesting bloke on the train coming home, and he give me a lot of food for thought. Nick, his name was. Had a fascinating chat with him. Turned out that until about a year ago he'd worked for a big firm of bookies. Said that, not everybody knew they haven't just got betting shops, they're in every kind of gambling, in like subsidiary companies. He told me when you see those games machines in pubs, they're all rented out, pubs don't own them. And it's big business, buying and selling machines like those fruit machines, one-arm bandits we used to call them, renting them out, employing engineers, money collectors, big office staff keeping tabs on it all on computers, all that. Course I never let on I was police and naturally knew all about that. I could have told him many a time we'd been called in to settle disputes and investigate how a thumping great gaming machine could disappear from a pub full of people without anyone noticing. And all that.'

Derek let out a big sigh, so Alfie started talking faster.

'Anyway, this Nick, he said he got one promotion after another, till finally he got sent to work for a few months in a casino in Atlantic City. In America. Like training for moving on to Las Vegas. So then he told me, he learned a few things he wished he hadn't, and him being so smart, his bosses thought he wouldn't mind being a bit outside of the law. But he told me he was that one-in-a-million, an honest grafter. So he said. And the band played on, believe it if you can. What he said he done then, he just walked out, come back to England fast as he could, changed his name, enrolled at university as a mature student and hoped he'd disappeared as far as they was concerned. What was it he'd found out, I asked him. He said he didn't dare tell anyone any details, but he could say it wasn't just a rumour that the Mafia runs all that in America, and they've got a good finger in the pie in this country, and all. You can imagine what I did then.'

'No, what?' Derek was hooked by this time.

'Well, told him I was police, thinking maybe I could help him. Like get him some protection. But he must have took fright, because he run off and hid, I suppose in the lavvie. Last I see of him I just caught sight of him as the train pulled out of Milton Keynes. He was scuttling down the platform, with his collar pulled right up round his face.'

'And the point of this fascinating anecdote?' Derek asked. I think we were both feeling a bit let down. It was turning out to be one of Alfie's long pointless stories, after all, like the one about the Australian who'd thought he saw his twin.

'Well, see, I thought from the start that the Gilmore case was something to do with the Mafia,' Alfie offered, all eager. 'So what this bloke Nick told me, got me thinking, how do we know Kate Dunkerley was telling the truth when she confessed she'd done that bit of post-mortem surgery on Gilmore? Maybe she was in with the Mafia and covering up for them. We don't know enough about the Mafia to work it out yet. But one thing we do know is that they're all Italians, the Mafia, and we've got a Colombian on our case. That's a connection, for a start. Stands to reason.'

We couldn't help it. I'm sure we didn't mean to be unkind to Alfie. But we both burst out laughing at his weird geography, connecting Italy to South America, and then we just couldn't stop. He was all put out, and was just about to go stamping off to the canteen when the phone went.

Listening, Derek went quite serious.

'That was Camden Town nick on the line, Alfie,' he said. 'They've got your twins there, and they suggest you should go along and see about them.'

'My twins? Why? See what about them? What have they done?' poor Alfie stammered.

I couldn't imagine Carole and Neil breaking the law.

Alfie and Betty might have had personal problems with them, but I was sure they'd never do anything actually illegal.

Derek spoke kindly.

'You'd better nip along there, Alfie. Go and see what you can do. Never mind about anything here. Do you want us to phone Betty and tell her to meet you at Camden Town?'

Alfie looked as if all the blood in his head had rushed to his nose. It looked all hot and throbbing.

'Oh God, no,' he said. 'For God's sake, don't tell Betty anything. Let me go and find out what it's all about first.'

Chapter 18

Because of Alfie's sudden departure for Camden Town to find out what was the problem with his twins, and him wasting our time telling us pointless anecdotes, we hadn't had a chance to tell him our own news.

With one of his bursts of brilliance, Derek had got someone from the Colombian Embassy to come and talk to Garcia. What with Garcia refusing a solicitor or an interpreter, and bursting into tears every now and again, it had been impossible to get anywhere with him. But when Derek got this Mr Consuelo to help with the persuasion, somehow between the two of them, they convinced Garcia to say that he'd asked us to keep him in protective custody.

Then they called me in.

'Will you accept that Señor Garcia did not mean to shoot at you, Detective Sergeant Pusey?' Consuelo asked.

'That's a bit difficult,' I said. 'When a man has a gun in his hand and he points it at you and pulls the trigger, what might he expect to happen?'

'Ah, but you see, it was a grave misunderstanding. He mistakenly thought you were part of some gang which was trying to kill him. So of course he tried to defend himself. But I must also point out to you, Detective, that as you were told at the time, it was not a real gun, but in fact a starting pistol.'

'Looked real enough–' I started, but Derek cleared his throat loudly and gave me one of his superior officer's looks. I got it. We were striking a bargain. I shut up.

'So there's a possibility that the magistrates would

accept that it was a misunderstanding, and let Garcia off with a warning,' Derek said, smooth as high-gloss paint.

I was baffled. What about Garcia breaking into Gilmore's flat? And what were we up to, anyway? Why should we want to be so lenient with him? For all we knew, he could have been the key to the whole mystery, and we were trying to arrange to let him go. But there was no time. We were due in court. All four of us piled into a squad car and set off with the sirens going. That was about Derek's hang-up about punctuality, not because we were late or anything. It wasn't very comfortable anyway, with Derek and me and Garcia and Consuelo all silent because we couldn't talk in front of the driver.

So we got to court early, and then had to sit around for ages like a plateful of lemon tarts. I still thought the hearing might be a bit interesting, but it was dead boring. After a bit of haggling with the counsel from the CPS, the Embassy man did all the talking for Garcia, with the excuse that his English was better. It certainly was.

'On the night in question,' he said, 'the street door to the flats was unlocked. When, inside the building, Mr Garcia couldn't get an answer at the door to Mr Gilmore's flat, having come there for an appointment with him, he became anxious for his well-being and broke the door down. Seeing Gilmore dead, he became afraid and ran away.'

'And the other incident?' prosecuting counsel asked. 'When he ran from the police?'

'How it appeared to Mr Garcia was just that some strange people came to his lodgings, and he was even more apprehensive. The reason for his fear was that he thought they might have been the murderers of his colleague Gilmore, and they'd traced him and come to harm him. After this misunderstanding was resolved, and he finally comprehended that they were actually the police, he begged them to take him into custody for his own safety.'

One of the magistrates asked the nature of Garcia's business with Gilmore. Back came the prepared answer: it was to do with precious stones, hence Garcia's anxieties. Some of his fears appeared to be well-founded, because his passport, which he'd given to Gilmore for safe-keeping, had disappeared along with all the dead man's own papers.

The lady magistrate said, 'And may I ask why Mr Garcia is on crutches? Has this anything to do with our reason for seeing him here today?'

Still slick, Consuelo said, 'No, there's no connection at all. It was an unfortunate accident. Mr Garcia had been balancing on the edge of a lavatory in the police station, and lost his footing. He fell with one foot in the pan and broke his ankle.'

After a surprisingly short deliberation, the Court decided to dismiss all charges against Garcia provided he stayed at the Colombian Embassy. Not a word of enquiry as to why anyone should have been balancing on the edge of a lavatory. Prosecuting counsel looked daggers at the Bench, but kept his lips pursed.

Thanking the magistrates, Consuelo said, 'You have my assurances that Mr Garcia will not leave the country until the police agree that they no longer require his presence as a material witness.'

What a smoothie! And he looked just as much a swarthy shifty crook as Garcia himself, too. Still, if it was OK with Derek and the Court, it wasn't up to me to argue. And Derek must have cleared the whole business with Mr Moon before he came to this arrangement with the Embassy man. Just the same, I had to have a go at him when we got back to Shady Lane.

As soon as we were alone, I burst out at him, 'Do you mind telling me what good all that's going to do us? I can't see the point of letting Garcia get off like that.'

'No, I don't suppose you can,' he said, at his most cold and condescending. 'But can you tell me what good it was going to do to get him charged with breaking and entering and assaulting you with a deadly weapon? How was that going to help us with this case if we got him a nice long sentence, tell me.'

We could have gone into a long argument about crime and punishment and what the police are for anyway, and what use it might be us getting any criminals banged up, and all the rest of it, but I decided to let it go. Anyway, Garcia had gone off with Consuelo to the Colombian Embassy, and now it turned out that somebody was needed to escort him from the Embassy to his digs in Hendon to pick up his gear and take him back again to the Embassy. And I was the muggins selected for this errand.

'Why me? Why not uniforms? Or Fred or Kevin? Or Alfie, when he gets back from whatever's happening to him and his twins in Camden Town?'

'Because I think you might like the opportunity to mend some fences with Garcia. I don't know – and I don't want to know – what you or Alfie might have said to him to make him desperate enough to try suicide. But I think it would be a good idea if he stopped being so scared of you. So you can do this little job and take the opportunity to get him to trust you a little.'

Can't argue with the boss, specially when you're trying to get him to fancy you. So off I went.

No hitches picking the little bugger up and taking him to Hendon. Far from 'mending fences' as Derek had optimistically put it, we didn't speak a word to each other, the whole journey. It was when we arrived at 142 Dickens Road, Hendon, that the fun started.

Sleazy Sue greeted me warmly enough.

'Ow, Sarge, wot a pleasure to see you again. Alright, are you?'

Then she peered behind me. She took a deep breath and I could hear all her seams straining. She looked like an over-filled ice-cream cone – or a pair of them.

'On yer own?' she said, ignoring Juan Garcia balancing on his crutches. 'Nuthink wrong with Sergeant Alfie, I ope. Only e said e'd be back to see me soon, and I was goin' to, like, make im a nice tea.'

'He's busy.' I didn't see any need to tell her more than that. 'And I've brought Mr Garcia to–'

She didn't seem at all pleased to see him. She gave him a very cold, 'So you're back again then, are you, Juan?'

I didn't give him a chance to answer.

'He's leaving. I've just come with him to pick up his things, then he'll be staying at the Colombian Embassy.'

She looked thoughtfully at his crutches. 'Ad a accident, did e? Fell down some stairs at the station, somethink like that?'

I wasn't sure if she thought she was joking. I hardly knew the woman. So I gave a big hearty laugh while she was shoving Garcia towards the stairs. 'Up you go, then, and get cracking with the packing.'

Fretfully he said, 'I don' know what is cracking, Meeses Sleepworthy.'

But she ignored him and said to me, 'I expec' you'd like a cuppa while you're waiting for im, then? We can ave a chat. P'raps you can tell me wot's appened to Sergeant Alfie. E was reely keen to see me again. 'E'll prolly be disappointed you come instead.'

I bet he will, I thought.

Leading the way to the kitchen, she threw an afterthought over her shoulder, 'Or ave you got to keep a watch on that Juan? E done a runner on you oncet before, I remember. An you come a cropper, an all.'

Now I was sure she was mocking me, but by this time I

was sort of hypnotised by the way her bum was twinkling along in front of me. I'd never seen one like it. I had to admit to myself, I could see what Alfie found fanciable about her. If you liked that sort of thing – and I knew he did – she looked as if she was up for anything.

'No,' I finally remembered to answer, 'he wouldn't get far on crutches, and anyway we've come to an arrangement. Just a cup of tea for me, please, er, Mrs Slipworthy, is it?'

I didn't get a sip of that tea, and no chance to start questioning her about a few things I had on my mind. Suddenly there was a whole series of bumps and crashes from the stairs, with a lot of what sounded like Spanish swearing, and we both rushed out to see what that Colombian idiot had done this time.

Nothing terrible, as it happened, but it certainly put a stop to any chat I might have had with Sleazy Sue. Garcia had tried to get himself, his crutches and his suitcase all down the stairs at the same time. The crutches and the case made it, but Garcia was left hanging on to the banisters with no visible means of support, as it says in the manual.

'Come on, Juan,' Sue shouted, 'just sit down and bump down one stair at a time on your bum.'

While he was doing that, with a lot more groaning and his usual carrying-on, Sue poured him a cup of tea and got out a few chocolate biscuits. Well, I was surprised that hadn't put Alfie off. Right away, that was a big difference between Sue and his Betty. Sue might have had more tight overfilled dresses, but shop biscuits! There was nothing like that in Alfie's house. His Betty made fresh cakes every day. And to Alfie, there was nothing in the world more important than his tummy. So maybe I was wrong, and he wasn't having a little how's-your-father with Sue after all.

'It is Mrs Slipworthy, isn't it?' I asked. 'I noticed that
Garcia called you Sleepworthy, but I suppose that's just
his accent, and not a reference to your way of life.'

I knew it was a bit bitchy, but I hadn't forgotten that
crack of hers about Garcia falling down the stairs at the
Station.

Coldly she said, 'Yes, Susan Slipworthy is my proper
name. An it is *Missis* Slipworthy an all. I did once marry a
man called Slipworthy, so I kep' to it, bein' my legal name,
even if he's not with us any more.'

'Oh, I'm sorry to hear that, I didn't realise you were a
widow.'

She laughed, but not in a jolly way. She'd quickly
forgiven my crack about her morals.

'Wouldn't mind if I was a widow, between you an' me,
Sarge. Nah, e's inside. Your lot copped im.'

I grabbed the chance.

'Well, at least he left you with this house. Do you have
many lodgers?'

'Snot my 'ouse. I just work ere. Ousekeeper landlady,
like. I don't ave no say about lodgers, neither. Wouldn't
ave ad that little bugger Garcia if I 'ad any say. Bloody
nuisance e is.'

Dead on cue, the bloody nuisance hopped and thumped
his way into the kitchen.

'Is make very tire, the crotches,' he complained.
'Especial on stairs.'

I didn't bother to point out he could have left the case
for me to bring down the stairs for him. Some people aren't
worth telling anything.

'Sit down then,' Sue said, quite kindly, 'I'll make you a
cup of coffee, I jus' remembered you don't like tea. They're
not civilised, you know,' she explained to me, 'don't know
the blessin' of a nice cuppa.'

'I do, for sure,' I said, sipping mine. 'So who does own

this house and tell you who to have as lodgers, then?'

'Werl, I never met im, it was all done through a third party, as you might say,' she said, 'but course I do know is name. Mister Leonard Gilmore, it is.'

Gilmore! Why did he need this place? For a moment, I thought she was having me on. Then I realised, of course, she didn't know he was dead. Maybe she wouldn't have been so ready to tell me he owned the house if she'd known. But there'd been no publicity, we'd made sure of that. How would she know? Clearly Juan Garcia hadn't seen fit to tell her, and who else was there? Possibly Kate Dunkerley knew her and might have let her know, but why should she? Well, it certainly wasn't up to me to tell her she'd lost her boss. But there were more surprises coming.

'Not that e's ever told me imself oo to take in,' Sue went on. 'No, not Mister Igh and Mighty. E wouldn't talk to the likes of me. And as for comin' out ere, not im. E's never set eyes on the place. Don't suppose e ever leaves Up West. Proberly lives in Mayfair, I wouldn't be surprised. But that Kate, she's a nice friendly girl. I get on all right with er. She come ere that day, you know, when you and Sergeant Alfie come looking for im,' she nodded at Garcia, who was sipping moodily at his coffee. 'In er leathers, she was, so she must of come on er motorbike.'

That rang a bell, but I left it for now. I wanted to follow one line at a time. By this time I was really wishing that I'd waited until Alfie could have come with me.

'So is it Kate who tells you who you've got to take in as lodgers?'

'Ner, my instructions was, when somebody comes ere and says, Mister Leonard Gilmore says you're to take me in, I as to give them a room. Ooever they might be. Even shifty little foreign types. And board too, if they wants it.'

'Well, that's a funny kind of arrangement. I hope you get a decent wage, as well as all found.'

'Oh yes, mustn't grumble about that, I get a good screw out of the job alright,' and she suddenly gave a suggestive wink. 'You'd be surprised. Only yestiddy, the latest one come.'

What! I thought. How could that be? Because, by then, Gilmore was already dead!

Chapter 19

I couldn't understand how another lodger could have been sent to Sue Slipworthy yesterday. Surely whatever operation Gilmore had been running must have come to a halt at his death?

'Yestiddy it was she come,' Sue confirmed, not noticing my dropped jaw. 'Pretty young thing she is. Irish, I'd say by the funny way she talks. But timid, you wouldn't believe! Will she come out of that room? She will not. I can't make out if she even goes to the bathroom. P'raps she pees in er washbasin. Wouldn't be the first to do that, I can tell you. But she won't come down ere for er meals. I ave to take it all in to er on a tray.'

Irish! I thought. Christine Smith! I've found her. No, couldn't be. How could she be here, in Hendon, in what was obviously a safe house owned by Gilmore. Or why. That was the question. Why.

'Maybe I could have a word with that girl, Mrs Slipworthy. She might be the one we've got half the Service out looking for—'

'No disrespeck, Sergeant, but that's ridikerlous. Ow can you tell she might be the same one you're looking for. I never even tole you er name, so ow can you know oo she is?'

'Well, if you don't mind, I'd better check up, just the same. Show me to her room, please, and I'll try to get her to come out and talk to me.'

Grumbling, 'You're wastin' your time there, I'm telling you,' Sue got up and led the way to a downstairs door.

I didn't want to admit it, but she was probably right. I was just jumping to conclusions because I wanted to find her.

I knocked loudly.

'Miss Smith,' I shouted, 'Miss Christine Smith? I am Detective Sergeant Greta Pusey, you know me, we've met. I need to have a word with you. Please don't be afraid, I just want to protect you.'

Except for a little mouse-like rustling, not a sound. Suddenly Sue decided to help.

'It's me, Miss,' she called out, 'it's true, she's a police sergeant, she won't do you no arm.'

A longer silence. Then the key turned and the door opened a crack. An eye that I recognised looked out.

'What more do you want from me, Sergeant, darling?' a husky voice muttered. 'My life is in danger, you must know that. You know I saw a murder–'

And the door slammed shut again before I could take a step to hold it open. With a lot of thumps and crashes, Juan Garcia joined us. Who invited him?

'Mees, Mees,' he called, 'thees wimmin is good. Ees better to be fren with her. Otherwise you be sorry.'

'Well, thank you very much, Juan,' I said bitterly. 'That was a big help. Why don't you keep out –'

Right and wrong. For some reason, it did the trick, and she unlocked the door and opened it again. She didn't actually come out, but just stood there and looked at us. Of course it was Christine. I'd known that as soon as I'd seen that unmistakeable eye peeping out at me. She wasn't looking quite so beautiful, but still pretty stunning, I was sorry to see. There were too many good-looking women in this case for my liking. If only I'd been a 'lesbeen' like Alfie's Carole, I'd have been like a stud in a harem! As it was, I just felt plainer and plainer.

'We had a safe place all prepared for you in Hemel

Hempstead,' I told her. 'Why did you go and run away like that?'

'Leonard Gilmore gave me this address and told me if I was ever in trouble, this would be a safe place to hide. "Hide," says I, "now why in the world would I want to do that?" "Well," he said, "you never know." '

'He was right there,' I agreed, 'you never can tell.'

'Yes, now we know what we know, right enough. At the time I'd no idea what he might have meant, and I don't suppose he did himself, either. Now I'm thinking to myself, how could he judge he was talking about his own murder, the poor man.'

Christine couldn't have guessed that one of us knew nothing of Gilmore's death, or maybe she wouldn't have come out with it quite so directly.

Sue had gone white while Christine was talking.

'Murder!' she screeched, nearly deafening the lot of us. 'Was you talking about im? Mr Gilmore been murdered, as e! Ow Gawd!'

Then while we were all standing there gawping at her, she got her breath and turned to Garcia. She gave him a great thump round the head, and yelled at him, 'I suppose you done it, you bloody foreign little git, you!'

Well, sorting out that lot certainly made a long day longer. First I had to take a statement from Sleazy Sue about her arrangements with Gilmore. As I thought, it turned out that he'd used Kate as his runner to give instructions and sort out problems, so that he never needed to come to Hendon himself.

Then I finally gave up trying to persuade Christine to come with me to Hemel Hempstead. I had to threaten her that if she wouldn't come voluntarily, I'd have to arrest her as a material witness to a crime. That settled that. I called in to Derek and put him in the picture, and he agreed to send Fred and Kevin to pick up Garcia and take him back to the Colombian Embassy.

I handed Garcia over to them and took Christine to Hemel. I was dead beat by the time I got back to Shady Lane. All that excitement was more tiring than an evening of karate, but at least I'd achieved something to make up for the mistakes I'd made earlier over Christine.

*

It turned out that Fred and Kevin had done a good day's work while I'd been out. They'd found out the name of the holding company that owned Robin Hood House, and that the same company owned the estate agents who managed it. It was a private company, so they hadn't got the names of the directors yet, but they were sure they'd root them out by tomorrow.

More interesting was that these estate agents didn't handle any other properties, so it was just a front for handling Robin Hood House. And taking into account that the shop on the ground floor had always been empty, and the only occupied flats were those three (Kate, Gilmore and Winkelhorne), well, that all came to something pretty fishy. Some kind of a set-up there, and Derek was about to move right into it.

And when Fred and Kevin heard about Gilmore owning the house in Hendon – that would give them a whole lot more to chew on. Some of the questions were: How did he buy it? Through that same bogus agent? And how did he come to employ Sleazy Sue to run it?

'We found out a lot more about Winkelhorne, too,' Derek told me. George Axel Winkelhorne–'

'–what, was that his real name? Winkelhorne?'

'Oh yes, maybe it was easier for him to use his own name while he was posing as a woman.' Derek didn't seem to think it was even slightly funny. But I'd have jumped at the chance of changing my name if I'd been stuck with one as bad as Winkelhorne.

Anyway, he went droning on, 'We found his passport, driving licence, private investigator's licence – all American, of course. He even had his initials, GAW, gold-embossed on his briefcase. So even though Kate says he was already there when she moved in, he must have been there to keep an eye on her and Gilmore. Why else would an American private detective have been the only other person in that little block of flats? Clever way to follow people, that – knowing where they were going before they did themselves, and getting there first!'

'Yes,' I said, struggling to keep my eyes open, with my brain going soggy, 'a trick like that could be handy for us sometimes. But we know how Gilmore and Kate were directed to those two empty flats, don't we. By the way, any news about Alfie and his trip to Camden Town to see about his twins?'

Derek shook his head.

'He called in to say he'd got it sorted and he'd be in tomorrow, but he didn't tell me what it was all about. Anyway, not much more about Winkelhorne. Nothing in his flat to show who he was working for. Oh yes, he comes from New York State. It was on his driving licence, Wappingers Falls, NY.'

'What about the pm?'

'He died from injuries commensurate with falling – or being pushed – out of a second-floor window. He was already dead when he was dumped in the canal. We'll have a few questions to ask the bogus Agent Simon Goldfeather about that, if we ever catch up with him.'

We both brooded quietly for a while, then Derek asked me, 'Did you find out from Christine Smith what she did with the gun? Once you confronted her, did she admit picking it up?'

'Oh yes, she said she chucked it over the bridge by Bushey Arches, into that little stream. I suppose we'll have to get a search going for that?'

'Yes, but not now. Let's go. You look as bushed as I feel.'

It was only when I got home and fortified myself with a little refreshment that I remembered Derek hadn't told me a thing about his day. Specially his visit to the American Embassy with Mr Moon, and their meeting with the real Agent Goldfeather. I thought I'd call him on his mobile to ask, then I changed my mind. I didn't even know where he was kipping by this time, but wherever it was, he wouldn't want to be pestered with questions at this time of night. He'd probably had a still harder day than I had.

*

Even next morning, when the three of us met in the canteen for early breakfast, Derek still didn't seem to want to tell us anything about his visit to the Embassy. Before I had a chance to ask him, he was saying to Alfie, 'I hope it was nothing serious about the twins. How are they now? Everything OK?'

Alfie looked glum.

'Learned their lesson, I hope,' he rumbled, as usual spraying crumbs all over the table, his beard and my hand, which happened to be next to my plate at the time. 'Bad enough,' he went on, 'getting into a fight in one of them bent Camden Town clubs. But then starting up again in the nick right in front of me, and if that wasn't bad enough, in court the next day too! You'd think they'd know better, the way we brought them up.'

'But what was it about?' I asked. I was trying to seem sympathetic, but really I wanted to get this story out of the way so as to get on to what happened to Derek.

166

Of course, Alfie was only too glad to get it off his chest.

'They went to this club, and my Carole started making eyes at someone, but this someone thought that Neil was looking sideways at them, and give him a swipe, and that started the whole free-for-all.'

By this time I was trying not to laugh and even Derek, who'd been looking really down till now, started to twitch around the smile area a bit.

'Pardon?' I said. 'Could you clarify that statement for us a little, Detective Sergeant Partridge?'

Alfie sighed, spraying more crumbs which I managed to dodge this time. Derek wasn't so lucky, but didn't say anything, just wiped his cheek in an absent-minded sort of way.

'Well, I may as well tell you the whole thing,' Alfie said. 'Fact is, recently our Carole told me and her mother she's a lesbian, see, and this was a lesbians' club they'd gone to. And Neil looking like he does, neither one thing nor the other, this dyke what Carole fancied thought that Neil was one too, otherwise what would he be doing there? So there was a bit of sort of what you might call rivalry and argy-bargy. But course our Neil didn't know why this les give him a knock, so he got a bit aggravated and one thing led to another. And it turns out that when she found Neil wasn't one, she thought he was taking the piss, so it started up the whole frackarse again in the nick, and then all over again in front of the magistrates.'

'But I take it you sorted it all out?' Derek asked in an off-hand sort of way. I could tell he couldn't care less, just thought he ought to show an interest. Alfie didn't spot that, though.

'Yer, course,' he confirmed. 'Once I said I'd see they'd be of good behaviour and the beaks knew who I was, they was just bound over. Then I got them both back to Carole's place and give them a good talking to, and there'll be no more of that. My Betty doesn't know anything about it, so you won't mention it, will you?'

He must have meant me, so I reassured him and then at last turned to Derek and asked him what happened at the American Embassy.

'What was the real Agent Goldfeather like?'

'Nothing like the bogus one. Nice chap. Not tall dark and handsome, just an ordinary middle-aged sort of man you'd pass in the street without a second glance. It was a bit embarrassing at first, because I had to tell him what had happened and what the fake Goldfeather had told us. And after he'd taken the trouble to send us an Embassy messenger with photocopies of his identification, complete with photographs, he might have cut up nasty about it.'

Alfie and I both muttered things about anyone making a mistake, and he shouldn't blame himself, but he just sat there, stony-faced, waiting for us to shut up so that he could go on. Now that he'd wound himself up to tell us, he couldn't wait to spill the whole thing.

'He was a real gentleman. Not a word of reproach about my stupidity in accepting someone entirely different in his place. I'd had enough of a rollicking from Mr Moon about that, so I really didn't need another lot from Goldfeather,' Derek sounded bitter.

But he went on, 'He just sat there and listened, and lit a pipe. Can't remember the last time I'd seen anyone smoking a pipe, and it nearly finished poor Mr Moon off. I could see him trying not to cough. It certainly didn't make the whole interview any easier for him.'

Alfie couldn't wait any longer. He burst out, 'But did he tell you anything? Was he any help to us, after all that?'

'Yes, he told us that the Art Redondo story was a combination of truth and lies. He certainly was kidnapped, but his release was arranged after a three-way negotiation with the kidnappers by the Colombian Government and who he called "his people". But Redondo hadn't been investigating a black market in human organs, hadn't had a kidney removed himself, and positively didn't murder Jack Roc. He hadn't even made a false confession about it. Goldfeather reckons that if Gilmore didn't do that murder himself, he probably had a big hand in it.'

Alfie came up with one of his red herrings.

'I'm surprised,' he said, 'that anyone can smoke in the American Embassy these days. They're so against it.'

Derek didn't bat an eyelash.

'Well, by this time Goldfeather spotted that Mr Moon was going a bad colour and having trouble with his breathing, so he put his pipe out. That made it easier for Mr Moon to speak. He asked Goldfeather for an opinion about what this phoney agent was up to. Goldfeather was all ready with an answer. He said it was a hypothesis, but I think he really knew. He said from our description, he thought the man impersonating him was really Jack Roc's nephew who lived in Hollywood. They wouldn't send anyone from New York, because Kate probably knew the whole family there. Apparently this fellow was trying to get into films, but he occasionally did a few odd jobs in California and Las Vegas for Jack Roc. His name is Roberto Panteolini, but he calls himself Bobby Panther.'

'But–' I started, but Alfie was ahead of me.

'–you still haven't told us what he wanted,' he pointed out.

'Agent Goldfeather thinks that if it really was Panteolini, he was sent by the Roc family to get some of their business back from Gilmore. When he arrived and found Gilmore was already dead, he tried to improvise. First he had a go at Winkelhorne, and that went wrong. Then, possibly, he tried to seduce Kate Dunkerley, on the grounds that she's apparently susceptible to handsome men. Of course he didn't know what a chance he was taking, impersonating an American Federal Agent. But he thought the real Goldfeather was still in New York working with the NYPD investigating the Roc family there.'

'So Agent Goldfeather thinks this man's whole purpose was just to get information, ready for an all-out bash at getting the Roc family business back?' I asked. 'He must have known who Winkelhorne was, then, if he tried him first.'

'Right. Then Goldfeather asked us if we knew who was employing Winkelhorne. And did we have any leads on the murder? And I had to admit although we've got two eyewitnesses to the actual crime, we're nowhere near being able to give him any useful answers. It was all extremely embarrassing, and Mr Moon is not pleased.'

'But surely it was a help, what you got from this Embassy man?' Alfie argued.

'Yes, but we look a right load of incompetents,' Derek said bitterly, and looked angrily at me, as if it was all my fault.

So I was out of favour again, and this time I had no idea why.

Chapter 20

I'd made up my mind to get in before Alfie next morning, to try to get Derek alone and ask him what I'd done to make him so angry with me.

But just as I was about to put it to him, Mr Moon came wandering in. That was enough to startle us. If he wanted us, why didn't he send for us? What was worse, he looked awful. His face was a nasty colour again, and he had great bags under his eyes. We both jumped up, almost to attention, and I thought for a moment Derek was even going to salute. I knew we were both worried about how we stood with the Super, what with letting that bogus Goldfeather and his mate handcuff us together while they got away, on top of Derek not knowing he wasn't Goldfeather anyway. And of course I was still scared spitless that he'd find out it was my fault Garcia had tried to top himself.

Mr Moon flapped his hand at us in a weary kind of way.

'It's alright,' he said, 'you can sit down. I was just on my way in and I thought I'd drop by to see if you needed any advice. But I can see you're busy, so I'll leave you to get on with things.'

He started to go, then said to Derek, 'OK about the search warrant?' and when Derek just nodded, he wandered off, looking even more haggard than when he'd arrived.

Derek said, 'Well! That's the sort of boss to have. What a considerate man.' But somehow there was something in his tone of voice that seemed to be saying the opposite. And after all, having seen Mr Moon in one of his rages, I wasn't sure what I thought, either. If I'd been asked what sort of boss he was, I'd have said variable, maybe.

Anyway, there was still time before Alfie came crashing in, so I quickly asked Derek, straight out, 'Are you angry with me about anything? You keep giving me these looks–'

'No, why should I be angry with you? I don't know what I'd do without you on my team.'

That wasn't exactly what I wanted to hear, but it would do for now, so I left it, and picked up on work.

'Are we getting a search warrant for Kate's place? Or the house in Hendon? Or both?' I asked. 'And does Mr Moon think we should bring Kate in again?'

'The fact is, Greta,' Derek went on as if I hadn't spoken, 'I'm in a funny situation with Mr Moon. He keeps going all fatherly on me and asking about my personal life and giving me his vile whisky to drink and trying to chat about Alfie and his twins. And I'd rather he was just a proper Superintendent and businesslike and, even, purple in the face with rage when we get things wrong...'

I couldn't see what that had to do with me, or if he really was angry with me about anything at all, so I tried again to steer him back to talking about the case.

'You didn't tell Agent Goldfeather all the details about how the bogus one got away, did you? I mean, he must think we're a right load of useless prats anyway.'

'No, at least Mr Moon saved me from that.' Derek sighed, then brightened. 'But Mr Moon did make another suggestion on the way back from the Embassy that I forgot to tell you yesterday. He thinks we should get a proper firm to install an entry video at Robin Hood House to replace the voice-only entry-phone, with screens in all the flats, and a CCTV as well. Like we thought was being done when the workman turned out to be the bogus

Goldfeather's accomplice. Turns out that Kate thought we'd arranged to have that done, and I thought her greasy lawyer had fixed it up. Still, the real thing's already in hand. So we can know all the comings and goings without wasting any man-power.'

'What, will there be one in your flat too?' I asked in my most innocent voice, thinking this was a way to find out if he really was moving into that empty flat in Robin Hood House. If he was, it could only be with Mr Moon's permission and it also must mean he'd been to the fishy agents who were handling the place. He might even have picked up some info there.

'No,' he said glumly, 'I haven't had a chance to do anything about moving in there yet. What with one thing and another, who knows when I'll get a chance to get around to it. And Mr Moon keeps on at me about it's time I settled down–'

Just as the conversation was getting a bit more interesting, of course Alfie came bouncing in, full of the joys of spring. His life seemed to have improved, at least, even if the rest of us were in the dumps. It's not that I'm not fond of him, it just didn't seem fair. So I had a go before Derek even got a chance to say 'Good morning, Alfie'.

'Well, Alfie,' I said, 'what do you make of it all now?'

I could see some of the juice beginning to leak out of him. He got a cautious look.

'You mean the case?' That was a brilliant start. 'Well, it's all gone a bit pear-shaped,' he said. 'It's my opinion it all ties up somehow or another, and all the bits that seem nothing to do with each other will turn out to fit together. But there's a key piece missing.'

'That's very good,' I teased him, while Derek just sat there, shtum. 'But where should we be looking for the key piece? Is it to do with Gilmore's weird set-up? Or that Jack Roc, who Gilmore took over from? Kate lived with him, too, didn't she, till he ended up so suddenly dead. Or is the key whoever employed Winkelhorne to follow Gilmore and Kate? And he followed them from in front, too. How did he do that? And what about the house in Hendon run by your friend Sleazy Sue Slipworthy?'

'I've got no friends in this case, where she's concerned I'm neither partial nor impartial,' he claimed. I noticed he didn't even flinch when I called her 'Sleazy'. 'Anyway, I can see all you're doing is trying to confuse me, so let's just drop it. What now, Guv?' he asked Derek.

'Incident Room, bring things up to date, then you and Greta and I will go to Robin Hood House again. But this time we'll have a search warrant, maybe we'll see what our little Miss Dunkerley has been hiding.'

'What about Fred and Kev?'

'They can go on with their ferreting into background stuff on Gilmore and Robin Hood House and the dodgy agents who manage the flats, and whatever they can get on the house in Hendon.'

On our way back to Kate's flat, Derek said I should try to get her aside for a girlie chat, but I was more interested in what we'd find there.

Wouldn't you know it, the first thing we found was that the smooth Mr North was there again, supposedly still protecting his client's rights. Funny how he managed to be there at all the crucial times.

'No ill effects from your adventures with the bogus Agent, I trust, Inspector?' he asked Derek in his syrupy way.

Derek's face went dark red. I could see he felt like hitting the oily bugger, but instead he went all pompous.

'No, certainly not, Mr North, everything is proceeding, I'm glad to say. We are hopeful that we shall soon get our hands on the man who was posing as an American government agent, and also his confederate. You will have seen that we now have an authentic workman putting in the video entry-phone for Miss Dunkerley and in the other flats, too. Hopefully that will help her to feel more secure.'

I thought Derek won that round. But then we got down to business, and we found absolutely nothing of interest until we got to the safe. Of course it was well hidden, behind the suitcases in the cupboard in the little lobby between the sitting room and the bedroom and bathroom. And boy, did it have some fascinating stuff in it.

Eight passports, for a start. Three each for Kate and Gilmore, a Colombian one for Juan Garcia (so he'd told the truth when he said Gilmore took it from him) and a US one, which could have been Garcia's too. Anyway, the photograph looked a bit like him, and the name on it was Glicco.

Then there was a canvas bag holding several bunches of keys, all with labels attached. It was a pity the labels were in some sort of code, so they stayed a puzzle. No surprise that there was also lots of jewellery, some cash (about a thousand pounds and as much in US dollars) and some bearer bonds. But the most interesting item, as far as I could see, was an address book.

'This could tell us the meaning of the labels on the keys,' I said to Derek, all glowing and excited, thinking he'd say, 'Well done, Sergeant,' for the benefit of the watching and listening slippery Mr North. All he said was, 'Just have a word with Kate about all this, will you?' and went on rummaging in drawers and cupboards.

I plonked myself down next to Kate. She wasn't looking her best.

'Well, Kate, what about all those passports, eh?' I started.

'I'm sorry, Greta, I can't tell you anything about them. I was as surprised as you were when you opened that envelope and they all fell out. I never looked in any of those envelopes or bags or anything. I had no idea what was in them.'

'Oh? How did you happen to have them, then?'

She sighed, and pulled her fingers through her hair as if she'd just realised she hadn't combed it that morning. That wasn't the only thing wrong with her looks that day, though. She answered in a lifeless kind of voice, as if she really couldn't be bothered about the whole thing.

'Well, you see, Len didn't have a safe in his flat, so he just gave me things to put in mine, and I didn't know what they were.'

'Not the keys? You didn't wonder what was in that canvas bag? And you didn't even know you had three separate passports of your own?'

She sighed again and shook her head.

'No, what would I want with three passports? There's nothing wrong with my English one. That's what I've always used. I don't know anything about keys, either. I never even looked in that bag. I didn't care what was in it.'

'What about the address book?'

'I never looked at that either.'

'You see, Sergeant Pusey,' North butted in, 'my client simply cannot help you with these matters. As she has told you, she is as puzzled as you are. But there is one thing which Miss Dunkerley would like to tell you which may be of interest.'

'Oh yes,' she said, suddenly all wide-eyed innocence. 'I forgot to tell you, I hardly ever went to Len's flat. He always came up here, because it was so much more comfortable. That awful night, when, you know, when it happened, that was the first time I'd been down there for about a year.'

In my most sarcastic voice I said, 'Well thank you both

very much. That was a great help. But you've never told us why you had to have two separate flats.'

North got in the way again.

'That's a personal matter, Sergeant, and my client doesn't have to answer such questions. It can have no bearing on your investigations, I assure you.'

And we left soon after that, Derek having carefully given North a receipt for the items we were taking with us.

'So much for him and his formalities,' he said, not all that happily. I thought we'd done some good there, but he was as fed up as ever. What was it going to take to cheer him up, I wondered. We didn't know yet what we'd found, but it was a start, surely.

When we finally got back to Shady Lane, Fred and Kevin were waiting to talk to Derek.

'Good news bad news, Guv,' Fred said. 'Which do you want first?'

'Give me the bad first,' he said gloomily. 'Let's get the worst over.'

'Well, Guv, we can't seem to get to the bottom of this company that owns Robin Hood House. We've got the names of the directors, and well, they're all, like, nobody in particular. We've checked them up and they all seem to be just ordinary employees of the company. But the trouble is, we can't unravel who the major shareholders are – it's like a maze, Guv, every time we think we've got something, it turns out to be another company, and we can't get any names. And they're all private companies.'

'Oh great,' Derek groaned, 'so what's the good news?'

Fred and Kev both started beaming. We could tell they were really pleased about this next bit, but blowed if I could see why.

Fred said, 'Well, Guv, we already knew this company owned Robin Hood House and the estate agents who manage the property. But what we've found out now is that the same company owns a night-club right here in Watford, called the Knight Owls.'

There was a silence.

'So?' Derek said.

Fred looked a bit squashed. But he went on. He was always the one who did the talking. Kevin was a man of very few words, preferring action. He left all the explaining to Fred.

'So Kev and I thought we could along there tonight, unofficially-like, just as ordinary punters, you know, and see what we could find out.'

Derek was at his most scornful.

'Great,' he said. 'Marvellous. That was the good news, was it. Well, how exciting. Yes, all right, go to that club tonight as ordinary punters, and don't run up too much of a bill on expenses. I expect you'll have a good time, but don't feel too bad if you come back no wiser. Which of you two is Sherlock, by the way, and which is Holmes?'

Poor Fred and Kevin slunk out looking discouraged, and I gave Derek a bit of a fishy eye. What was he being so moody about? We'd picked up some interesting stuff from Kate's flat, and Fred and Kev were keen, so he should have been a bit more cheerful. No chance. I noticed that Alfie was looking at him like a dog with his eye on a ham sandwich, hoping he'd get better treatment than Fred and Kev.

All we got from Derek was, 'OK team, you've got plenty to get on with now. I've got to go out for a while, and I hope you'll have good news for me when I get back.'

Alfie and I emptied the bag of keys on to Derek's desk and pawed over them. We read the labels over and over, and I tried writing down what was on them and jumbling them up on a bit of paper. It was a mixture of letters and numbers that just didn't seem to be in any kind of sequence. What made the frustration worse was Alfie coming up with one of his terrible jokes.

'I'm sure we've got the key to the whole mystery here,' he said in his daftest voice, and then looked puzzled when I threw my notebook at him. 'What's up with you, then, girl? You're a bit touchy today. Derek's not a bundle of laughs, either. What's wrong? Had a tiff, have you?'

This time he knew why I threw a telephone directory at him, and was ready to duck as it came his way. Then he got a bit serious.

'No, but listen, Greta. I do crosswords sometimes, and the hardest bit is the anagrams. You know, when they jumble up the letters in a word and you have to sort it–'

'–yes, brilliant,' I interrupted. 'Specially when there's figures mixed in with the letters. What sort of words have got numbers mixed in with the spelling, Alfie? And will you please stop calling me girl,' I barked at him, surprising myself as well as him. I hadn't realised how ratty I was feeling up to that moment.

Anyway, we both shut up after that and just kept shuffling these damned labels around, getting nowhere. Then I started looking through the address book, and that was even worse. I couldn't make out anything except that the names were all in numbers. By the time Derek came back I was ready to bite his head off. Or any other bit of him I could get hold of. It didn't help my mood that he'd suddenly gone all cheery and pleased with himself.

'It's all fixed,' he announced. 'I can move in whenever I like.'

'What's that then, Derek?' Alfie asked, always ready to be friendly.

'I've got a flat in Robin Hood House. That's where I went, to see the agents who deal with the tenants there.'

'Oh, find out anything interesting?' I asked. 'Were they suspicious at all about you specially wanting that particular flat?'

'No, I just said I'd been past that empty shop in Squash

Court Road and wondered if any of the flats above them were available to rent. There's no board out, so I asked another estate agent and they sent me to that one. She didn't ask any questions, didn't want any references, just asked for three months' rent in advance. Pretty reasonable rent, too.'

'She? So a woman was running it? Was she in charge?'

'Seemed to be. Nobody else there. She even offered to be at the flat to receive my furniture when it came out of store. Said she was glad of anything to do, she was so bored. Is that how she seemed to you, Alfie, when you went to tell them about the death of one of their tenants?'

'Now you come to mention it, she looked more upset than you'd expect when I told her about Gilmore,' Alfie said, stroking his beard thoughtfully. 'I thought at the time, she must have known him personally. But from what we've heard about him and women, he'd at least have had a try there, her being such a pretty little blonde. She was the only one there at that time too, but I never thought anything of it. Didn't seem busy, either.'

'Right then, Greta, I want you to go there and nose about, see what you can find out. Something's not right about that place. Pretend you're looking for a shop to rent – a boutique or something.'

'But just a minute, listen, didn't you think Kate looked awful when we saw her earlier? She looked quite ill, and all scruffy, didn't you notice? I thought I'd go and have another word with her–'

'No, she looked OK to me. Off you go then, estate agents, never mind what Kate looks like.'

I did something I'd never done before. I disobeyed a direct order, and went to see Kate again.

Chapter 21

The thing was, I'd got the feeling when I was talking to Kate that she was really cracking up. Except for the odd moment when she did the wide-eyed bit, she'd looked absolutely done in and as if she couldn't be bothered any more. Maybe Derek had been so taken up with the search that he hadn't looked at her properly, but I'd actually talked to her, and it seemed to me if Smoothy North hadn't put his oar in, she'd have just folded up. She might even have given up more information.

And it wasn't just that she looked a mess. Her clothes looked grubby, her hair needed doing, and she had no make-up on. None at all. I knew she'd acted all kinds of parts since we'd first come on the scene, but I could see she wasn't putting it on this time. I suppose if I'd told Derek that, he'd have said maybe it was too early in the morning for her. And he might have made some crack about all women having their off-times, even me, specially first thing. But there was something else, too. When I sat down next to her to question her about the contents of the safe, I'd noticed that she was a bit niffy. Sort of a mix of BO and dirty knickers, like some of the tarts I'd had to deal with when I was in uniform. You don't forget that smell.

So I thought I'd see. She'd had plenty of time since our search to doll herself up again and look – and smell – a bit more like dainty little Kate Dunkerley. But I was beginning to suss that she was more than a bit wobbly in the top storey. Which personality was she going to treat me to this time?

It didn't take long to find out. As soon as I was in the door she started on with some rambling story. She certainly hadn't had a bath since our visit that morning. In fact she hadn't fixed herself up at all, looking and smelling even worse.

'Oh Greta,' she burst out, 'I'm so glad you're here. Terrible things have been happening. First I heard some people talking in Len's flat, and I knew it couldn't be you because you'd all finished in there.'

In my most hard-boiled voice I said, 'Well, why didn't you look through your famous spyhole in the floor?'

'I did, I did. I thought it might be the killers come back for something, you know, and I thought I'd phone you and you'd come and arrest them. But when I looked, there was nobody there and it was all dark. But I could still hear them talking, a man and a woman, it was. Then I recognised their voices, Greta, it was Len and that Irish woman.'

This was too far over the top, even for Kate. I tried to soothe her.

'No, it's alright, Kate,' I said, 'it's just your imagination. You've had a very stressful time, and you're a bit nervous and emotional.'

But then it got really spooky. She just went on as if I hadn't spoken. She honestly didn't seem to hear a word I'd said.

'They were talking about me, and saying what they wanted to do with me. But I beat them,' she suddenly looked very cunning. 'I put my hi-fi on very loud for an hour. That shut them up.'

'So that was alright then–'

'–but after they'd gone, I heard that bogus Goldfeather outside my front door, calling to me to let him in, in his lovely chocolatey voice.'

I couldn't help it, I gave a sudden shudder. But it didn't matter. She didn't notice, just went droning on.

'I looked through the peephole in the front door, but I couldn't see anyone there either, so I didn't open the door. But I wanted to. He was so handsome, and I know he fancied me, too.'

'Why didn't you phone me, Kate?' I almost shouted this time, trying to make her take notice of me.

It worked. She seemed to come out of this kind of trance she'd been in while she was telling me all this loopy stuff.

'Oh, er, yes, Greta, well,' she started stammering. 'It's that Mr North, you know, my solicitor. He said not to speak to you, not just you, any of the police, unless he was with me. Would you like a drink?' she suddenly put on a kind of false bright hostessy voice.

'No, thank you, I just dropped in to see how you are. You didn't seem very well this morning. I hope we didn't upset you,' I improvised.

So then, of course, muggins had to make this nutcase a cup of coffee which naturally she didn't drink, and finally she said she was going back to bed and that gave me the chance to scoot out of there.

'Oh, yes, Greta,' she called after me just as I was nearly out of the door, 'I meant to tell you. We met this young blonde estate agent on the QE2 coming over from the States, course Len fancied her and she told us about these two flats in the same block...'

Her voice died away and I saw she was out of it before she even got to bed. She probably went to sleep right there on the floor.

So had the young blonde running the estate agent's office been planted on the QE2 to try to direct Gilmore and

Kate to the two flats in Robin Hood Court, where Winkelhorne was already in residence? That seemed a bit far-fetched and complicated. So what, everything about the case was difficult to believe. Specially for Watford, not usually the crime centre of the world.

Just to make life a bit more difficult, the estate agents' office was closed when I got there. Derek was still at his desk when I got back to Shady Lane, so I had to confess what I'd done. He didn't seem as cross as he'd a right to be, but listened carefully to what I told him about Kate and her creepiness.

'Well,' he said, 'I admit it all sounds a bit spooky, hearing voices. On the other hand, we both know what a little liar she can be. So maybe she's just spinning you another yarn. And that bit she threw in about the blonde estate agent on the QE2, didn't she tell us something like that before? Did you believe her? Who knows what she might be up to.'

'No, honestly, Derek, I really think she'd going round the bend.'

'You may be right, but I still think it could be an act. We'll just have to wait and see what develops. Anyway, now that I've got the OK from Mr Moon and I've made the arrangements, I'll soon be moving into that empty flat across the hall from Gilmore's. So I'll be able to keep an eye on her. And if she *is* having some sort of breakdown, I'll be there on the spot to take care of her. Or if she's up to one of her crazy tricks, perhaps I'll be able to nip it in the bud. What's up? I thought you'd be glad that I'll be there, but you look as if you've lost a swan and found a duck.'

I was ashamed of myself. There I was, trying to be a tough guy, with my karate black belt and my career ambitions and everything, and I was being soppy. Just because he seemed to be fancying himself as Kate Dunkerley's rescuing hero.

I tried to act all cool and detached. Didn't really work.

'None of my business,' I managed to mutter. 'If you fancy Kate Dunkerley, even if she is a half-barmy gangster's moll. If you feel you've got to protect her, just because she's little and dainty and pretty and blonde, who am I to pass an opinion?'

And I left very rapidly, before I gave myself away any more. As I rushed out, I saw his mouth had fallen open, but I didn't wait to hear if he was going to say anything.

*

After a night of troubled dreams I wasn't feeling my brightest next morning, but it turned out I wasn't the only one.

Alfie was waiting for us both to arrive, anxiously combing his beard with his fingers, always a sign of severe strain for him. He wouldn't talk to me, just paced up and down waiting for Derek.

Seeing the state he was in, Derek greeted him with a snappy, 'Now what, Alfie?'

No 'Good morning' for either of us. So it looked as if none of the three of us was on top of the world.

'Got time for a word, Guv?' Alfie rumbled, sitting down and standing up again. This had to be serious.

'Go on,' Derek muttered in a long-suffering voice, flopping down in his chair and putting his hand over his eyes as if he couldn't stand the sight of either of us.

'Well, see, Guv, I thought I'd pay a call last night on that house in Hendon, not officially, you know, er, socially, like. See, that lady what's been looking after the house for the late Gilmore, she's a very nice friendly person, Sue Slipworthy her name is, and she sort of made it clear that she'd like us to get to know each other better. And things being a bit strained at home on account of our Carole upsetting Betty about being a lesbo, and our Neil not coming out as anything, I was glad to get out and, er, visit her.'

Derek got on his high horse.

'Sergeant Partridge!' he thundered, giving a fair imitation of Superintendent Moon in his most purple-faced rage. 'Do you mean to tell me you've been socialising with somebody who's probably criminally involved with a case we have currently under investigation? Do you realise what this means, Sergeant?'

Well, I thought, he's a fine one to talk. And why's Alfie being such a fool as to tell him all this. If he hadn't said anything, Derek would probably never have found out about it. It wasn't like Alfie to be so stupid, for all his faults. I should have guessed there was something special coming, not just a confession of straying.

'I have to tell you that I found that little Colombian git, Juan Garcia, hopping around the premises on his crutches,' Alfie blurted out very fast like someone trying to get the worst over as quickly as possible. 'I apprehended him and Sue, er, Missis Slipworthy and I questioned him, and he said he had something hidden for Gilmore and he had to find it. It so turned out that the item in question had already been discovered by Missis Slipworthy and I now have it in my possession.

'Sir,' he added as an afterthought and probably, he thought, a way of showing respect to a superior officer. Bit of a change from all first-names, our normal way of talking to each other. 'Guv' was usually the most formal we ever used to Derek.

It certainly wasn't the 'sir' that changed Derek's attitude. I could see he was as excited as I was at getting hold of something that might be real evidence, at last.

'Come on, then, man, let's have it,' Derek yelled, almost losing his self-control. I could see it was getting more and more difficult for him to keep a grip on himself.

Alfie hoisted a suitcase out from behind a chair where he thought he'd hidden it. Actually I'd spotted it the moment I'd got in, but hadn't realised it was important.

'It's locked and I didn't know if you'd want me to bust it open,' he muttered. We could see he was still feeling bad about it all, because he hadn't noticed the change of atmosphere.

'Go on, Alfie, open it,' Derek directed him, and we could see by the way he slipped a screwdriver under the lock and forced it off the case that he'd been ready and hoping for this order all along.

All three of us rummaged around among all kinds of packing materials before we got to the important section and found the vital contents of the case. And it wasn't Garcia's spare shirts and socks.

Unless it was icing sugar, we had hundreds of thousands of pounds-worth of cocaine there.

'How in God's name are we going to explain this to Mr Moon?' Derek groaned, but we could both see that, groaning or not, he was really overjoyed. And Alfie was double-thrilled to know he had Derek on his side again, to save him from the Wrath of Moon.

Dead on cue, The Man himself walked in. He was beginning to make a habit of this.

As if we'd rehearsed it, all three of us managed to put ourselves between Mr Moon and the open suitcase on Derek's desk, without falling over each other. Mr Moon was so full of what he had to say, he didn't even notice that we were all lined up as if ready to salute.

'Well, troops,' he said, 'we've got a lot to thank our friends in the US Embassy for today. They've come through with all kinds of useful information. Of course, this won't solve our case, but it's bound to help.'

We all stood there trying to look eager and keen.

'Winkelhorne,' he said. 'Private investigator planted

187

beforehand in the little block of flats to which Gilmore and Dunkerley had been cleverly led. But before that he'd been employed to report on all he could get on Dunkerley – no interest in Gilmore except his connection with her. Winkelhorne had no criminal connections in the US, and no family, just a partner.'

'Is his partner still running the detective business, then?' Derek asked, for no reason that I could think of.

'Ah, er, no, not a business partner, a, er, what our American friends call a "significant other".'

Alfie gave a groan, which he managed to turn into a cough. He was probably thinking he didn't want to know any more about the gay fraternity. I nudged him to keep quiet just as Mr Moon turned to him.

'You're very good at handling formalities, Sergeant Partridge. Perhaps you'll see about Winkelhorne's body being released by the coroner for shipping back to the, er, the mourner.'

'But who employed Winkelhorne?' Derek burst out. 'All this complicated spying, then manoeuvring them into taking two flats in Robin Hood House where he was already in place, that takes some doing.'

Mr Moon sighed.

'Patience, lad, patience. Winkelhorne was employed by a firm of attorneys in New York, who of course are not obliged to tell the law who they were acting for. But here's a clue: the New York firm has a link with a practice in London called Abel, Levi and North. Familiar name, eh? Also, Special Agent Goldfeather's superiors have decided he should work with us in uncovering Gilmore's activities.'

'Work with us?' Derek said in panic. 'How?'

'Well, by pooling information, of course. To start with, he's told me Gilmore was a married man with three grown-up children. I wonder if our Miss Dunkerley knew that, eh?' he said with a sort of naughty twinkle. It didn't suit him. He wasn't really the twinkly sort. 'The legal tangle of what happens to his estate need not concern us,' he went on, 'but it's going to be interesting. There's the house in Hendon. Not to speak of whatever iffy businesses he'd been running, apart from his legal importing of emeralds... You're a lucky feller, Derek, to be involved in such a complicated case. It can be the making of your career.'

And he bounced out, looking much less haggard and really a bit pleased with himself. Derek wasn't.

'It can be the making of your career, Mr Moon says,' I pointed out, trying to cheer him up.

'Yes, or the opposite,' he said glumly. 'I still don't know how we're going to explain how we got hold of this suitcase. And you haven't told us where Garcia is now, Alfie. How about it?'

Chapter 22

Alfie stood there, looking awkward, and Derek stood in front of him, looking up into his red face. This was all a big mistake. Usually one or both of them sat down so that Derek didn't have to feel self-conscious about being so much shorter than Alfie. Specially if he was telling him off, which I could see was going to be the case here.

'Shall I take this to Forensics?' I asked, picking up the suitcase and trying to break the tension. It didn't work.

Derek suddenly yelled at Alfie, 'Where is he? What have you done with him? You haven't let him go, have you?'

Trust Alfie to make an awkward situation worse.

'Course, I'm not daft,' he grinned, 'I wouldn't let that little Colombian git go, would I. I might of made a slight error of being friendly with Sue Slipworthy, but I'm not completely barmy. As if I'd let him go!'

Not really listening, but seeing Alfie shaking his head, Derek started to calm down a bit. He took a deep breath, and we could both hear it whistling through his tubes. Maybe he thought Alfie hadn't twigged he'd crossed the line himself by taking Kate Dunkerley out to dinner early on in the case, but it must have caused him a bit of conscience when he rebuked Alfie for doing something not quite the same with Sleazy Sue.

I started to be glad he'd ignored my offer to take the evidence to Forensics. This was going to be an interesting conversation. But I did wish they'd both sit down.

'Sit down, Alfie,' Derek finally groaned, as if he'd read my mind, 'and tell me everything from the beginning. Don't worry about disciplinary measures. Just blurt it all out.'

'What, you mean about things being a bit strained at home? Well, it started with my Carole telling my Betty–'

'No, *no*, NO!' Derek shouted, getting all wound up again. 'This isn't the time for your domestic problems, Alfie. What I want to know about is from when Garcia came hopping in on his crutches during your, er, visit to Mrs Slipworthy. First of all, how did he get in? Did he still have a key?'

'Right, Derek, got you now. No, Sue got his key back from him a while ago, but you know what a dab hand he is, he just slipped the lock on the front door and tried to creep in, but course we heard his crutches going thump thump thump up the stairs, didn't we, so we run out into the hall and there he was, just about to hop into his old room. Sue let out a scream, "Wot you doing up there?" she yells, and he got such a fright he nearly fell all down the stairs again. I've never known a villain having so many accidents, you'd think he'd give it all up by now, wouldn't you.'

Derek bared his teeth in what I could see wasn't meant to be a smile. 'Get on, get on with it,' he sort of growled at poor Alfie. This case wasn't doing his nerves any good, we could see.

'Well, anyway,' Alfie went on, not a bit bothered by Derek's edginess, 'to cut a long story sideways, the long and short of it was, I run up and fetched him down and give him a cuff or two round the head, and then he said he'd left this other suitcase in his room and he wanted it for more clothes, and Sue said when she was clearing up the room she took his case and put it in a safe place, namely the garden shed. When he heard that, he let out a sort of howl and said something about the damp, and all this while we thought it was clothes we was all talking about. But when Sue lugged this case in, I got suspicious about it being so heavy, and said I'd better take possession of it, and that Garcia, he got very distressed, sobbing and carrying on and so forth. So I asked Sue if she had a specially secure place where we could keep him for a while, because I didn't fancy bringing him back here to the nick, things being as they were, and I knew if I left him, he'd scarper back to the Colombian Embassy and we'd never get hold of him there.'

'Good thinking, Alfie,' Derek said quite warmly, and we could see he'd started to feel better about things. 'Where did you leave him, then?'

Alfie hesitated for the first time.

'Well, there was a bit of argy-bargy, Sue suggesting some ideas I didn't like and her getting rorty and saying she didn't need to co-operate with the police at all. Still, I don't suppose you want to know about all that. What it was, him being such a slick operator with the locks, I thought best to find somewhere really safe, so finally we left him in an old wooden chest with plenty of rope tied round the outside. And Sue's got his crutches.'

'Did you question him at all?'

'No, I thought you'd want to do that yourself when we knew what was in the case. Course, we still don't really know for sure, do we?'

'I think we do, you know. Anyway, you and Greta go back to Hendon and bring Garcia back here, and we'll see what he's got to say for himself this time. Oh yes, and you'd better get your friend Mrs Slipworthy to come back with you to give her statement about the suitcase, too. While you're gone I'll get the contents verified and checked in as evidence.'

'Anything happening about the stuff we got from the safe in Kate's flat?' Alfie asked. I could see he wasn't worried about Derek being off him any more.

'Not yet. Fred and Kevin have been having a go at deciphering the codes on the labels and in the address book. Those two lads are good at the backroom stuff, you know, Alfie,' Derek said, getting back to being quite friendly. 'Not as good as you and Greta at the real police work, mind you.'

As we were leaving to pick up Garcia from Hendon, I couldn't help laughing to see Alfie blushing right down to the roots of his beard at such unusual praise from Derek. On our way, I mentioned to Alfie that Derek had given permission for Fred and Kev to go to some nightclub that night.

'I hope they work something out about those keys before they go,' I said. 'They won't have their heads on straight enough tomorrow for that kind of puzzle.'

'What nightclub? What for?' Alfie asked. 'Don't you think there ought to be more communication between people working on a case, Greta? That's what we've got an Incident Room for.'

'Oh, nothing important enough for that, it's some red herring they're chasing. Load of rubbish,' I said as we arrived outside Sleazy Sue's house in Hendon.

When I saw where they'd got Garcia, I felt sorry for the poor little bugger. I reckoned he'd be pleased to come back to the nick this time, after being in that roped-up chest. It must have been poky and stuffy in there, not even as big as a coffin. It was a wonder he could even breathe in there. Sure enough, he came peacefully along with us. And Sue made no fuss either, saying, 'I ope I always know my duty, Sergeant,' with an open wink at red-faced Alfie.

By the time we got Garcia back, crushed and unusually quiet, the contents of the suitcase had been confirmed. Derek was beaming, and Mr Moon had sent his warm congratulations on a fine piece of detection. Turned out there were ten kilos of cocaine in amongst the mysterious packing materials, and with a street value of about sixty thousand pounds a kilo, that was quite a good haul we'd got. I wondered what yarn Derek had spun Mr Moon about how Alfie had got hold of Garcia and his dodgy suitcase, to cover up his real story. We'd have to check that with him before one of us put our foot in it.

Meanwhile, Derek was charging Garcia with possession of an illegal substance and asked me to be in on the questioning. He said Alfie could come too, as long as he kept his mouth shut.

'Do you want a solicitor? A translator? Your representative from the Colombian Embassy?' Derek asked Garcia, who shook his head sadly at each question, but didn't say anything.

'Do you understand the crime you've been charged with?'

Garcia nodded.

'Do you wish to make a statement?'

He nodded again. This was all a nuisance, because each time I had to record into the tape whether he was shaking his head or nodding. So things went quicker when he started talking.

'Am making statement,' he said. 'She,' he pointed at Alfie, 'chump on me, knock me down, make me injure. How you feel,' he suddenly got all passionate, 'how you feel if you have broke the leg, then is taking away your crotch, put in the box, tie up, no air. When I say, help, no breathing, all she say is shot op.'

I was struggling with all this, but Derek didn't even crack a smile. You have to admire a man who can keep a straight face after a statement like that.

'I don't want to know about any of that, Mister Garcia,' Derek said, 'I want to know about the suitcase with ten kilos of cocaine in it you had in your possession at 142

Dickens Road, Hendon. Did you bring it into the country with you? How did you get it through Customs? Where were you taking it? Who were you working for? Didn't you tell Mrs Slipworthy you were looking after that case for Mr Gilmore?'

'I don' know nothing about cocaine,' Garcia stated. 'Is nothing to do with Meester Geelmore, neither. I lef' a case of clothings and chews at thees address what you say, and when I go to get heem, these Meeses Sleepworthy, she sweetch for other case and say he is mine. Then thees man,' he pointed dramatically at Alfie, 'she chomp on me and put me in thees box I can't breathe.'

'But you told Detective Sergeant Partridge here and your ex-landlady, Mrs Slipworthy, that you had been looking after that case for Mr Gilmore.'

'No, I deeden say thees, is all lies.'

And that was it. Looked as if we were stuck again. Garcia told the same story over and over, however many times he was questioned, and he wouldn't budge. His word against Sue Slipworthy's. She said it was his case and he said it wasn't. He said she'd swapped it for a different one, she said she hadn't.

But then we were saved by the fingerprints on the case: Alfie's, Sue's, Garcia's and others. Alfie and Sue were agreed that Garcia hadn't touched the case after she'd got it out of the shed, so his prints must have got on it earlier. That made it clear there was no swap, it was Garcia's own suitcase alright. So we'd got him. His pal at the Colombian Embassy wasn't going to get him out of that.

Then we got more good news. I knew Alfie hated to admit it, but Fred and Kev really were good at solving puzzles. They'd deciphered the Gilmore keys and address book.

Fred said, 'See, when we sorted out all those keys, it turned out there were only three separate bunches, each with two keys that must have been for outer doors and the rest smaller, like for rooms or cupboards or filing cabinets sort of thing. Then we worked out three lots of addresses from the book that seemed to match the labels on the keys. So after that, all we had to do was puzzle out the addresses. Here we are,' and he handed a piece of paper to Derek.

Have to hand it to Alfie. He didn't mind showing he was gobsmacked.

'Is that all?' he said warmly. 'Bloody marvellous, I'd say. Greta here and me, we could have worked on that for a month and not come up with the answer, eh girl?'

I wasn't best pleased at being put in the same class of brainpower as Alfie, but I admitted that Fred and Kev had done a great job.

'So are you off now, lads?' I asked them, which gave Alfie a chance to ask them where they were going and why. He did know, he just wanted to hear them say it themselves. Maybe he was a bit huffy at having to be told about their club visit by me and not them.

They might have been brilliant at puzzles, but the way they both went 'Ahah' and went off sniggering together showed that they weren't ready for promotion quite yet.

Pity though that Fred and Kev weren't in the Incident Room when Mr Moon gave us our briefing for the following morning. They might have heard him praising the way they solved the riddle of the keys and their labels.

'Three teams,' Mr Moon said, 'will swoop simultaneously on these three addresses at six tomorrow morning. We will assemble here at five. I will head one team myself, Detective Inspector Michaelson will take another, and Detective Sergeants Partridge and Pusey will be jointly in charge of the third team.'

Chapter 23

Well, by the time we'd got through the briefing next morning and Alfie and I had got to our target address on an industrial estate in North Watford with our team, it was nearly seven o'clock. Any later and people would have started arriving for their normal day's work.

Not that it would have mattered, as far as we could see at first. I just hoped the other two teams had a more interesting result than we did. Naturally it wasn't like a regular raid, no shouting and battering doors down and all that. We just took the usual precautions with posting plods all round so no-one could slip out of a window or a back way, then calmly and quietly let ourselves in with the keys kindly provided by the management.

Just the same, it seemed to be a bit of a let-down. An ordinary legitimate business, with all the proper machinery, a little glassed-round office separated off in the corner, a hot and cold drinks machine, overalls hanging up, the lot.

'Well, Greta,' Alfie said, 'where does that get us, eh, girl? A print works, innit?'

'Yes, sure, but what do they print? A bit more than leaflets for local businesses, I think.'

'You're a lovely girl, Greta,' Alfie laughed, 'but you do sometimes let your enthusiasm get in the way of your common sense. Go on, I suppose you think it's a counterfeiting business. What do you think, bearer bonds or hundred dollar notes?'

I wasn't put out, I was used to Alfie. Some people would get huffy when he made fun of them, but not me. I just picked something up from a bench and showed it to him. It was a label, looked like something for one of those French scent bottles.

'Big business, Alfie,' I said. 'Ever been down Oxford Street where they sell cheap designer perfume out of suitcases? Somebody has to print the labels, don't they? That's one of our Len Gilmore's businesses accounted for. Let's start looking through their files and cupboards. Got the keys?'

I could see Alfie was a bit startled. When he'd made that crack about counterfeiting, of course he wasn't serious. So he was all the more surprised when it turned out that was what it was. We'd all been well briefed for quite a while about all the fake designer stuff: clothes, cosmetics, toiletries, everything you can think of, and all the money that was being lost – and made – in that business. And here it was, right on our doorstep, the print works that produced the phoney labels for their packaging!

'So *that* was one of the late Len Gilmore's criminal activities,' Alfie said. 'Funny though, how an American could come over here and set up something like that. I mean, you've got to have the connections, haven't you. Can't just put your sign up, like.'

By this time it was near on eight o'clock, so we decided to leave going through their files until later. We gathered the uniforms in from outside, re-locked the outer door, and we all settled down out of sight behind the machinery, dead quiet, to wait for the workers to turn up.

Quite soon we heard the door being unlocked, and a jolly-looking red-faced man let himself in, whistling cheerfully. He bustled about, putting lights on, humming to himself, and then let out a terrible squawk as I stood up and put my hand on his shoulder. Well, you've never seen colour drain out of a face the way it did with that poor man. One minute he was a happy-go-lucky working man, starting off his normal day, and then – bang! He didn't know what was going on. I thought he was going to pass out.

Naturally, he wasn't the boss, so we took him quietly into the office and sat him down and told him to keep his mouth shut until all the others arrived.

'What's this all about?' he stammered, but we told him he'd find out soon enough.

'That's if you're going to go on pretending you don't know,' I told him. 'What's your name, anyway?'

'Bond,' he said, and before he could say another word I put in, 'Oh yes? James Bond, I suppose? Got a licence to kill, have you? Just sit there and shut up until I tell you to speak, Mister 007.'

And I wasn't laughing, either. Nor was Alfie by then.

Well, by the time we'd collected all the workers, and got together the evidence, and sealed the place up and posted a plod to stand over it and got that lot back to the nick, it was well on to lunchtime, and of course Alfie was starving. Then we had to process them in, which is never very quick.

Finally Alfie said, 'Let's go and have a bite before we do anything else,' but I was too excited.

'I couldn't eat now, and anyway,' I said, 'we ought to report in to the Incident Room first.'

'All right,' Alfie said, very downhearted, 'but don't be surprised if I faint or something.'

At least that got me my first laugh of the day. I'd been so serious up till then, I could see Alfie couldn't make it out. We usually had a laugh together, but I'd been really tense this time. I was so anxious to do everything right and not overlook anything.

The man who said his name was Bond turned out to be

the foreman, and he claimed the factory was owned by his nephew, whose name, he said, was Jeremy Bond. His own name, he said, was John Bond. What a story. That was all he would say, though. I noticed his ruddy colour came back after a bit, and I thought that was a bad sign. You can always get more out of them when they go deathly pale, I've found. And it seemed to me he had plenty to worry about.

We'd got him dead to rights on the dodgy labels for the counterfeit designer goods, and if that wasn't enough, we'd found a couple even more interesting items.

Tucked away in a corner was a group of small machines nothing like ordinary printing presses. Turned out they were the special ones they used for cloning credit cards, electronic gadgetry and such. Very satisfying, finding those – tied up nicely with the blanks we'd found in Gilmore's flat. And we had to remember that the box holding them had given us the connection with Juan Garcia, too. So we had a lot more pieces of the puzzle, if only we could put them together in the right order.

The other thing we found was something even I couldn't explain, over-active imagination or not. It was a printing press, alright, but it was nothing like any of the others in the place, and we none of us could make head or tail of it. It was much bigger and – I can't explain, exactly – but it was simpler and yet more complicated.

When we were trying to describe it in the Incident Room, Mr Moon got so excited I thought he was going to start jumping up and down.

'Did it have a name, a name-plate, could you see a name on it?' he bellowed. 'Sergeant Pusey! Sergeant Partridge! WAS IT A HEIDELBERG?'

We both admitted we hadn't noted a name, and he didn't calm down, he got even worse. But when Derek explained, we could see why.

The premises Superintendent Moon had swooped on at dawn that morning was a small lock-up garage out towards Croxley, and at first it seemed almost empty and pretty disappointing. But then, tucked away in a corner, wrapped in layers of newspaper, they found some sets of lithographic printing plates. And so much for Alfie's scoffing at the idea of counterfeiting, these were plates to be used on a Heidelberg printing press to produce £20 and £50 forged bank notes. For some reason, they only used Heidelbergs for that.

And just to complete the picture, the other place, the one Derek had raided at the same time, held quantities of paper of bank note quality, complete with interwoven foil strips and watermarks. It was wonderful how neatly the whole story tied together. What a triumph that we in Watford, and not the Met, had picked up this whole operation. One in the eye for those people who sneered at Watford, eh. Edge of the civilised world, was it?

We were all dead pleased with ourselves, right up to when Derek said again what thanks were due to Fred and Kevin for deciphering the codes on the labels on the keys which led to all this. Gilmore's address book had given them the clues they needed, and the rest was down to their own cleverness at solving puzzles. We all looked round to give Fred and Kev a round of applause.

Where were Fred and Kevin? Nobody knew. We all trooped up to the canteen for a late lunch much less excited. What could have happened to Fred and Kev? They'd missed all the praise Derek had given them.

'We last saw them going off to some club or other, last night,' Alfie said, munching away.

I turned to Derek. 'What did Alfie say? All I got was a mouthful of spag bol.'

Derek looked worried.

'I let them go to that club,' he said. 'I think we'd better make enquiries there.'

'After lunch,' Alfie suggested.

'Was that all there was in your place, Derek?' I asked. 'Just that paper? I mean, of course that's important, but it didn't take much space, did it?'

'Oh yes, there were three motorbikes and two sets of leathers,' he told me, 'and if sizes are anything to go by, one set of leathers was Gilmore's, and the other belonged to our little friend, Kate Dunkerley.'

'Kate!' I said. 'On a motorbike? Hard to imagine… just a minute. Alfie, do you remember when we had our first run-in with Garcia, there was someone on a motorbike idling alongside us for a while? Could that have been Kate? How about you finding out something about that from your pal, Sleazy Sue?'

Alfie was probably only too glad of an excuse to look Sue up again, though he still couldn't see why anyone should call her sleazy. I expect she seemed a smart and well-set-up woman to him, just like his Betty must have been years before.

*

Alfie came rushing out of the men's locker room, panting and almost speechless.

'Boss!' he said, 'Don't I keep saying we ought to have a better mirror in our bog?'

I couldn't see that was any reason to get in such a state, and Derek seemed baffled too.

'What's up then, Alfie?' he asked in his kindest voice. 'Start from the beginning.'

Of course, Alfie being Alfie, he did.

'I was in there, trying to see if I'd brushed all the apple-pie crumbs out of my beard, and generally having a bit of a wash and tidy-up, when those two came staggering in. You wouldn't believe that men could look so changed in twenty-four hours.'

'Who?' I said. 'What two? What are you on about, Alfie?'

'Fred!' he said. 'Kev! I asked them what happened. Fred just groaned and leaned on the wall, but Kevin worried me much more. He started giggling, sort of like in a high-pitched hysterical way, and then he went on and on as if he couldn't stop himself. I couldn't make out what was the matter with them. Even if they'd got drunk at that club the previous night, that wouldn't account for it.'

Now that Alfie had actually started telling us what was up, he couldn't seem to stop. He went on, 'Whatever you might think about Fred and Kev as police officers, you've got to admit they always keep themselves looking spruce and decent, not like some of our younger plain-clothes lot these days. Some of them look scruffier than the villains they're after. But our prize pair, they looked as if they'd slept in a ditch in the rain: they're dirty, not shaved, their clothes are all torn and messy, they've got bloodshot eyes with great purple bags under them, their hair's all on end, and on top of that, they're both really daft-looking, as if they'd lost all their brains.'

'What did you do, then, Alfie?' I asked, while at the same time Derek was asking, 'Where are they now?'

But Alfie was caught up in his story, and had to tell it his own way.

'I told them to pull theirselves together. Have a bit of a wash and tidy up, I said to them, and I'll fetch you both a cuppa from the canteen before you go to face the boss. But Fred said they wanted to come straight to the Incident Room, they had a lot to tell, he said, then they could cut off home and have a bath and a bit of a kip. So the three of us went together, me fussing over them both like an old hen. You know, Greta, that's not like me, but I *was* a bit worried. Fact was, I thought they might both collapse completely before they got their information off their chests. Kevin specially went a really funny colour, bit like that Juan Garcia when he got scared.'

When we saw them in the Incident Room, I think Derek was as shocked as I was, too. I was glad to see that Mr Moon wasn't there, just in case the lads had done anything he shouldn't know about.

'On the way to this club, Knight Owls, Kev and me had a little chat about how to go about things,' Fred started his account. The poor blighter was nearly asleep on his feet.

'Yer,' said Kevin, suddenly coming to life. We knew Kev wasn't likely to say much more than that at the best of times, so Fred went on with the story.

'We thought best to act like we wanted to know about getting jobs as bouncers. So we went inside the club, ordinary-like, then after a while we come out and started chatting them up at the door. And we was really surprised them being so friendly. Unusual, that is, for club bouncers. So they said, you go in and have a good time, there's some well right birds in there, then when we pack up, we'll get together and have a bit of a chat.'

'I was worried about it, wasn't I, Kev,' Fred went on. Kevin nodded emphatically. 'I said to you, didn't I, there's something fishy about this. Do you think they've sussed us for the filth, I said to Kev. Maybe they've got evil intentions, pretending to be so friendly, I said. Didn't I?'

Kevin confirmed this, but then they both got droopy, and we had to give them cups of tea to revive them. It certainly looked as if those bouncers must have given them a bad time after the club closed. Poor silly lads, letting themselves in for something like that. They should have stuck to the backroom stuff we'd seen they were so good at. We were all on edge by this time, but after a while Fred took up the story again. Nothing like what we thought.

'See, you can be wrong about these geezers,' Fred said. 'They really were nice friendly fellers, and we had a lovely time with them.'

'Lovely!' Alfie burst out. 'Oh yes, lovely. We can see that for ourselves. That's just how you both look, like you had a lovely time.'

'No, honestly,' Fred protested, getting lively for a moment. 'We went back to Sean's house – I think it was Sean's, but it might have been Liam's – and they made us a great Irish breakfast, and then we all settled down for a game of cards.'

'Cards?' said Derek faintly.

'Yes, Guv, see, we thought we could get really friendly over a game,' he explained. 'Course, that meant they brought out the Irish whiskey to go with it, and we couldn't refuse, could we? But the important thing they told us was that there had been four of them on the door at the club until recently, and one night Ardal and Frank had been sent off to do some special job for the boss, and after that there was just the two of them. So we gradually got more of the story out of them, and it turned out it was the night Len Gilmore was killed. And when Sean and Liam called round on them next day, Ardal and Frank had packed their things and left word that they'd gone back to Ireland.'

'So then Kev got a bit over-excited, I suppose,' Fred said, giving his partner an un-matey glare, 'and started asking the wrong questions. What we should have done was say, well, so there's these two vacancies then, and how about it. You know, following up on our cover story. But I couldn't shut Kev up. He went on, like, trying to get Sean and Liam to describe Ardal and Frank, because of course we'd seen the descriptions of the two villains who'd done for Len Gilmore, and Kev must have thought we'd got the case half-solved. And, I mean, Sean and Liam were really nice guys at first, but you couldn't blame them for sussing us out, with *all those fishy-sounding questions*, so they got a bit rough with us.'

It was difficult to imagine Kevin getting over-excited, but that did at least explain why usually it was Fred who did all the talking for both of them. Suddenly Kevin found his tongue.

'Yer, and getting punched about after all that Irish whisky on top of bacon and eggs and colcannon and tomatoes and fried bread and baked beans,' he muttered, going that nasty colour again, 'does you no good.'

And he rushed from the room, to cheers and whistles and catcalls from the others.

Alfie never did tell us what all that had to do with him rushing out of the men's locker room carrying on about it needing a better mirror. But we left it. We had more important things on our minds by then.

Chapter 24

Derek thought it would be a good idea for me to go with Alfie next day to the Magistrates' Court for the Garcia hearing. On the way there Alfie took it into his head to share some of his troubles with me. The poor bugger probably didn't have anyone else who'd understand what he was on about.

'My Betty had a right old go at me this morning,' he said, 'while she was giving me my breakfast. I thought at first it was because I'd been telling her about that hearty Irish breakfast that Fred and Kev had, and I asked her if she could do this colcannon stuff, and what was it. Mind you, she's always been touchy about her cooking, and p'raps she thought I was criticising her or something. But it was even worse than that.'

'What's happening about those two Irish that Fred and Kev spent the night with, anyway?' I asked, only half-listening to Alfie's ramblings.

'Oh, the plods went round to pick them up. Spect we'll see 'em when we get back. No but listen, Greta, I'm telling you about me and Betty. See, she was scolding away at me but I couldn't pick up what it was all about.'

'What do you mean, she didn't say what was the matter?'

'No, she was like this,' and Alfie adopted a falsetto nothing like Betty's low voice, 'she says, "they're your responsibility as well as mine, and even if you are on the biggest case of the century, that doesn't mean you don't have to worry about your own family. You can't expect to forget all about us," she went, so I made a stab at it, and I says to her, was she still going on about our Carole's sex life, because if she was, there's no more I can do about it than she could. I told her, people these days just come out and say, they prefer women or men or sometimes one and sometimes the other, and there's no point going on about it, you can't change people's feelings.'

By this time I was getting a bit interested.

'Did that calm her down?'

'Not likely. Next thing I know, she's fetched me a right one round the ear.'

Picturing that scene, it wasn't easy to keep a straight face, but I managed, and Alfie went on.

'She said I hadn't been listening, she hadn't said a word about sex, she said that was my whole trouble, I've got nothing but sex on the brain. You know me, Greta, you know that's not true.'

I thought, quite right, sometimes he thought about food.

'Turned out she was talking about Freda and Muriel both being ill,' Alfie droned on, 'and Carole and Neil not bothering to come and fetch them to the vet. What with me working round the clock on this important case, it was left to her to take the two poor creatures round to the vet all on her own. Well, it's nearby, but just the same, Muriel in her basket, she's a big fat heavy cat, and poor old Freda could hardly walk, so Betty was practically dragging her on her lead.'

'Oh, I'm sorry to hear the animals are ill,' I said insincerely, 'so what was the upshot? Did the vet have to put them down?'

I'm usually a bit of an animal-lover myself, but I just couldn't take to those two. Also I didn't really give a hot damn about Alfie's domestic troubles. But he'd made up his mind to tell me the whole thing, and nothing was going to stop him. So on he went.

'Well, then I put my foot in it by asking was it just old age, and she give me another wallop, nearly put me off my breakfast I can tell you, and she says I'm a fine one to talk about old age, she thinks I'm going prenaturally senile. No, it's bronchitis, and she was that touchy because she said she'd been up all night nursing the pair of them while the twins and me was out gallivanting. No good arguing when she's in that mood. She didn't want to know I wasn't exactly enjoying myself. Anyway, once I found out what the trouble was I got on the blower to the twins and told them their mum was all overwrought and they had to come and look after their own pets for themselves.'

'Everything's OK now, then?' I said, trying not to sound bored. Then the penny dropped. 'Oh, I know what's the matter with you, Alfie Partridge. You're feeling guilty towards Betty, not about that blasted cat and dog, but because of your dalliance with Sleazy Sue.'

'Dalliance? What's that when it's at home? Borrowed Derek's dictionary, have you?'

Lucky for him we'd arrived at the court in Hendon by this time so I didn't have to pretend to swallow his sham innocence. He knew what I was talking about, alright, and he was probably looking forward to his next 'interview' with Mrs Slipworthy, his next assignment after he'd got through the formalities about Garcia this morning.

Derek had instructed him, 'Get every detail of every visitor from her, and find out how Gilmore set her up in that house in the first place.'

That job had made Alfie's eyes sparkle. But meanwhile we had to hang around waiting for him to be called to give his evidence to the magistrates about catching that little bugger Garcia red-handed with his case of coke. I thought we might take the opportunity to go over the whole case while we had nothing else to do, to give ourselves an overview of where we'd got to. But not Alfie, oh no. If he couldn't talk about his personal problems, all he wanted to do was sit and brood in silence. So I thought I might as well do the same.

We waited long enough to write a book. Nothing unusual about that, waiting to appear in court is always a time-waster. But it seemed worse this time, because there was still so much to do on the case, and I was busting to get on with it. Three hours we sat there. Well, of course we didn't sit all the time. We paced up and down. We got undrinkable drinks from the machine. We stood. Alfie went to the Gents for quite a long time. I went to the Ladies for a brief one. And all that time, I discovered, Alfie was turning over in his mind his home life and his flirtation (if that was all it was) with Sleazy Sue.

Suddenly he burst out, 'I've never been unfaithful or disloyal to my Betty. Fact is, I love her as much as I did when we got married so young – too young, our parents said. And even with all the trouble and how odd they are, I love our Carole the Les and Neil the Whatever-he-is. Likewise their funny pets. I mean, how many families have a dog called Freda and a cat called Muriel? But they mean all the world to me, the lot of them. So how could I have been so foolish about that Sociable Sue? She's a very friendly and obliging lady, and whatever you might think you know, Greta, nobody really knows if anything went on between us. But it's not worth taking a chance, definitely not. And now I come to think of it, I know I'm a fine figure of a man and still very attractive, but maybe I've been fooling myself. Does she really fancy me?'

I shrugged, but he didn't even notice. Now he was getting to the point, at last. As far as I was concerned, all this personal stuff was a way of filling our waiting time, only slightly less boring than staring into space. But to Alfie it was all desperate.

'Having all this time to turn things over,' Alfie said at his most self-important, 'it's come into my mind that p'raps

Sue had some purpose of her own in giving me the old come-on.'

I bit back the words 'No kidding' and instead gave him a few words of advice, whether he wanted them or not.

'So your best plan, Alfie, is to play along and seem to be as keen as before, to find out what she might be up to.'

He seemed well pleased with that, so it was quite likely what he'd been winding up to all along. And at last he got called into court. The hearing was as expected, Garcia only admitting his name, nationality and address, not kicking up his usual fuss. Of course Alfie had trouble describing the packing in the suitcase, and he was taken a bit by surprise when he was asked to state what he knew of the prisoner's injury. But it was all pretty much routine, and Garcia was remanded in custody, no more hiding in the Colombian Embassy for this slippery customer. He could kick his one good heel at HM's pleasure till his case came up.

'I'll drop you off at Sue's before I go back to Watford,' I said.

But Alfie pressed so seriously for me to come with him to talk to her, I finally agreed. As it turned out, the interview was almost formal. Sue wasn't wearing one of her half-in, half-out dresses, and she wasn't flirty at all with Alfie, though that might have been because I was there. She did give him a lovely big unhealthy fry-up for his lunch while she and I had a ham sandwich and a cuppa, but that was only reasonable.

The interesting thing, though, was that it turned out she'd kept her own records of each and every visitor who'd stayed at the house in the years she'd been running it, so all she had to do was hand her book over.

'No,' she said, 'Mr Gilmore never knew I kep' them records. Ow, you don't reely want to know ow I come by the job, do you, Sergeant dear? No, wot you want to know that for?'

I shot her my number one hard look, and she gave in.

'My Abe, see, e's a American, too, like Mr Gilmore, an e like arranged for me to ave this job while e's inside. Doing seven, e is, but e'll be out soon for good be'aviour. It's all connections, like, if you see wot I mean, Sergeant.'

I could see she didn't want to give any more details, and it didn't seem all that important, so I let it go.

On the way back to Watford, Alfie said, 'I must say, that woman knows how to put on a good spread for a fellow with a healthy appetite. And seems like we're still good friends, just not too intimate, if you know what I mean, Greta.'

'Satisfactory to both parties, then,' I commented, but it was wasted on Alfie. He never did understand irony.

Back at the nick, we went straight to the Incident Room, and I couldn't believe my eyes. With all the extra bods we'd managed to get, our full complement by now had got up to fifteen, which we'd reckoned was the best we could do. Nobody had said anything about scraping the bottom of the barrel, but there'd been a rumour about getting some plods seconded from North Watford.

But now, instead of our fifteen, the room was absolutely packed. Men and women were sitting on chairs, on desks and on the floor, and more were standing all round the walls in some places as much as three deep. What had happened? Who were all these people? I guessed there must have been about fifty people jammed into the room. And of course they were all talking and eating and drinking, and you couldn't think for the noise, nor breathe for the pong. It reminded me of that old American TV series, 'Hill Street Blues', except of course there was nobody there like that little mad one who bit people and was soft on his ma. I saw Derek, so I knew we hadn't strayed into the wrong place. He shoved his way through the crowd to us.

'Close your mouth, Alfie, you look like the village idiot,' was his greeting to Alfie. Not a word to me.

'But, what's going on, Guv? Who are all these people? What's happening? We haven't called in the Yard, have we? Just when we're doing so well?'

'No, of course not. But with all the ramifications–'

We didn't get a chance to ask about the ramifications. Superintendent Moon came in with three other important-looking people. I was pleased to see one of them was a woman. Without a word of command, everyone in the room shut up, and the eaters and drinkers stopped slurping and munching. I was impressed. You have to be really someone to make a roomful of noisy cops go silent and obey the rules without being told. Mr Moon introduced himself (so there must have been some people there who didn't already know him) and Assistant Chief Constable Janet Woods, and Detective Chief Inspector Mark Daniels, Drug Squad, and Owen Johnson, Customs and Excise. Mister Johnson didn't seem to have a rank or title, not that anyone gave a toot about that. We just wanted to know what the hell was going on.

Turned out that we were going to have a combined operation, because of all the different aspects the case had now taken on, covering practically every known crime except poncing, noncing and people smuggling. And for all we knew, they'd come into it sooner or later, too. Meantime, Mr Moon informed us, we were all going to have to work together, and with the CIA as well, because it seemed that there were connections with crime in the US, probably involving the Mafia.

At the word *Mafia*, Alfie straightened up and gave first Derek, then me, a big grin. I could see him thinking, who was it told him he was a fool right at the beginning, when he said it was to do with the Mafia? Clever Detective Inspector Derek Michaelson, that's who! He got no satisfaction there, though, because Derek's face stayed totally blank.

As for me, I was feeling like someone who'd just found something warm and nasty on the sole of their shoe. Or as if I'd lost my Black Belt and found a brown one. I was really choked. We'd lost control of the whole case. Now if it finally got sorted, who'd get the credit? Drug Squad? Customs? CIA? Not us, anyway. Not DI Michaelson, DS Pusey or DS Partridge. No chance.

Still, I did perk up a bit when Mr Moon called on Derek to give a complete recapitulation of the whole case, from the beginning. At least all these people would see who was in at the start.

Afterwards, I guessed Derek probably wanted to ask me and Alfie to come and have a quiet drink, but the whole mob joined us, and half of them wanted to buy Derek one, so the evening dragged on. Various bods kept coming up and introducing themselves and saying they'd never come across anything like it, and how well they thought we'd managed so short-handedly. So that was alright. But I saw that Derek was getting antsy, and finally he told me why.

'I'm just keen to get to my new flat and get myself sorted out there,' he muttered. 'Can you help me get away?'

I saw my chance.

'I can do better than that,' I told him. 'I can come with you and help with the unpacking and getting you settled.'

'You really are a splendid person, Greta,' he said, 'as well as a good copper. I feel I can count on you as a friend.'

He seemed to think he was paying me a big compliment, but it wasn't the sort of thing I wanted to hear. I didn't want to be his friend, or a splendid person, though of course being a good copper was great.

But what I wanted most was to be his...

I wouldn't even let myself think the word.

216

Chapter 25

On the way, I asked him what happened about picking up the two Irish bouncers who'd given Fred and Kevin such a hard time.

'What do *you* think?' he said, a bit snappishly. 'They'd gone without leaving a forwarding address. Irish doesn't necessarily mean thick, you know. Of course they'd seen through those two and got away. But what's up with you, Greta? You look a bit down. You don't have to come and help me, you know. It was your own idea.'

I told him there was nothing wrong and I'd be glad to help him, but I saw he didn't believe me.

'I'll never understand women,' he said. 'I learned that much from my situation with Erica. However hard you might try, you lot are just not like men.'

I didn't bother to tell him it wasn't the ambition of most women to be like men.

Anyway, when we got to his new place we set to, and in no time we had it more like a home and less like a dump. Not perfect, but liveable. Then, when I could see he was expecting me to say I was dead beat and wanted to push off, I offered to make us both a cup of coffee.

'Good idea,' he said. 'Fortunately, I've got decaf, so there's no danger of our not being able to sleep. We must get a decent night, we're going to have a heavy day tomorrow. And you've still got to get home.'

'Have I, Derek?' I said sadly. 'I thought you might like me to stay here, as it's so late.'

'But I haven't got a spare bed.'

Could any man be that slow on the uptake? Could I really fancy a man that dim? All I could do was try to make the silence heavy with meaning, without being too obvious. Then I actually saw the penny drop. I saw the wheels turning, and like a light came on behind his face. I held my breath.

He said, 'Oh.'

Then he said it in a different way. Like more drawn out. Like, 'Oh-oh-oo…'

Then he put his arms round me and kissed me. I kissed him back with much more enthusiasm than he seemed to be putting into it. The difference in our heights didn't seem to matter. When I came to think about it afterwards, which I did quite a lot, I guessed I must have bent my knees. I know I automatically kicked my shoes off. But at the time, we seemed to fit together so well that I was sure we both forgot that I was inches taller than him.

Anyway, it was as lovely as I'd hoped. More sweet and loving than heavy-breathing and passionate. But I was ready to settle for that. It was a start. And who knows how long we might have gone on like that, and even – with more than my usual luck – taken things further, if it hadn't been for the interruption.

An enormous racket in the hall outside made us spring apart and stand for a moment like a couple of dummies. It sounded as if the building was falling in on itself, and the debris was hurtling past Derek's front door and on down to the street level. I bounded to the door and was about to open it, but Derek pulled me aside and looked through the peep-hole.

'Not a thing to be seen,' he hissed, 'and now it's all quiet.'

Carefully he opened the door and peered out, just in time for us to see what looked like a small table go flying down the stairwell.

'Kate,' Derek called up the stairs, 'Kate, is that you? What's wrong? What's happening?'

It was Kate alright, but not a Kate we'd seen before. A distorted face, sort of yellowish, looked down at us from the banister above.

'I know you're there, you devil!' she screeched. 'You've come back, haven't you, to laugh at me! Well, you won't get me again, Len Gilmore!'

I pushed Derek out of the way.

'Kate! It's Greta,' I called. 'Let me come and talk to you. I won't let them get you, Kate. You know you can trust me. Can I come up?'

Long silence. Well, not exactly silence, but not like before. What we could hear was a lot of sort of snuffling and muttering, but no actual words. Derek hauled me back into his flat, not an easy thing for him to do, because I'm no lightweight and anyway I was resisting.

I did the obvious thing. I put my arms round him, gave him another sweet kiss, and before he could get his breath back, I'd started creeping up the stairs. I heard him take his own shoes off and follow, but I didn't let on I knew he was there.

Kate wasn't at the top of the stairs, so I went straight through her open front door. Derek hung back to give me a chance to do whatever I thought was best. I suppose he expected me to call out something soothing, to try to calm her down and convince her she had nothing to be afraid of. None of that. I knew a better way.

I stood just outside the doorway and called in an ordinary chatty sort of way, 'How about a cuppa for a poor hard-working friend, Kate?'

I knew I was taking a chance. She could have been armed and dangerous. We didn't know if she was alone, or if she had a gun, even though we hadn't found one when we'd searched the place. She certainly seemed off her head.

I could hear Derek behind me breathing heavily, and maybe he was wishing he had a weapon to back me up with.

But then I heard her sobbing, so I went straight in and saw her sitting on the open Murphy bed, crying like a little kid. I sat beside her and put my arms round her, and she leaned on me, buried her head in my shoulder, and blubbed and snivelled like a baby. Derek crept in and I mouthed over Kate's head the one word 'Ambulance' and he nodded and ran back downstairs.

One way and another, we didn't get much sleep that night, and it wasn't for the reason that I'd hoped for earlier. By the time we'd gone with Kate in the ambulance and dealt with things at Watford General, it was hardly worth thinking of going to bed, singly or together. Not for any reason.

*

Next morning having breakfast in the canteen, Derek said to me, 'I don't know how I could have been such a fool. The facts were all there, staring us in the face, and I still didn't believe what it was. That day in her flat, when she disappeared with her lawyer and came back so different, it did cross my mind, but I wasn't even convinced enough to say anything to you. And I certainly didn't want to mention it to Mr Moon. Even after Alfie caught Garcia with the coke, I still wasn't sure.'

'Well, Guv,' I said (I'd decided to be a bit formal with him after our near-miss the previous night), 'I don't think you need reproach yourself. We all saw how irrational she was, changing her personality like the rest of us change our clothes. And getting barmier, imagining voices and who knows what else. But I can tell you now, what I thought was, she was a schizo, and seeing Gilmore's murder had tipped her over the edge. I just didn't twig that it was coke. Even when she got violent I still didn't see she was getting worse because she needed a fix. So anyway, we're not going to get any sense out of her for a while, are we?'

'No, and once I get hold of that greasy brief of hers and tell him what's happened, I expect he'll get her transferred to a private clinic, and we won't be able to get near her.'

I knew I should have left it at that, but I couldn't let it go.

'You did fancy her at first, though, didn't you? Go on, you can tell me now, it won't do any harm.'

'No, honestly, Greta, I mean of course it was no hardship to take her out to dinner that night, but what I did think was that if I acted struck with her feminine charms, I might get more information than by the usual questioning. Not that it worked,' he added gloomily, while I tried not to look as pleased as I felt. 'In future I'll stick to the more orthodox lines of enquiry.'

'So what next?'

'Well, this morning I can kill two birds with one stone. I can use telling Mr Charles North that Kate's in hospital, and what condition she's in, to try to open him up a bit. Now that we've heard about the connection between his firm and the one in New York that employed Winkelhorne, maybe that might help to get something out of him.'

'And what am I doing?'

'Well, you never did go to those agents in Market Place as I asked you. Oh yes, I remember, you said they were closed when you got there. Well, try again. You know what I said, ask about a shop and say you're a friend of mine and when I moved in to a flat in Robin Hood House, you saw the shop was empty…'

'Then what? Ask who owns the property?' I argued. 'But we know the name of the holding company. I can't see where that's going to get us. What's the point?'

Derek was startled. I'd never actually argued about an order before. And even though I was right, I hoped he didn't think I was taking advantage of our little smooch the night before.

Before we got to crisis, we were saved by Fred Archer rushing in.

'Guv, Guv,' he panted, 'we've just heard that Roberto Panteolini has been detained at Stansted!'

I could see that Derek was glad of the interruption but less than thrilled about the message.

'And why is this of interest?' he asked in his silkiest voice. I could see I was going to have to help him out here. He'd forgotten.

'You remember, boss, we sent out the description of the false Goldfeather to all ports and airports,' Fred gabbled on before I had a chance to butt in. 'Course, we thought he might have got away already – well, he must have been lying low till now, thinking it'd be safe. And they've copped him at Stansted!'

'Roberto Panteolini?' Derek said in a baffled kind of way.

Time for a rescue from faithful Greta.

'Yes, Guv,' I said, 'you remember the real Goldfeather told you that the fake one called himself Bobby Panther because he wanted to get into films. But seeing he's Jack Roc's sister's boy, his real name is bound to be Italian. Roberto Panteolini to Bobby Panther sounds right, doesn't it. I expect Jack Roc's real name must have originally been something like Guiseppe Rocco.' I thought for a minute. 'You know what, we made fun of Alfie when he said it was all to do with the Mafia, but maybe he wasn't so far wrong, eh?'

'Come on Greta, you know he said that because of Gilmore's cock being stuck in his mouth. And we do know who did that, and why,' Derek added. 'Not the Mafia.'

'No, why?' Fred asked.

'Because she's out of her head with dope, poor little cow,' I told him. 'Let's go to the Incident Room and catch up. Not everybody's heard Alfie's report from his interview with Sleazy Sue Slipworthy.'

On the way, Fred muttered to me, 'I don't know where we are with the whole case after the guvnor's so-called recap yesterday. P'raps you can give me a run-down later, Sarge.'

I answered, sharpish, 'You must be dumber than I thought, then, Fred Archer. It was perfectly understandable, and perhaps you didn't know the Super congratulated him afterwards on its clarity.'

The same mob was in the Incident Room, and I wondered what Derek was going to do with all these bodies. Good thing it wasn't my problem, I couldn't think of a thing.

Derek gave a brief account of Kate's condition, then it was Alfie's turn. This was where his long experience showed. He was perfectly professional, and there was not the slightest whiff of anything going on between him and Sleazy Sue.-

'I obtained a complete list from the housekeeper, Mrs Slipworthy, of every visitor to the house since she was put in charge. A copy of this list is posted on the bulletin board, but unfortunately none of the names – except of course the Colombian Juan Garcia – are known to us. It's more interesting to know how she got the job. We knew her husband, Samuel Slipworthy, was in HM Prison in Brixton, but till now we didn't think it was a priority to look at his record.'

'Why not?' one of the bods at the back shouted out rudely. Alfie wasn't put out. He went on smooth as you like.

'At the beginning of this case, we were a very small team, and we were forced to concentrate our efforts on the main enquiry. It wasn't till later that Gilmore's ownership of the house in Hendon, and the reason for it, came to light.'

I whispered to Derek, 'Good old Alfie! I've never heard him sounding so polished. Do you think he's been rehearsing?'

Derek shook his head and smiled. What sort of message was that? I was confused and shut up. Alfie was still holding the floor.

'Sam Slipworthy came over here from America about twenty years ago when things were getting a bit hot for him over there. He settled down in Brixton, made friends with some Yardies, got himself a rep for being a general handyman. He was a useful heavy, bit of GBH, some B & E, and was well known to the local cop-shop. They couldn't get enough on him to please the CPS till about five years ago when he got a bit careless and they got him bang to rights using a knife in a rumble with another gang and put him away for seven. That left his missus wondering whether to go back on the game, like she'd been doing when they got married. But Slippy Sam had kept in touch with some of his old buddies back home, so that was how she come to run that house for Len Gilmore. More respectable than her previous job, he reckoned.'

Derek stood up. 'Well done, Sarge,' he said, 'that's tied up some of the loose ends.'

'There's more, though,' Alfie grinned, full of himself as usual. 'Mrs Slipworthy told me it was through her husband that Gilmore bought that print shop as a going concern. Previously owned, it was, by a elderly feller from Cyprus who was retiring to his homeland. He'd been running the shnide business for a long time, but he'd only been doing the designer labels and all that. Gilmore developed it into the currency counterfeiting and card cloning. More profit in that, wasn't there, than just printing labels for phoney scent and T-shirts.'

Alfie sat down, beaming through his beard, pleased with himself and waiting for praise.

Even if his connection with Sleazy Sue had been a bit dodgy, it had paid off in the end.

But maybe he hadn't realised that the question now was, were we going to arrest his little friend? If we did, would he still be so satisfied with what he'd done with her, whatever it was?

Chapter 26

Back in Derek's office, he flopped down with a big sigh.

'Where are we now, Greta?' he asked me, as if I'd know any more than he did. 'The Drug Squad's dealing with Garcia, Customs are winding up the print works and taking care of everyone they can lay their hands on who's connected with it, everything seems to be going like clockwork. We've got all these extra people but we're still busy. Yet what is there to do?'

'What do you mean?'

'Gilmore was the kingpin. He's dead. We haven't got his killers, but we've got a lead on them. Kate, who might or might not have been his partner in crime as well as in sex, is safely tucked away taking the cure. We know who Winkelhorne was and why he was here, and the same goes for Panteolini. So what's left of our case?'

I didn't know what to say, so I suggested a cup of tea. Bit feeble, but better than admitting that we still didn't have a clue what was behind it all. Even if we got the actual killers of Gilmore, we still had no idea who'd employed them or why.

In the canteen, Alfie was jawing away at Fred Archer and Kevin Burton, doing his fatherly act.

'That was good work you done, lads. You'll do well with us, what with being whiz-kids on the Internet and wading in like that at that night-club. Bit foolhardy, though, getting yourselves roughed up. Caution is what you still got to learn, my opinion.'

'That's very nice of you, Sarge, to take an interest,' Fred said. He always did the talking. I didn't remember ever hearing Kev say more than two words at a time. They were good mates as well as partners, and Fred being their mouth-piece seemed to suit them both. 'But listen Sarge, seeing you seem to have time for a bit of a chat, we'd like to ask you a favour.'

'Go on then.'

'See Sarge, it's like this,' Fred went on. 'When Detective Inspector Michaelson gave his summary of the case so far, when the big nobs sat in on the briefing, and all those others were crowding the place out, well, he explained everything brilliant, didn't he?'

We knew that Alfie could see we were near enough to hear, because he'd caught my eye and got the wink from me a few times. He didn't let on, though. But Fred and Kev had their backs to us and we couldn't tell if they knew we were there or not. Alfie kept a straight face.

'Well course, our guv'nor is exceptionally good at his job, came in on the Fast Track, and prob'ly better educated than us. You expect his statements to be crystal clear. So what's your point?'

'I'm not saying I didn't understand, I wouldn't pass no judgment on the DI, but if you wouldn't mind just running over the more complicated bits for us, it'd be a big help, if you'd just explain some of the details, you know. I mean, us lower ranks, we don't have to know everything, and anyway, we wasn't in on it from the beginning.' Fred was really being a bit of a creep. 'But you got to admit it's proberly the most interesting and complicated case we're likely to come across, and you've been on it from the first. And with all your experience an' all, if you can spare the time, Sarge…'

Derek and I exchanged looks. I could see he was thinking we ought to go and leave Alfie to it. I expected

Alfie to tell Fred and Kev to go about their business and not be so stupid. His vanity got the better of his judgement, though, and I saw he was settling down to spell out the whole thing, right from the start. Well, it might be interesting for Derek and me to hear his version, find out how different it was from ours.

'Well, tell you what, lads,' Alfie began. 'I think we'd all have a better understanding of the whole thing if we didn't just look at our case, as such, but if we started further back, before Gilmore's murder. Look at the history of it all, like.'

'What, you mean, before we come on the scene at all? You're not going to do that stuff about going soft on villains because they come from a broken home, are you, Sarge? All that background rubbish like what the do-gooders say?'

Alfie gave Fred a hard look.

'You know me better than that, DC Archer. No, course not. What I mean is, a lot of this case started before Gilmore's murder. Kate Dunkerley was living in New York with this Jack Roc, a well-known villain, and she says she didn't know he was a wrong'un, but obvious she must have, because you can't live with the Mafia and not know it.'

Derek silently mouthed the word 'Mafia' at me with a big grin.

'Then he got murdered,' Alfie went on, 'and all of a sudden she's took up with this Gilmore, who turned out to have been Roc's deadly rival. All the while, this private investigator Winkelhorne has been employed by a big firm of lawyers to keep watching her. But we don't know who they're acting for. Nor why. Like, who's the big boy in all this, see? What's the private dick watching her *for*?'

Kevin startled us all by speaking. 'Cor!' he said. We waited for more, but that was all he had to say. It did at least show he'd been staying awake and paying attention.

'Who's behind this watching of Kate Dunkerley? My

opinion, it's the key to the whole case. It must be important to someone. They've spent a fortune on it – look, Winkelhorne was flown over to take up a flat in Watford, while Gilmore and Kate come over on the QE2. On the boat, a woman was planted to get Gilmore to move into that same building where Winkelhorne was. Just so as Winkelhorne could go on watching. Obvious, this mystery person what's behind all this is the owner of the building, and the agent works for him an' all. Then there's the nightclub you found where the two missing bouncers are prob'ly the ones who done in Gilmore. But our mystery man hired the Irish girl to get close to Gilmore too. What did he do that for? And if he wanted Gilmore done away with, why did he have to do it so complicated? If he had Gilmore killed, did he have Jack Roc murdered too? What for? What's his interest in Kate Dunkerley, having her watched all the time, in New York and Watford? See why it matters that we know what happened previous?'

'No, Sarge, I'm sorry, I don't,' Fred said forthrightly. 'We've got a case to solve here. We've found out a lot of what Gilmore was up to, and I reckon we done a good job there. But why should we care who done the murder of some gangster in New York? Isn't it just our job to apprehend the murderers of Gilmore and Winkelhorne, what happened on our patch, and get all the proof what they done so the CPS can bring a proper case against them? We don't care who wants to watch Kate Dunkerley, do we, long as it's not illegal.'

Kevin made one of his contributions. 'Yer,' he said, 's'right.'

I could see Alfie starting to simmer a bit.

'Do you want to hear a recap of this whole case, or what? And while you're making up your minds, you can go and get me a cuppa and a bit of pie.'

'OK Sarge. Peach or apple?'

I'd been wondering whether Alfie was going to go into detail about his friendship with Sue Slipworthy, and how he came to catch Garcia red-handed with the coke. His version of events had been interesting, but not really a help to my thinking, and probably not Derek's either. I thought I'd suggest to Derek that we should go, when Fred saw us and came straight up to our table. He started to apologise to Derek right away, in case he'd heard and thought Fred was criticising him.

But Derek cut him short by saying he thought we should all sit together to hear the rest of Alfie's account of our case. Alfie of course wasn't the least bit put out by us joining them.

'Now about Agent Goldfeather,' he went on through a mouthful of peach pie. 'There was this chap who first presented himself as the son of Mrs Winkelhorne–'

'Just a minute,' Fred interrupted. 'Who is Mrs Winkelhorne? Did this private detective bring his wife with him?'

Alfie bored on for a few minutes about Winkelhorne's disguise having fooled Kate for three years and us for about three hours, and how we'd found out in the long run that he wouldn't have had a wife anyway because he was gay. Not that it had anything to do with the case, but maybe Alfie still had the subject of homosexuals in general on his mind because of his family problems.

Then he spoke about Winkelhorne's death and reappearance naked in the canal in Rickmansworth. When he explained about how we'd all been fooled by this false Agent Goldfeather, who turned out to be the nephew of the murdered Jack Roc, I thought it was sweet the way he was so discreet about it really being all Derek's fault for not looking at the folder Mr Moon had put on his desk.

'So why did he kill the private detective then?' Fred asked. 'What did he have to do with him?'

231

'Who?' Kevin asked.

We all let that one go. Life was difficult enough.

'Well, you know, we got the bogus Agent Goldfeather, and we'll be able to question him thorough as soon as he gets here,' Alfie said. 'But he can't hardly deny it, because we got him nearly red-handed on that. Sergeant Pusey here and PC Brown practically saw him chuck that Winkelhorne out of the window and drive off with the body in a private ambulance.'

'What's that got to do with our case, then, Sarge?' Fred asked.

'Buggered if I know, lad,' Alfie admitted, and we all turned and looked at Derek.

'I think the main factor that confused us all from the start,' Derek started slowly, 'was that none of us realised the extent of Kate Dunkerley's instability. From the time she confessed she was the one who'd cut off Gilmore's penis, we should have realised she was the wild card in the whole affair. I think she must have been quite deranged for some time, and then getting hooked on coke pushed her right over into fantasy-land.'

'You mean,' Fred asked, his eyes bugging out, 'you think she's our Mister Big?'

I couldn't help it, I just had to chime in.

'What, and employed an expensive American private detective to have herself watched? Get with it, Fred.'

Derek picked up.

'No, anyway, she's too unbalanced to be in charge of her own life, never mind managing a little empire of crime. What I mean is, her behaviour kept putting us off the track. When we first saw her, she was trying to look like a plain older office worker, said she hardly knew Gilmore. Next she'd done herself up as an expensive tart and came marching in here to Shady Lane to make a statement, she said. She told us she'd hacked off his tool because she was

232

so angry with him for getting himself killed. Then she put on a little-girl act for Greta here, and told her a sob story about her childhood. And now she's gone right over the edge with delusions and hearing voices – probably because she hasn't been able to get any more stuff since Gilmore died.'

'Course, that's it!' Alfie said, all excited. 'If we take her out of the whole thing, what we've got is Gilmore with a legit emerald import business as a cover for a lot of different counterfeiting lines. Garcia delivers the emeralds from Colombia. Then Gilmore tries to take over the coke business where Jack Roc left off, using Garcia to bring in the stuff with the emeralds. The Roc family send over Roc's nephew to put a stop to it, and he does that by bashing Gilmore to death and then chucks Winkelhorne out of the window because he susses what's happened!'

Alfie beamed round at all of us, so pleased with himself I thought his shirt buttons would pop off. I was glad when Fred picked up, so that neither Derek nor I had to be the ones to burst his balloon.

'But Sarge,' he said, 'even if we leave Kate Dunkerley out of it as being an unreliable witness, we've still got that other girl who says she saw Gilmore being killed. And it was nothing like you said. It was like Dunkerley said it was. Me and Kev, we think we've sussed out the two fellers what done it, those two missing bouncers. And if that's right, it's got nothing to do with drugs or counterfeiting, because we're back to our mystery man who employed the Irish girl to have it away with Gilmore!'

Kevin made a lengthy statement. 'IRA,' he said. 'All Irish, aren't they.'

This was even better than Alfie's Mafia theory.

'What Kev means,' Fred explained, 'is that those two bouncers are both Irish, and the girl was Irish too. No, Kev,' he kindly advised his partner, 'I think you've got a hold of another red herring there, mate.'

'It is just possible,' Derek suddenly said, 'that there've been no real murders at all, in the legal meaning of the word. Maybe those two heavies didn't mean to kill Gilmore, and Panteolini killed Winkelhorne by accident too.'

By this time I'd had enough of this conversation, and was longing to do something more useful than sitting around chewing the fat and watching Alfie stuff his face with peach pie. I'd hardly said anything all the time anyway, so I thought it wouldn't matter if I was the first to leave. I stood up just as one of the many anonymous bods who'd been seconded to us came panting in.

'Important message for you, sir,' he said to Derek.

I was impressed. It was a long time since I'd heard anyone call Derek 'sir'. Alfie and I sometimes called him 'Guv', but that was as far as we'd go in showing respect.

'They've just come in with Panteolini, sir, and thought you'd like to know right away,' the bod said. 'And we think we might have got a line on those two missing Irish bouncers from the night club!'

Chapter 27

Coming down from the canteen, we found that some of our spare helpers had been busy while we'd all been idly sitting around nattering.

One of them told us, 'We've been checking up, and none of the bouncers at the Knight Owls club are on record as registered doorkeepers.'

Like a fool, rushing in all bossy because I thought Derek and I were real mates by now, I said, 'Well, I reckon it's OK for me to put in an application to have that place closed down then.'

But Derek didn't see things the way I did. He was icy.

'I see, Sergeant. You don't think you need to check this with me first, then?'

That made me look silly in front of some strange detective constable who'd been seconded to us for the duration. But I pressed on.

'No, well, I thought you were busy, so it would be a help if I–'

'Yes, alright, get on with it,' he said, turning to the DC who was still hovering about. 'What else?'

Seeing me on the receiving end of the old put-down, the poor guy was getting a bit nervous, but he ploughed on bravely.

'Well, Guv, we took it on ourselves to bring in the manager of that club, see, because we thought you'd want to question him about using non-registered bouncers. And he might have some thoughts on where they'd all disappeared to. He's waiting in Interview Room 2. That Panteolini is in IR1.'

'Yes, let Panteolini sit around for a while, let's have a go at that manager, eh, Greta,' he said with a sudden change of mood. 'He might even know who he works for, you never know. Leave that paperwork for now, come with me to talk to – I suppose you got his name,' he said to the DC, who promptly gave it to him on a scruffy bit of paper. Not bad.

Bright, quick lad. Maybe we ought to see if we could get him permanently on our strength, I thought. But I wasn't going to make any more suggestions to Derek, who seemed to be blowing hot and cold in a very temperamental way just then. Maybe he was worried about us getting too close. Just as well I'd decided to keep my mouth shut, because Derek changed his mind again.

'No, tell you what, Greta, we'll get Alfie to interview this, er–,' he looked at the bit of paper he was holding '– Sevinson, and we'll go and charge Panteolini and then we'll interview him together. You–' he said a bit rudely to the DC who was still hovering around, '–go up to the canteen and tell DS Partridge and DCs Burton and Archer to interview this club manager and see what they can get out of him. Come on, Greta, let's give this false Goldfeather the works.'

We had quite a good time charging Panteolini, what with him being implicated in Winkelhorne's death, impersonating an officer of a foreign government, and attacking us all in Kate Dunkerley's flat. This Roberto Panteolini, alias Bobby Panther, alias Simon Winkelhorne, alias Agent Goldfeather, looked quite worried at the end of the formalities.

Privately I didn't believe the one about impersonating an officer of a foreign government was a legal charge, but I could see by this time what was really bugging Derek and making him so snappy. He was still smarting at letting himself be fooled because he hadn't looked at the dossier

Mr Moon had left on his desk about the real Agent Goldfeather.

If I hadn't twigged his problem, it would have been clear by the way he spoke to Roberto. Not his usual smooth style at all. More like one of those American TV cops coming the rough stuff. It worked, though. The man soon got worn down, although he tried bluff at first.

'I'm telling you,' he said, 'I don't know what was wrong with the guy. He just threw himself out the window before I could stop him.'

'Oh sure,' Derek sneered, 'just one look at your handsome face was enough to make him say good-bye to the world, right? And what about that ambulance you had waiting? That was just in case he hit you, I suppose, and you needed medical attention.'

'No listen,' Panteolini was beginning to sound a bit desperate, 'I don't know bubkes about no ambulance. It was nothing to do with me. I'm a stranger here. What would I know about getting an ambulance?'

'That won't wash. We know you've got connections here. And you knew from the start that Winkelhorne wasn't a woman. You knew he was a private eye watching Kate Dunkerley and Len Gilmore, didn't you?' Derek snarled. I could see he was starting to enjoy himself. 'Come on, Bobby Panther, the American authorities have told us all about you and your uncle, Jack Roc. So you wanted to find out what Winkelhorne had on Dunkerley and Gilmore.'

'Yeah, well, sure, I wanted to ask him a few things,' he admitted, getting a bit sweaty. 'I didn't know he was going to attack me like that, though. I had to defend myself, didn't I?'

'He didn't attack you, you lying scum! You had a private ambulance waiting to take him away to somewhere you could hold him until he'd talk. Come on, you may as well tell us the truth, we know most of it, anyway.'

After sitting quietly for a bit, every thought in his head showing on his handsome face like a slide show, he decided to come clean.

'OK, I'll tell you. My family thought Len Gilmore had my uncle Jack killed so that he could take over some of his business, so they sent me over to see what I could find out.'

'Three years later? You mean Gilmore had only just started to take over this branch of the drugs business after three years of lying low? So you got some help and beat him to death, right?' Derek snapped.

Roberto was gobsmacked. His shock showed on his stupid face. For some reason, it hadn't entered his empty head that he might be accused of Gilmore's murder. Finally after we'd watched the wheels going round for a few minutes, we could see him deciding that just denying everything might work.

'Nah, you're not gonna get me on that! He was already dead when I got here. That was why I thought the private eye was my best bet. I thought the quickest way was to question him, know what I mean? So I was going to take him somewhere quiet in this ambulance we had ready. But I didn't know he was going to be such a tough guy, I was taken by surprise. So we had a real heavy struggle. He tried to push me out the window, which by the way was closed. I mean, he was going to throw me right through the glass, if he could. And during this contest, by accident it came about that *I* threw *him* out the window. Listen, by this time I was fighting for my life. What could I do? Was it my fault? He died. It was an accident. By the time we got him away in the ambulance, he was already dead. I was in a foreign country. What could I do? I hid.'

He looked at us, first Derek, then me. Maybe he thought he'd get some sympathy and understanding from a woman. This was a man not over-loaded with brains who'd relied on his looks to get by. No such luck. How was he to know he was wasting his time on me. I wasn't a soft touch like most of the women he was probably used to.

'And then you tried to leave the country,' was my smart comeback to his pleading look. I gave a quick glance at Derek to see if he minded me joining in, and he gave me a little nod. He was over his dodgy temper, then. So I went on.

'And how do you account,' I asked, 'for the man's naked body being found in a canal some miles from where the so-called accident took place? What about that?'

'Oh shit,' he answered bitterly, 'how the hell should I know? These were local guys who were supposed to be helping me. I got out the ambulance a few blocks away, and they drove off. I don't know what they did after that. Like that guy, he was one of them, who was supposed to help me when he was pretending to fix the entry video at Kate's flat,' he went on, so full of whingeing that he forgot who he was talking to, 'his idea of back-up, waving a gun around at a roomful of cops. Who was that moron, anyway? Did you ever catch up with him?'

He suddenly realised he'd said too much, and shut up. But it was too late, he'd told us everything and we had it taped. We'd got him. One good result, at least. Still, there was a bit I was curious about.

'But why did you put on that act of being Agent Goldfeather and spinning that yarn about the journalist in Colombia and the black market in human parts? What was the point of that?'

'Oh well, I guessed the real Goldfeather was still in New York, and I thought maybe Kate would open up to me if I told her all that crap. I got the story from a script I've been developing with a freelance producer back in Hollywood...'

When we'd got him through Custody and banged up, Derek said to me, 'Jack Roc's family certainly didn't choose the brain of the century to represent their interests in England. Maybe once it's fully got into his thick skull how much trouble he's in, he'll give us some more about his accomplices. I don't swallow his pretence at not knowing their names, do you?'

'No, of course not. But what about the real Agent Goldfeather? Do you think he might want to get his mitts on our Roberto?'

'We'll have to ask Mr Moon to sort that out for us. But either way, at least the killing of that private detective, Winkelhorne, has been solved. Now, Greta, after lunch, what do you think about coming with me for another talk with the charming Mr Charles North of Abel, Levi and North? You never know, we might get something out of that greasy customer if we both have a go at him.'

This was very promising. It seemed as if Derek was beginning to treat me as a partner. Even if that was only at work, it might lead to an off-duty partnership of one sort or another. I crossed my fingers and gave him my best glowing look.

Then I had lunch in the canteen with Alfie, Fred and Kev, and Derek disappeared from view. I uncrossed my fingers.

Still, we did meet up in his office later and go together to see the sleaze-ball lawyer. By this time I wasn't in the best of moods. Hacked off, I was. I felt like a ping-pong ball in a match with the Koreans. Was Derek just my boss or did we have a stronger connection than that? Maybe I'd never find out how he really felt. Mind you, wriggling about in the car and fiddling with my seat belt, I did feel his eyes rest for a moment on my body in what I hoped was a more personal way than usual. Specially the part that Jim the Long-Distance Lorry Driver always called my best two belongings.

Derek leapt right in at the deep end as soon as we were shown into North's office.

'Did you know Kate Dunkerley was a drug addict?' he barked.

North didn't even blink.

'Inspector, I think the time has come for me to make my position quite clear to you,' he said.

'I would say the time was long past,' Derek positively snarled. He seemed to be taking up snarling in a big way recently.

North sort of agreed with him.

'Possibly so, quite possibly you may be right,' he said, smooth as ever. 'Allow me to rectify that matter now, if you will.'

'Get on with it, then.'

'Some time ago,' North started, like someone reading a fairy-story to a kid at bedtime, and I expected him to go, 'in a land far away', but of course he didn't. He went on, 'We were notified by our affiliate in New York that an eminent client had instructed them to employ a private detective to watch over Miss Dunkerley, who was then residing in New York. I must emphasise, Inspector, that the key phrase is "to watch over". This implied that it was a caring, rather than a spying brief. One might almost say that the detective was more of an unseen bodyguard than anything else. You realise it was made clear to him that he was never to make himself known to Miss Dunkerley.'

'Pretty unusual directive,' I put in my two penn'orth.

'Yes, indeed, Sergeant, but perfectly legal, you will agree,' he batted back at me. I shrugged, Derek nodded, and North went on.

'This only became of particular interest to us when, due to events of which you are aware, Miss Dunkerley's circumstances changed.'

'You mean when her lover was murdered and she took

up almost immediately with his arch-rival,' Derek said in his most sarcastic voice.

'And so arrangements had to be made for Detective Winkelhorne to continue his operation here in England,' North went on, not a bit bothered by Derek's interruption. 'For the first few years after Miss Dunkerley arrived in Watford, apparently all went smoothly and we had no active role in her affairs. However, after her latest companion, Mr Gilmore, was also killed, it became necessary for us to introduce ourselves to her. And after the regrettable death of Detective Winkelhorne himself, our client specifically requested that we take over the duty, as it were, of guardian of the unfortunate lady.'

'And has Watford General Hospital informed you, Mr North, that the unfortunate lady, as you call her, is now in a demented state due to drug abuse?'

'Yes, I am afraid that is the case, Inspector. However, we arranged for her immediate transfer to a private clinic, and this has been effected.'

'I presume your mysterious client is paying for all this? The cost of the private clinic, not to speak of your own fees? Very generous, I must say.'

'Yes, indeed, Inspector. A person of means, of course. But such benevolence doesn't always go hand-in-hand with wealth.'

'OK, Mr North, I think we've done enough sparring. You know very well I have to press you to tell me the name of this philanthropic person.'

'And you know, my dear Inspector, that this is privileged information, and I cannot possibly tell you.'

I thought it was time I put in a few more words before this conversation got too stupid. They were beginning to sound like one of those old-fashioned music-hall double acts that my Gran had been so fond of, and we were getting nowhere. I turned away from North and spoke directly to Derek.

'Would you say Mr North is obstructing the police in the course of their enquiries in a major investigation, Inspector?'

Before Derek had a chance, North jumped in with, 'I think you will find that is a fruitless line to take, Sergeant. And now, if you will excuse me, I have another appointment.'

And to cap it all, when we got back to Shady Lane, there was a message that Superintendent Moon wanted to see Derek, whatever time he came into the office. Derek had a moan to me before he went upstairs.

'It's late,' he said, 'and I was looking forward to going home. I thought I'd listen to some soothing music. Maybe get rid of the day's frustrations with a glass or two of good wine.'

He sighed and shook his head.

I looked at him hopefully, all but wagging my tail. Was he going to say he'd been going to ask me to join him?

He stamped up to Mr Moon's office without another word.

Chapter 28

On my way home, I called myself a few rude names. Fool and softy were the politest. No question, I wasn't the hard nut I'd always thought I was. I was really gone on my boss, and I had no clue how he felt about me. Finally I had to admit to myself, I almost cared more about him than about my career ambitions. Who would have believed it? Tough Sergeant Greta Pusey, more macho than most of the fellers, hard, heartless, unfeminine, was keen on an undersized inspector who wasn't as clever as he thought he was! What a fool, I was scolding myself as I got to my front door, and what am I going to do about it?

For the moment, the question had to hang fire. Because from out of the shrubbery there arose, like a ghost from the past, Jim the amorous Long-Distance Lorry Driver, who I'd nearly forgotten about. He hurled himself at me, and if it hadn't been for my quick reflexes, he might have done me and himself some serious damage. At least that part of my identity hadn't been lost. I was as fast on my feet as ever.

'Jim!' I shouted, shoving him back into the bushes. 'What the hell do you think you're doing? I thought I'd got rid of you. What do you want now?'

As if I didn't know. He was probably after another night's free lodging and a good bunk-up. And I certainly wasn't in the mood for either of those. Turned out I was wrong. I'd made a bad guess there.

'Greta, darling,' he snivelled, 'I've left, I've given everything up, I can't live without you, please take me back.'

'Oh shit,' I responded, 'Jim, I don't want to know. Why don't you just bugger off and leave me alone.'

'No, please, give me another chance, I know you love me really. I'm sorry I treated you so badly, sweetheart. Please forgive me,' and he went on grovelling and whining like that. So I pushed him out of the way and, letting myself in the front door, quickly slammed it in his face. I stood there in the hallway, sweating and cursing with everything in my extensive vocabulary, and wondering what the hell to do next. Call the police, right, that's what we advise the public in this kind of situation. Very funny.

Oh, I don't know, I thought. Maybe that's not such a bad idea. After all, even if he was temporarily fed up with me, Derek owed me a favour or two. I'd been a good friend to him, one way and another, apart from gazing at him bug-eyed whenever I thought he wasn't looking. Jim shouting through the letterbox helped me to make up my mind, and I phoned Derek. Lucky for me, he'd just got home.

When I poured out my tale of woe, his tone went quickly from languid to brisk. 'Sure,' he said, 'I'll just get some clothes on and I'll be right round.'

I was so taken up with going all soppy at the thought of that taut little body with no clothes on, that it didn't dawn on me right away what I'd done. Jim was my height and twice as wide. He'd make mincemeat of my darling Derek. How could I have put him in such danger!

Turned out I wasn't such a fool, and neither was Derek. Just as I was beginning to fume at him for taking such a long time, and thinking he wasn't going to turn up after all, he arrived. But not alone. The clever little devil had been delayed because he'd gone to pick up Alfie first! Talk about reinforcements. They both came striding up the path, and even through the letterbox I could see how pale Jim went at the sight of them. I had to admit that Derek on his own wouldn't have impressed him, but with Alfie – six foot four and built like a brick shit-house – that was enough to scare anyone.

I flung open the door with a flourish, and in my most ladylike voice I went, 'Oh, good evening, Inspector, and good evening to you, Sergeant Partridge, how good of you both to come. This man–' and I pointed to where Jim had been a moment ago. There was a space there, but we could all see him hot-footing it down the road.

I invited the two of them in for a drink. I thought I ought to, after them both turning up trumps like that. Sorry to say, the wrong one accepted and the right one muttered an apology and left. So I was left with Alfie Partridge sprawled all over my sofa, swigging my beer and telling me his troubles, while the apple of my eye went back to his bachelor pad. All alone. At least, I hoped so.

Well, at first it was a bit of a bore, with Alfie bumbling on about his Betty and his twins and their pets, and how friendly that Sue Slipworthy had been, and all that. I did brighten up a bit when he mentioned about his Betty giving him another one round the head – that must have been a sight worth seeing! Betty Partridge must be the only living being who'd have the nerve to fetch him one without fear of getting a few back.

But then, somehow, we got to reminiscing about our earlier days at Shady Lane, before Derek or Mr Moon came there, when I was still a WDC, as we called them then, before sexlessness came in and I became a DC. And I recalled how Sergeant Partridge had taken me under his wing and helped me become a sergeant myself.

'Do you remember Gladys Trulove?' I asked Alfie.

'Do I not! Your first murder! And those names! It ought to be part of the history of Watford,' he chuckled. 'And I've never seen you look like that, before or since.'

'Like what?'

'Bit of everything, you looked. Green at all the blood, disbelieving at what she told you, and aggravated when you thought she was having you on. Regular one-woman show, you was, girl.'

For once I didn't mind him calling me 'girl'. Looking back, it was quite funny, although at the time that was far from how I felt.

'Well,' I answered, 'bad enough she'd stabbed that poor old tub of lard because she thought he'd been unfaithful to her with two other women in the same street – as if he could have managed that, the poor thing – but when she told me, in all seriousness, that his name was Jules Verne, that was the last straw. Specially with her name being Gladys Trulove, you couldn't blame me for not believing a word of it.'

'Extra specially, haw-haw,' Alfie laughed delightedly, as if the whole thing had happened yesterday, 'with him being married to Gladys's best friend, and she not knowing that their name was really Varney, after all those years of having it away with him and going to the bingo with her. Julius, his name was, wasn't it?'

'Yes, but the most amazing part was when I told her that Jules Verne was a famous French writer who'd been dead for years, and all she said was, had he been done in for being unfaithful, too.'

By this time, we'd both had a fair amount to drink and it was getting pretty late, so we ended up laughing quite a lot more than we would have done normally. We were making such a noise that we didn't hear at first that the phone was ringing and also that someone was banging on the front door at the same time.

That calmed us down. I answered the phone and waved Alfie to the door to see who it was. I didn't mean him to open it, just to look through the letterbox, but I suppose he didn't think of that. At his size, you don't have to be cautious.

I was just getting excited at hearing Derek's voice on the phone, when I heard a yell and a crash at the front door. I dropped the phone and dashed to see what was up. I should have guessed, it was that stupid Jim again. He must have been hanging around all this time, waiting for Alfie to go, and then decided to try his luck anyway. Of course, Alfie hadn't given him a chance to say more than a few words before giving him a big shove which sent him flat on his back halfway down the path.

'Don't think he'll bother you for a while now, girl,' Alfie grinned. 'I'd better get off home anyway, otherwise I'll be for it with my Betty again. Tara for now.' And he was off, still chuckling to himself, either about the persuasion he'd used on Jim, or the recollection of Gladys Trulove and her faithless lover, Jules Verne alias Julius Varney.

I'd never told Alfie that I went to visit Gladys a few years later at Holloway, and gave her a book by Jules Verne. By that time, she was even more confused than she'd been when I'd arrested her. Well, actually, it was only technically an arrest, because she'd phoned the nick to ask for someone to give herself up to. She thought I'd given her the book as a keepsake of her dead lover, and she was so touched by my thoughtfulness that I left it at that.

Compared to the Len Gilmore case, it was straightforward, but the background story was just as sad. I didn't want to dwell on that now, though. I rushed back to the phone, and was thrilled to find Derek was still patiently hanging on.

'What happened?' he asked, and I said that Alfie had hung around in case Jim came back, and he had, and Alfie had seen him off.

'But that's not what you phoned about, is it?' I asked hopefully.

'No, I thought that was all dealt with,' he said. 'I phoned because it occurred to me that I'd been a bit rude in refusing your offer of a drink, and I wanted to apologise.'

I was over the moon. He cared! He didn't want me to think he was rude! My opinion mattered to him! He wasn't off me about anything.

'Oh, Derek, does that mean we're friends again?' I cooed at him. 'Would you like me to come round and help you sort out your books and records? Can I do anything to help you? It must be very quiet in that building now that you're all alone there.'

He laughed.

'That's very kind of you, Greta, but do you know what time it is? It's nearly two in the morning. I'll see you in the canteen for breakfast, OK?'

I wanted to say that for my part, any time of day or night would be a good time for us to be together, doing anything at all. But I knew I mustn't rush him. He'd only just got over one bad experience, and I'd have to chase him slowly and patiently.

But I'd get him in the end. I'd made up my mind.

What he told me over breakfast next morning didn't make his feelings any clearer, though. He wanted to tell me about his session with Mr Moon the previous evening, after the rest of us had gone home.

'He's taken to calling me laddie, you know, and it's not like when Alfie calls you girl, it's sort of more fatherly. And he keeps giving me great dollops of that whisky of his. Slurps quite a bit of it himself, too.'

'Well, what's wrong with that?' I asked. 'Better than being in his bad books, isn't it?'

'Yes, I suppose so. But last night he started telling me about his personal life. He started off by saying, all chummily, "You've met Mrs Moon, haven't you?" and waited for me to say something complimentary about her.'

'Well, that shouldn't have been too hard. She's not a bad-looking old girl. It's when she stands next to him that they look a funny couple...'

'Yes, like a sort of cartoon of a giant letter **b**, she about six foot tall, about your height, Greta, but not shaped like you, she's like a collection of sticks–'

I was thrilled he'd noticed my shape, and interrupted, 'Yes, she's really skinny, and he being short and fat–' because I wanted Derek to see that we wouldn't look so comical together. But he didn't seem to have thought of making that comparison at all.

He went on, 'Yes, last Christmas, you could hear some of the ruder oiks making ribald suggestions about how they'd managed to have five children. But when the Super and his missis pushed off the dancing together, they were both so light on their feet and so obviously still keen on each other, you forgot all about how odd they looked together.'

'Yes, but what's that got to do with what he was talking to you about last night? Don't tell me he was asking if you thought they looked a funny couple!'

'No, worse than that. He started telling me about their early life. When they first met, can you believe it, *she* was an inspector and he was only a sergeant. And I must have looked surprised when he said that, because he laughed at me and said did I think he was born a superintendent. I expect you knew, Greta, that he was only made up to Super just before I got my transfer to Shady Lane. And he said he didn't start getting fat until after their fifth child was born.'

'So?'

'So then he said that whatever success he'd made of his life, he owed to the fact that he met a woman who was so determined to marry him that she resigned from the Job. Then he didn't say anything for a while, but he kept giving me these meaningful looks. Finally I stood up and thanked him for the chat and the drink but I thought I'd be on my way, and just as I got to the door he called after me, in a casual sort of way, "She's a fine girl, that Sergeant Pusey of yours." And I bolted. Do you think he's actually trying his hand at match-making, Greta?'

God bless him if he is, I thought. But I could see Derek was panicking at the whole idea, so I played it cool. I stood up.

'I certainly hope not,' I said, trying to sound indignant, 'what a cheek! I can't see him as Cupid, can you? I think I like him better when he gets so angry we all think he's going to do himself a mischief. Come on then, Guv, back to the old grindstone.'

Chapter 29

After that fairly satisfactory breakfast, Derek went off, dragging his feet a bit, for another long session with Superintendent Moon. I made a stab at writing reports and stuff, anything really to keep me in the office. Not that I could think of anything to go out for, unless Derek had been serious about sending me to those people in Market Street who'd been managing Robin Hood House. I couldn't honestly think of any good I could do there, but of course if it was an actual order, I had no choice.

Finally, just when I was getting a bit worried about him being up with the Moon for so long, he came back, looking pink and pleased. I didn't have time to wonder whether to ask him about it. He could hardly wait to shut the door before it all came out in a rush.

'Mr Moon is really pleased with the way we've been handling this case, Greta, and if we can close it all satisfactorily, he's going to put me up for Chief Inspector!'

'Oh, Derek, how–'

He didn't give me a chance to congratulate him, before going on, 'And he wants me to talk to you about promotion, as well. What's your ambition, Greta? Do you want to be made up to Inspector? Do you think you can pass the board? No worries about passing the exam, of course. But how do you feel about it?'

If he'd asked me that when he first joined us, of course I'd have leapt at it. No cop, male or female, was ever as ambitious as Greta Pusey. I'd always had a dream of being

253

one of the first women to get to the very top, or at least a Deputy Assistant Commissioner at the Yard. And I had everything going for me. Young enough, good appearance, intelligent, hard-working, fit, fairly popular – all I needed was a bit of luck. And this case could have been the break I needed.

But this was before I went so soppy. I'd managed to get to within sight of my thirtieth birthday without ever falling in love, although of course I'd had my share of encounters of all kinds. Jim the Long-Distance Lorry Driver was far from my first, and I'd never had any intention of him being my last.

Then along came Derek, and God knows what it was about him that got me in such a stupid state, but whatever it was I was a changed woman. I could look at him in a detached kind of way, and say to myself, 'He's a short, touchy, rather difficult, only fairly handsome sort of feller, what can a woman see in him?' And then he'd look at me with those big brown eyes, or give me his rare smile, and I'd go all silly and get a bit damp in places where I'd rather not, and sense had nothing to do with it.

So now the question was, did I want to try for promotion to Inspector? If I did, would I still be working with Derek? I had to admit to myself, that was an important part of the decision. I could hardly believe I could be so daft, but it was true. I was even willing to give up my big chance of onward and upward if it meant I wouldn't be on Derek's team. But if he was going to be Detective Chief Inspector, maybe he would have a Detective Inspector and a Sergeant (Alfie, of course) working with him. And I didn't know how to ask that question, without making a complete idiot of myself. He might have guessed by now that I fancied him, but he couldn't possibly have any idea how strongly.

I hate love. It gets in the way of real life. But I was buggered if I was going to let on to Derek that it was more than just the hots I felt for him.

Meantime, while all this was going through my addled head, he was patiently waiting for an answer, and beginning to look a bit puzzled at how long I was taking to react. Naturally, he was expecting me to be leaping about with joy and talking about premature celebrations. I could just imagine how he was at this very moment making up little speeches about not jumping the gun, and having to close up this case first, hurdles to be got over, exams to pass, and all the rest of it.

That was another thing I couldn't understand. He had all these characteristics that would have had me calling him a pompous little prick, if I hadn't fallen for him. No wonder I'd always been so scornful of love, if that was what it did to your judgement.

Finally, I mumbled, 'Yes, well, Guv, let's get the case closed first, before we start getting excited about promotions and such.'

He gave me his lovely smile, and I felt little beads of sweat popping out here and there. Oh, I could have picked him up and run out with him under my arm that very minute.

'I must say, Greta, that's a very mature attitude,' he said. Of course he didn't have a clue that he was cooling me off several degrees in as many seconds by being so bloody condescending. But then he didn't know how hot I was in the first place. 'This case has done a lot for both of us,' he went pompously on. 'And I think Alfie has learned something from it, too, with his little bit of dallying with that Sleazy Sue.'

For the moment, my indignation overcame my other feelings, and I burst out, 'That's so patronising of you, Derek! Typical! Has it ever occurred to you that there might be some things you could learn from Alfie? He might not have your education, but he's got a lot of experience on our turf here, and maybe he's brighter than you think.

He thinks a lot of you, and maybe you should give him a bit of respect in return.'

There was a silence, while I wished I'd had a tonguectomy before queering my pitch like that. Just when Derek was feeling pleased with me and himself and we were getting into a bit of mutual admiration, too. Or maybe something even better. Big mouth! I ticked myself off. I was just beginning to put together a miserable apology, when Derek surprised me again.

Quite calmly he said, 'You know, Greta, you're very good for me. Nobody else would give me home truths like that. And you're probably right. I must try not to be such an intellectual snob. But I think now we should get back on the case, don't you?'

Phew, that was a relief. I thought I'd really done it there. But there you are. He might be little in height, but there's nothing wrong with his stature. That's deep stuff. I must be getting a bit intellectual myself.

Well, after all that, I could hardly make an argument when he asked me again to dress up and call on those so-called estate agents who managed Robin Hood House. He had an appointment with the real Agent Goldfeather to sit in on the next interrogation of Roberto Panteolini, which would surely take up a good bit of his day. And he reminded me that we were all in court the next day, and to be there bright and early, and off I went to go home to change into something to make me look like a businesswoman. Whatever that might be.

I did cast a longing glance back at him as I left, but he had his head down and didn't even notice. I'd been hoping he'd say something about getting together in the evening. Off I went then, on this daft and pointless errand.

Except that I never made it.

I knew as soon as I let myself in my front door that there was someone in there. It wasn't a sound, exactly.

And I certainly didn't hear any heavy breathing or anything like that. It was just – sort of a feeling in the air that seemed wrong. When you know your home well, there's a kind of atmosphere about it, mixed up of your own stuff, what you drank last night, your soap, your shower gel and shampoo, even a faint trace of the detergent you put in the washing machine.

You try it, go on. Sniff when you get home, and sniff when you go to someone else's home. Home smells like home. And this felt strange. Yet there was no sign of a break-in. I slipped my shoes off and crept silently into the sitting room. And that was the last thing I remember.

I've got a gap in my life now, which I can only fill with hearsay.

Sad to say, it wasn't my little hero who found me. It seems that Alfie had been worrying about me for some time. Of course, he'd got a completely wrong idea about what to worry about. He'd mistaken my lovesick mooning about at Derek for something completely different, and later on he was so embarrassed about it that it took some probing to get him to confess.

Seemed he'd got hold of the idea that I was pregnant by Jim! – of all people! – as if I would! And he'd built up some daft scenario in his head about Jim being noble enough to leave his wife and marry me on account of 'the little one on the way' but I'd wanted an abortion, and he thought that Jim was getting so overwrought about the situation that I'd become afraid of him. The bit he did get right was that I was keen on Derek, but then he also thought that I was scared that Derek would get wind of the situation and it would put him off. What a complicated bit of theorising! Nearly as good as his idea about it being the Mafia that cut off Len Gilmore's cock and shoved it in his mouth.

Anyway, the upshot was just as well. Alfie thought

he'd just 'pop round to see if I wanted a quick drink' on his way home. And he found me, still spark out, lying in the hall with the front door wide open.

I must say, pretty damn caring neighbours I must have. And I'd always thought I was on good terms with them, too. Not a soul seemed to have spotted anything wrong. But Alfie got me to the hospital, pronto, and sent for Derek and Betty, and if Derek hadn't stopped him, he was going to send for Superintendent Moon as well! Turned out he thought I was a goner, and he didn't know what to do, knowing I had no family. Derek told me afterwards that Alfie was beside himself, pacing up and down and muttering to himself for hours. Goodness knows why he sent for Betty. Probably to give himself moral support.

When Derek told me all this, much later, I asked him, 'And what about you? Why weren't you pacing up and down and muttering? Didn't you care? Weren't you worried? Weren't you afraid of losing me?'

'Of course I was afraid,' he admitted, giving me a little buzz. 'But I can't show my feelings the way Alfie does. You must know that by now.'

It was true. When I finally returned to this world, I thought at first I was still dreaming. My hands were being held and stroked. My right arm was in a cast. The hand at the end of the cast was in the moist grip of Alfie's wife Betty, which was strange enough. But even more amazing was that my left hand was being held and patted by none other than my little dreamboat, my Guv, DI Derek Michaelson! My vision was still fuzzy at that stage, so naturally I thought what I was seeing wasn't real. But he saw my eyes open, and he gave me that wonderful smile, and I looked into those lovely brown eyes, and I liked what I saw.

Once I started to be myself again, I was furious at what happened. Just as we seemed to be wrapping up this bugger of a complicated case, there was this development. And the trouble was, we couldn't tell if I'd been assaulted by someone connected with the case, or if it was someone or something entirely separate.

'Don't worry about it, girl,' Alfie said. 'You just concentrate on getting better. That was a rotten crack on the nut you got, and a broken arm is no joke, either. Let us do the detecting this time, OK?'

I wasn't actually in the hospital for long, once I'd got a bit patched up. But I got a brief visit from Mr Moon before I went home, just long enough to tell me that he didn't want me back at the nick until the quacks said it was all clear for me. So I had to kick my heels at home and be bored for a couple of weeks, while that lot in Shady Lane tried to figure out what was going on.

Chapter 30

Even while I was still in hospital and a bit woozy, Alfie came and got every single detail I could give him about Jim.

'It can't have been Jim,' I protested feebly. 'He wouldn't hurt me. He loves me. He's left his wife for me.'

'You gave him your key,' Alfie accused.

'Yes, but, no, hang on a minute, I got it back from him, days ago. That was after you saw him off. But then, nobody's got the key except me, and it wasn't a break-in, so how…?'

'I told you, don't worry about it, leave it to me,' Alfie said. 'Now that I know you're not pregnant, I can deal with Master Jim Robinson. It was just when I thought he was the father of your child that I wasn't sure, you know, like, how you wanted him handled.'

'I still don't know why you were so sure I was up the spout,' I yawned, feeling the painkillers kicking in again.

Just as I was nodding off again, from far away I heard Alfie's boom, 'Because you were acting so barmy, just like my Betty was when she was expecting the twins.'

Barmy? Was I? Yes, probably this unusual, unwanted and unexpected strange feeling I had for Derek was like a sort of barminess. Hard to imagine stolid Betty acting like that, though.

I slept again.

Times like this, you know who your friends are. Derek

and Alfie together took me home and settled me down on the couch, tenderly tucking a blanket round me. (Oh, Derek, I thought, you looked so sweet when you fell asleep on this same couch.) Betty brought enough food to last me for three months, some in the fridge, some in the freezer and some heating up.

'Now,' she instructed, 'if you can't manage to put this stuff in the oven and take it out with one hand, you just send for me or Alfie and we'll come round, quick as a shot, and see to it for you. And don't you try no washing-up, neither, you'll get that plaster wet and then there'll be trouble!'

'Don't worry, Mrs Partridge–' Derek started, but she interrupted him with, 'No formalities here, young Derek, we're not at the police station now.'

He gave her his lovely smile. I saw that it got to her almost as soppily as it affected me. She didn't mind his size, either, nor the fact that she was a good many years older than him. He was just so scrumptious.

'I was just going to say, Betty,' he said, 'that I live quite near, so I'll be popping in to see that Greta's OK and doesn't need anything.'

Oh boy, I thought, it was worth a black eye and a broken arm and even suspected concussion. He'll be popping in! I must make the most of this. Perhaps he'll feel like helping me to have a bath some time? Could I kid to him that I couldn't manage dressing and undressing on my own? My imagination ran on...

The next time I saw Alfie was a few days after he'd helped bring me home from the hospital. He'd been busy. He and Derek came to see me together, and Derek said it wasn't strictly a social call. Alfie was gloomy.

'It definitely wasn't your Jim-lad,' he admitted. 'We've checked and double-checked, and his story was OK. He really was in the Channel Tunnel with his lorry at the time you were attacked, with half-a-dozen of his mates as witnesses. I could have sworn we'd get him for it, too. He was quite upset that you might think he would do such a thing to you, especially when I told him your assailant had given you a black eye, concussion and broken your arm. He cried,' he added in disgust.

'Yes, isn't it creepy,' I said, 'he's taken to doing that lately. He never used to be like that. I always used to think he was one of those tough unfeeling sort of blokes, and now I don't know if I had him all wrong, or he just changed completely after I gave him the boot.'

Derek was serious.

'The thing is,' he said, 'it wasn't this Jim fellow, and it was obviously personal and not a break-in, and anyway nothing was taken. So if you can't think of anyone else it might have been, then it has to be something to do with the Gilmore case.'

'How can it be!' I argued. 'There's no way anyone connected with the case could possibly know where I live. Why should they go for me, anyway? And it's even more unlikely that any of them could have somehow got hold of my front door key.'

'Can't you think of anyone, Greta? I suppose you haven't, by any chance, had a row with any of your neighbours?'

I shook my head and we all sat and looked at each other blankly. In my mind I ran through all the people connected with the case, but couldn't think of a single one who might have a personal grudge against me. Unless, of course, it might have been someone who was mentally disturbed...?

'Kate!' Derek and I exclaimed in chorus. He'd been thinking through the list as I had, and together we'd come up with the only possibility.

'No,' Alfie said. 'She's safe under lock and key at that private clinic. And anyway, she couldn't do all that to

Greta. She's too little and scrawny. Look at the damage. She hasn't got the strength. Even if she wanted to. Never mind why she should want to in the first place.'

'But she *is* nuts, you know,' Derek said, 'and I suppose she could have got someone to do it for her – she's got plenty of money, and she's probably got more connections than she wants us to think. There's still the puzzle of the key, though.'

'Derek, would you let Alfie go up to Darlington again?' I asked. 'When he went he only saw Jim and some of his mates. And I just wonder, I mean I've got nothing to go on, and I can't really justify the expense, but do you think it would be worth while to interview Jim's wife?'

Alfie got excited. 'What, you think Jim got all his pals to lie for him? Well, if he managed that, why should his wife be the one to shop him?'

We could see that Alfie really fancied Jim for this job, and I knew he'd do all his best ferreting on that account. Derek dithered for a while, wondering if he ought to clear it with Mr Moon, but finally he agreed that Alfie could go the next morning.

While he was in a giving mood, I thought I'd cash in with another request. I wanted to visit Kate.

'Not as DS Pusey, not in connection with the case, Derek,' I pleaded. 'I don't think the poor little thing's got any friends or relatives, and I really feel sorry for her. I know she might still be out of it and not even know me, but if they'll let me just sit with her for a while, maybe hold her hand or let her cry on my shoulder or something, it might do her some good.'

'You do amaze me sometimes, Greta,' he smirked. 'You always crack yourself up to be so hard and tough, and then you give yourself away as being as soft and kind as any normal woman–'

I still had one good arm, and I used it to chuck a cushion

at him. This was good. We were getting really informal.

'Speaking as a normal woman, I'll take that as a yes, then,' I grinned. 'Will you drive me there tomorrow?'

*

In the meantime life had been going on without me. In the intervals of rallying round with practical help and trying to solve the mystery of the assault on me, Derek and the others had been to court for the preliminary hearing of the charges against Roberto Panteolini. The real Agent Goldfeather had got his Embassy to put in for him to be extradited back to the USA. But it was a bit feeble, because they had no proven case against him back there, whereas we had a good heavy lot against him here. So that was turned down, and the CPS was well pleased that we'd get him for a bundle when the case came up at Crown Court.

I thought that was pretty satisfactory, but Derek was in a fret because he'd hoped to get a lot more out of Panteolini about his connections over here, and it was all no dice.

On the other hand, it turned out that the missing bouncers from the club – which incidentally the magistrates had refused to close down – were from Belfast, and not Eire as we'd feared. So there was a fair chance that they'd be tracked down by the cops over there, and at last we might get our hands on the actual killers of Len Gilmore. This didn't mean that we'd decipher the whole riddle of who was behind it all, and why, but at least we'd be a step nearer.

If the CPS was happy with the result they anticipated with Panteolini, they were in seventh heaven about the counterfeiting case, and you could almost hear the grunts of satisfaction as they got their snouts into this banquet of red-hot stuff.

The drugs side wasn't so good, though. With Juan

Garcia only being the courier and Len Gilmore not being available for questioning, it was kind of open-ended.

*

In an effort to be helpful, Derek almost queered my pitch with Kate. He'd phoned the clinic in Lisson Grove to ask about her condition and if she could have visitors. When he'd said who he was, they gave him an emphatic NO. But then I got the number off him and phoned myself and got them to ask Kate if she'd like a visit from her friend Greta. I was told she'd be delighted to see me. Although that put his nose out of joint, my dear boss still sweetly agreed to drive me there.

Our friendship was getting warmer every day. I was hopeful that it would grow into something more physical, but thought I'd better wait until I had two good arms to scoop him up with – and anyway, my face still didn't look its usual attractive self. No makeup was thick enough to hide the last of the bruising.

I took it for granted Kate was going to look pretty awful, so I got a happy surprise at first when I walked into her room. I could see she'd just had her hair and nails done, her make-up was perfect and her clothes were casual but smart. But then I looked more closely, and I saw that under the clever make-up her eyes were dull and sunken and red-rimmed, she'd lost a lot of weight, and she was droopy and listless. But at least she knew me.

'Oh hallo Greta, nice to see you,' she said in a flat monotone which was entirely the opposite to her actual words. Then she looked at me properly and I saw her eyes focus for a moment.

'What happened to your arm?' she said in that same dull voice.

So I told her about the assault. She didn't seem to be

listening. Then I launched into an account of my affair with Jim, making the most of him going so silly and how funny it all was, right up to Alfie thinking it was Jim who'd attacked me. I really worked hard at trying to make her laugh, or at least smile, or anyway pay attention to what I was saying. But it was all a waste of time.

'Shall I ring for some tea?' Kate said. 'Can't offer you anything stronger.'

Well, at least that was a sign of life. Over tea, I asked her if she'd had any other visitors. That got something like a little animation out of her.

'That FBI Agent Goldfeather wanted to see me, or CIA or whatever he is,' she said. 'What a cheek! After all that carry-on at my flat...' her voice trailed away and she drifted back into her grim dream-world again.

'I don't think it was that one,' I told her, 'the one at your flat wasn't the real one, he's in custody now. He's Jack Roc's nephew. I think the one who came here was the real Agent Goldfeather.'

'Jack Roc's nephew?' with a jerk she suddenly became almost alert. 'What was he doing here? Was he after me?'

I tried to reassure her, but she was becoming quite tense, and now at last she seemed to want to talk. So I let her. For some reason, she suddenly felt she had to tell me the whole history of her time with Jack Roc, from when she'd first met him at the casino where she was working. It turned out that, at that time, her ambition in life was to be a croupier. She'd managed to get a job in the cloakroom at a gambling club, thinking this would be a stepping-stone. Well, no surprise, Jack Roc saw this dainty doll-like little blonde as a trophy to take back to New York with him, especially as he was so taken with her English accent.

I wondered what she'd been doing between running away from her foster home at fifteen and accepting Jack Roc's offer (when she'd applied for a passport at eighteen, as Alfie had discovered). But I was afraid to butt in with questions in case it switched off her flow of reminiscences.

'I thought I was a toughie, and I'd just have a good time and get lots of money and clothes and jewellery and stuff,' she whispered, 'but I soon found out I was too stupid and innocent for Jack's world. He wasn't a nice man at all. I didn't like him. It was a miserable three years. But he wanted me to be happy and cheerful and laughing all the time, so when I got droopy and sad and wanted to come back to England, he gave me nose-candy to sniff. That was OK because he said that made me better company and more sociable. Then he didn't mind so much when I wouldn't do everything he wanted in bed.'

She gave a deep sigh, and I thought, poor silly little bitch, she's even thicker than I thought. But she brightened up a bit and became almost lively for the next few minutes, when she spoke about Len Gilmore.

'But then Jack got killed and Len brought me back to England, and I really loved him, Greta, honestly I did. He was nothing like Jack Roc. I know you think it was awful what I did after he was killed, but I was so upset, and I didn't know what to do, so I braced myself up with a good big snort, and after that everything seemed to make sense.'

Then she drooped again, and in a flat voice she said, 'The trouble was, that was the last of my stash, and I thought that idiot Garcia was going to let me have some more, and he didn't, and since then everything's gone to hell in a handcart.'

She started to cry, quietly at first, and I tried to put my one good arm round her, but she shoved me away. Then she started to scream. I made for the bell to get the nurse, but Kate started throwing the tea-things at me. I dodged the cups and saucers, but when I saw a half-full teapot sailing towards me, I thought I'd better get out fast.

But the door was locked on the outside, so I had to do a

fair bit of ducking and diving before I could get to the bell and lean on it, hard. They came quickly enough, give them that, but the room was a mess by that time. And so was Kate. All her careful make-up was ruined, and her pretty little face was a wreck. She screamed and howled like a kid, her mouth in that square shape that babies' mouths go.

It took two big strong attendants to hold her down while a nurse gave her an injection.

'I suppose I'd better go,' I muttered to no one in particular.

'Greta,' Kate screamed, suddenly finding words. 'Greta, tell him I won't ever give him away. I won't! I never would!'

'Who?' I asked, but she'd gone. Out like a light.

Chapter 31

I nearly dropped the phone. 'I don't believe it, Alfie,' I gasped. 'A bodybuilder? You mean a weightlifter? A wrestler? You're kidding! Go on, tell me more.'

'Course not a wrestler. I'm telling you, girl, she told me herself, she's been going to bodybuilding classes since she was at school. She's your height, same as my Betty, but no fat like her, no feminine curves like you, all muscle, hard.'

As I started to laugh, he added in his most serious voice, 'But you should see her face. She looks so young, like a kid, except for her size you'd still take her for a schoolgirl. I can't understand it. I haven't asked her age yet. She's got three kids and another on the way, but she doesn't seem old enough. Mind you, you can see she's really strong.'

'So where are you phoning from?' I asked, though that wasn't the question I really wanted to ask.

'I'm at her place, I mean their place.'

'What, with Jim and her and the three kids?'

'No, Jim's away, and she's taking the kiddies round to her mother to look after them for her.'

I thought, Alfie must be the last remaining person in the world to use the word 'kiddies'.

'Why?'

'Because she wants to come back to Watford with me,' he explained. 'That's what I'm phoning to tell you. She's confessed. She was the one who beat you up. She's told me the whole story.'

I wasn't all that surprised, really. Who else could it have been? There was nobody else to suspect. But the details: how, why and why now?

'But, Alfie, if you've arrested her, how could you let her go out of the house? How do you know she won't run away or hide or something?'

'I haven't arrested her. She's coming to Watford on her own accord, voluntary. She says she wants to apologise to you. And maybe, Greta,' he added at his most preachy, 'maybe you owe her an apology, too. Trifling with her husband like that.'

Trifling! Where does Alfie get these expressions? But I wasn't trifling anyway. It was a mutually useful affair, and neither of us took it seriously, until that thicky Jim suddenly took into his head to make a romance of it. Mind you, it was interesting to know that while he was saying he was dying for love of me, his wife was expecting their fourth child. How recently did that happen, I couldn't help wondering. Before or after he discovered his great love for me?

Just the same, I thought, I'd like to know the details of how she found out who and where I was, and managed to do me so much damage. But look on the bright side, I told myself, being set on like that was worthwhile in one way: it got me closer to Derek. And that counted for me.

Anyway, Alfie wasn't due back in Watford until that evening, so I had plenty of time to think about how I'd behave to Jim's wronged wife and what I should say about the injuries she did to me. And the harm she thought I'd done her, I supposed.

When Derek popped in at lunchtime, as he'd been doing regularly, I told him about Alfie's call, but his response was quite casual.

'I suppose we should have guessed,' he said, 'once your lorry driver was in the clear, and we knew it couldn't be to do with the Gilmore case, it could only have been his wife.'

'You don't know that,' I said. 'For all we knew, it could have been to do with the Gladys Trulove case.'

He gave me a hard look, and then realised that I wasn't serious.

'Yes, sure,' he said, 'but I'm much more interested in your visit to Kate. Tell me about that.'

So I had to accept that the case still meant more to him than my relationship with Jim or that I'd been bashed about by his jealous wife. Another disappointment. I gave him one of my sexy looks and a big sigh, but it was all wasted. He was just waiting for me to get on with my report. We were DI and DS again. Inspector and Sergeant. Guv and Sarge.

'Who do you think Kate meant,' he asked when I'd finished, 'when she said, "Tell him I'll never give him away"? Do you think she was hallucinating again about Gilmore?'

'I was wondering the same thing myself. But it's too difficult to guess. It could even have been Jack Roc – or come to that, someone in her past who we've never heard of.'

There was a silence while we both considered.

Then suddenly, taking me completely and happily by surprise, Derek put his arms round me, very gently, so as not to put any pressure on my bruised bits. He kissed me very softly. I tried to respond enthusiastically, but it doesn't work when the other half isn't so much into it. That sort of thing is only any good when the kisser and the kissee have the same end result in mind.

While I was still mentally cursing at the one-sidedness of it all, he said, 'You know, Greta, you've always meant a lot to me. And since you were attacked, I've come to realise that I see you as more than just a friend and colleague. When you were still unconscious in hospital, I got in a dreadful state thinking I might lose you. And even with a black eye, you looked so pretty lying there.'

All I could say at this thrilling news was 'Oh Derek!' *What a soppy response,* I was thinking at the same time, *but I can't help it.* I felt all slushy and moony, and gazed at him with what must have been the soppiest look. He had a lot more to get off his chest, though, and it hardly made any difference what I said. He'd obviously rehearsed this little speech to himself, and was going to deliver it whatever I said or looked like.

'So I've got something serious to ask you, Greta, and I hope you'll think it over carefully before you give me your answer. It's very important to me, you see, and I hope it will be to you, too.'

By this time I was nearly fainting with the buzz of what he might be going to ask me. Not a proposal, surely? No chance, but I'd happily settle for a proposition. Or anything, just as long as it wasn't about that damned promotion problem again.

'Will you consider coming with me some time soon,' he went on, 'to see an opera? I know your taste in music is very different from mine...'

I knew his voice went on for some time after that, but by that time I'd tuned out completely. It was such a letdown. I understood that the whole subject of music meant a lot to him, and had been the reason for at least some of his quarrels with Erica before they finally parted. But he couldn't have known what a disappointment it was to hear him going on and on about it, when what I'd hoped to hear was something so different.

By the time my breathing had got back to normal, and my heart had stopped thumping, and I'd got control of my facial muscles again, he'd stopped droning on about comparative tastes in music and how important opera was to him. He was looking at me expectantly. No, more than that. Hopefully. Like a dog who wanted to be taken for a walk.

'Oh Derek, that would be wonderful,' I gushed, in a voice and manner so unlike my usual way of talking that he started to look at me suspiciously. That wouldn't do. I couldn't have him thinking I was taking the piss. 'I'd really like that, I've always wanted to see an opera, but I don't know anything about it. What can we see? Will you explain it all to me? When can we go?'

So I convinced him that I meant it, and he started to bore on about this and that composer and opera and singer, but then he suddenly looked at his watch and realised it was time he was back at Shady Lane.

'We'll talk about it more this evening, must go now.'

And he was gone, leaving me to brood at how stupid I'd been to imagine he was going to say something really exciting. How could I love someone like that? I couldn't think of an answer to that, except that I really must do, if I could see all the reasons why I shouldn't, but still didn't get put off by them.

*

The first thing I thought was, she's nothing like the real famous Anne Robinson. Till then, I hadn't even known she had the same name. The terror of the quiz shows, the one who scares everyone to death on 'The Weakest Link' is a little, slim, fierce redhead – and not all that young, either.

Jim Robinson's wife had close-cropped blonde hair and was built like a brickie, but with the face of a little girl. A very strange combination. Maybe that was why he fancied me, being so normal and ordinary. But the thing about this Anne Robinson was that, if you saw her from behind, you'd swear you were looking at a man, and a hefty one at that. No wonder she was able to do me so much damage, specially catching me by surprise. Those were my thoughts in the first few seconds of our meeting. But I didn't let on.

I just looked at her very coldly with my sternest sergeant's face, and said, 'Well? You wanted to speak to me?'

She went bright pink, looking even more like a kid.

'I never meant to hurt you so much,' she said. Or I think she did. She had such a strong northern accent, it wasn't easy to make out, and also she mumbled. She went on muttering away, something about being sorry, and what sounded like she hoped I was too.

'Look at me,' I said in my hard police voice. 'Wouldn't you be sorry to be in a state like this? And I was unconscious for hours, I lost a lot of blood, and I could have had concussion. What the hell did you do to me? I won't bother to ask why, I can guess.'

Then it all came out in a rush. As far as I could tell through that accent, she'd found my key in Jim's pocket and had it copied and then hired a private detective to follow him to find out where he was going! What a performance. Would have been easier to ask him, I reckoned. Considering her build and level of fitness, she could have knocked the truth out of him, no trouble. Jim's a big fellow, but like most lorry drivers, a bit soft and unfit. Not a trim figure of a man at all. I suggested that to her, in an offhand sort of way, but she seemed quite shocked.

'I wouldn't hit my Jim!' she declared in the most accent-free statement I'd heard from her so far. Then she lapsed back into the semi-scrutable.

'I didn't reckon you'd be home when I used the key to let myself in,' I think she probably said, or something like it. 'I just wanted to see what sort of place it was, to get an idea if I could alter our house to look more like yours.'

'What! What for?'

'To make him like it as much as yours,' she explained. 'He's always saying I don't know how to be a proper housewife, and I've got no taste, and it's time I grew up and made a proper home.'

What a fool! So she had a child's brain to go with the face! No wonder Jim got a bit bored of her.

'But then when you came in, I panicked,' she went on, 'so I knocked you out with the first thing I picked up, and you fell down and there was a lot of blood and you looked dead. Then I got really angry, so I jumped on your arm. Then I was frightened, so I ran away and went back home.'

'So you got angry, did you?' I snarled. 'What, you were angry with me because you thought I was dead? That would have been a rotten trick for me to play on you, wouldn't it, being dead! And how do you think I feel now,' I ranted on, waving my plastered arm at her, 'don't you think *I* should be angry now?'

She'd gone very red during all this, and kept her eyes down to avoid looking at me, and when I finally came to a breathless halt, she just muttered, 'I'm sorry, sorry, sorry... but–'

'But what?' I shouted. 'But it was all my fault? Is that what you mean?'

Alfie had stayed quiet all through this idiotic conversation. I couldn't remember any other time when he'd been silent for so long. Calming down after giving vent a bit to my feelings, I turned to him now.

'Come on, Alfie, advise me,' I asked him. 'We can see she's not very bright. I think Jim must have learned his lesson by now. They've got three kids and another on the way. What shall we do?'

He still didn't say a word, just gave me one of his meaningful looks. I got his message. It was easy to tell what he wanted me to say.

'Go home and look after your husband and your kids,' I told this other Anne Robinson. 'There'll be no charge against you. Just give me back my front door key.'

Alfie nodded and spoke.

'I'll run you to the station,' he said to Mrs Jim. 'See you later, Greta,' he said to me, poker-faced.

Hopefully, that meant I'd never hear any more of the Darlington Family Robinson. I'd had to go through a lot to get rid of Jim, but maybe it was worth it.

Derek was a bit disapproving when I told him about it.

'You know the law, Greta,' he said. 'You should have charged her with at least common assault, if not B & E. And now I'm going to have to explain it all to Mr Moon, somehow. I don't understand why you let her go like that.'

'You wouldn't say that if you'd seen her,' I explained. 'The poor creature was almost retarded. Oops, sorry, we mustn't use that word any more. I mean she had special needs. Even when she saw me, she didn't really seem to understand how much damage she'd done me. And it was so pathetic, the way she said she wanted to see my home so that she could make hers more like it. As if Jim fancied me because of my decorations or furnishings!'

Derek eyed me up and down in a manner so meaningful that there was no mistake what was in his mind. He'd never looked at me like that before.

'Nothing wrong with your furnishings,' he murmured, taking me in his arms.

Whoopee! I thought.

Chapter 32

Derek had been busy while Alfie and I had been mucking about with Anne Robinson, and he'd had another interview with Juan Garcia.

'I had to keep it low-key, but it was worth trying to get something out of the little bugger,' he explained to me and Alfie.

We both listened eagerly. Alfie specially had always believed we could get more out of Garcia, and had reminded us countless times that Garcia had said he was supposed to have phoned his boss's boss here in England, but had forgotten the number since Alfie had 'chomped' on him. Well, sure enough, my clever Derek had managed to give him a good grilling. But the outcome was disappointing.

'He said he'd lied, and he simply didn't have a boss's boss here in England, so that was a complete dead end. But it was worth a try, and I suppose we'll never know which time he was lying. He'll do his time, then he'll go back to Colombia, and let's hope we never see him again.'

It might have been my imagination, but I thought Alfie looked disappointed. Maybe he thought we'd have been able to get more out of Garcia, with me as the Bad Cop. Well, win some and lose some, is what he'd always told me himself.

'Then again,' Derek was going on, 'that Garcia business was only one of the loose ends we'd left hanging about. There's still Christine Smith. I want you both to be there while I interview her again. All that stuff about being hired anonymously to pick up Len Gilmore and have an affair with him! I don't know if either of you believed it, but I certainly didn't. I know there's a fine line for girls like her between being a model and being a tart, but that story never rang true. So we'll put some pressure on her.'

'Go on, Guv!' Alfie exclaimed, eyes bulging with admiration. 'That's not your usual style. What will you threaten her with?'

Derek got all haughty.

'Threaten? I don't do that sort of thing.'

Then he dropped the dignified senior officer act with a broad grin.

'Come on then, let's do it.'

He seemed to have forgotten that I was officially not back on duty yet, and I certainly wasn't going to remind him and miss something.

Christine Smith looked round apprehensively at our three grim faces.

'Would it be something else you were wanting to ask me?' she tried to smile, but the charm wasn't working.

'Well, there's certainly something we should tell you,' Derek said in his sternest voice. 'You don't seem to understand the seriousness of your position. Your story about what happened the night Gilmore died just doesn't ring true. It's just a matter of time until we pick up those two bruisers who killed him. And if the Crown Prosecution Service decides that it was murder, then you could be charged as an accessory.'

She started to cry. I could have told her she was wasting her time, but Alfie and I were both acting dumb and letting Derek get on with it.

'Ah, Inspector, darling,' she sobbed, 'what is it you're wanting me to say? I don't know what to tell you.'

He handed her a tissue. 'How about the whole truth?' he suggested. 'Right from the beginning. Forget the line you were told to take, and tell us everything. Start with who hired you to pick up Len Gilmore in the first place. Just don't keep giving us that story about not knowing all the time who your employer was.'

We could see her making up her mind and bracing herself to come out with it. She was never cut out to be a liar. I'll never know whether Derek and Alfie had already guessed, but I certainly had. They both listened without a flicker, and at the end, all Derek said was, 'We'll get that typed up for you to sign.'

'D'you see, Inspector, I'd already done a bit of work for him, so it wasn't as if it was some stranger asking me to do this unusual job,' she explained. 'You'll know that I'm not the type of girl to pick up a stranger and have a flirt with him on the say-so of someone I've never met. So when he offered me a lot of money to do this for him, and ask no questions, it never crossed my mind that there was crime involved, he being so famous. And a lovely man, in himself, as anyone will tell you that knows him.'

'And when the two men came to pick you up and go with you to Gilmore's flat on that last evening? What did you think then?'

'Why, just what they told me,' she explained. 'It wasn't exactly true that they didn't say a word to me on the journey. What they said was, Mr Curleigh wanted me to introduce them to Mr Gilmore, to put a business proposition to him. How was I to know it would end the way it did!'

And we left her crying.

'What do you make of it now?' Derek asked us both.

Alfie spoke first. 'Obvious, he sent them two bouncers to give Gilmore a good hiding, never mind all that guff about a business proposition.'

'But in that case, do you think it was anything to do with Gilmore playing around? Did Curleigh send those two to beat Gilmore up just because he thought Gilmore was making his kid sister unhappy? The kid sister, don't forget, who he'd never even seen for all those years. Never tried to get in touch with her, just left her alone.'

'No, Guv,' I said, so strongly that they both looked at me a bit popeyed. 'I don't believe any of that, and I don't think you do, either. Curleigh must have had some other reason, much stronger than worrying about his sister being mucked about. And even if those two thugs didn't take a weapon with them, we've got no way of knowing whether they'd been told just to beat Gilmore up, or to kill him. All that stuff about Gilmore surprising them with a gun, do we swallow that?'

I didn't bother to mention the fact that now we all seemed to be ready to believe that Curleigh really was Kate's brother, after all. Now it seemed too obvious, really.

*

Well, finally the day came when Kate was formally discharged from the clinic, and we were to interview her at her flat. Of course her solicitor would have to be there, with a nurse nearby on call. What a performance! Apparently the chief consultant at the clinic had explained to Superintendent Moon that she was still in a very frail condition, and needed to feel protected. So Mr Moon had warned Derek to take it easy.

When we got there I was quite pleased to see how much better she looked. She'd gained a little weight, her skin was a better colour, and her eyes showed that there was someone in there looking out at the world in a functioning sort of way. I wanted to give her a friendly pat on the shoulder or something, but I knew Derek wouldn't approve, so I just said a big hallo instead. She seemed pleased to see me, too. As expected, her pompous prat of a lawyer was there, but he said he was only an observer.

'Someone else will be joining us who will be of more interest to you, Inspector,' he added, with his usual oily smile. 'My client has accepted your invitation to speak to you informally today.'

So Derek's ploy had worked, and Curleigh was going to come clean! I don't know which of us was more amazed. There were certainly dropped jaws all round. Even Derek himself hadn't really believed his message would get a result. He'd just sent an email to Curleigh's office, asking him to come to the meeting and warning him that Kate was liable to be arrested if he didn't. No explanation, just assuming he'd know what it was all about.

'He won't get into trouble, will he?' Kate asked. That deep blush swept up her face and neck again, but this time it wasn't because of fancying someone like the dicey Bobby Panther. She knows who North's client is too, I thought. She's known all along.

'Don't worry about it, my dear,' Charles North said.

And then he arrived. In person. Curleigh, the famous designer, really was Kate's half-brother, just as she'd said. He was different from how he looked on TV. Older, not as good-looking, slimmer – well, positively skinny, in fact. Something else. Oh yes, no charisma. You'd have passed him on the street without a second glance. Definitely no glamour.

He ran across the room and swept her up in his arms in an actorish kind of way. They both hugged and kissed and cried and made wordless noises for what seemed a very long time. None of us had the heart to interrupt. Let them have their moment. It was almost touching enough to bring a tear to Derek's cold eye. It didn't, of course, but I had to blow my nose a few times. Specially knowing what was coming.

Finally, we all settled down, and Kate said earnestly to

Curleigh, who was holding her hand, 'Dunkie, I never told. You should have known I never would.'

'I know, sweetie,' he said. 'If only I'd believed that all along, we could have always been together instead of you living with those men.'

'Don't say that, Dunkie,' she protested. 'You shouldn't say "those men" like that, as if Len was as bad as Jack. I loved Len.'

Curleigh looked disgusted, and started to argue. Whatever he'd been going to say was drowned in a loud coughing fit from Charles North. Derek and I exchanged looks. This wasn't going to be easy. Pity we couldn't get rid of that damn brief. He'd stop his client saying anything we wanted to hear, if he thought it might be incriminating.

'Mr – er – Dunkerley,' Derek said, 'were the two men who killed Len Gilmore in your employ?'

'Yes,' Curleigh admitted over North's protests, 'and I may as well tell you now how all that came about. Look, Charles,' he said to North, 'if you're going to try to stop me every time I speak, you may as well go now.'

Some of the commanding personality came out as he spoke to North then, and you could see the empire-builder wasn't just a design genius.

North shrugged and sat down again, making a small sort of mocking bow in Curleigh's direction. Evidently this meant that he would stay and hold his tongue. Curleigh went on.

'I hired Christine Smith, who'd done a bit of modelling for me, to pick up Gilmore and have an affair with him. I had some wild theory at the time that eventually she'd tell him she'd been paid to string him along, and make him feel a fool. Then I thought that might shame him into not going on being serially unfaithful to Kate, because it must have been making her unhappy.'

'But you must have seen what a crackpot idea that was!'

I exclaimed, and then shut up at a stern look from Derek. Still, I thought, how crazy to think that was a way to stop a man having it away with anything likely-looking that offered. But of course it was well known that Curleigh was gay. Maybe that gave him an unrealistic view of heterosexual men's sex lives. No, just a minute. He didn't really think that at all. That was his fallback cover story. I mustn't get muddled.

'Yes, that was why I changed my plan,' he said coolly. 'I sent those two bouncers from my club to go with Christine and explain to Gilmore why he shouldn't carry on with his way of life. I couldn't guess how Kate would react. Of course, at that time I didn't know about her addiction problem. I never found out why Winkelhorne didn't tell me that – maybe he didn't know himself. Perhaps he wasn't such a good detective. He should have been, he cost enough. If I'd known that, I think I would have taken a completely different course of action.'

'But Dunkie,' Kate said, 'how did you know Len went with other women? I mean, how did you know anything about him and me at all? And what did Winkelhorne have to do with it?'

Curleigh licked his lips. He was entitled to be nervous. His situation was distinctly dodgy.

'Winkelhorne,' he said. 'Winkelhorne worked for me, watching you. In New York and then back here. And so did the woman you met on the boat coming over from New York who got Gilmore to take those two flats. We already had Winkelhorne planted here.'

Kate looked shocked.

'You mean you'd been having me watched for years? You could have spoken to me any time in the last five years. But you didn't.' Then I could see she had another, even worse thought. 'Did you have anything to do with Winkelhorne being killed?' she whispered.

'No, of course not, Katie darling. It was that Bobby Panteolini.'

There was a silence while we all digested the implications of Curleigh knowing about Bobby Panteolini. What else? What did he also know about the death of Jack Roc?

'When you say you sent the two bouncers to "explain" to Gilmore, what precisely do you mean?' Derek asked. 'Are we to take you literally?'

'Yes, indeed,' Curleigh answered earnestly. 'That was exactly what I'd wanted. But then Gilmore surprised everyone by pulling a gun, and the two men panicked, and the result was the tragedy we all know about.'

'And where are those two men now?'

North interrupted.

'My client doesn't necessarily know the exact whereabouts of the two men. And even if he did, I have advised him not to reveal such information until he can be assured that you understand and accept the true facts of the incident, Inspector.'

Another silence while we all had a further ponder. Suddenly Derek turned to Kate and barked, 'And what was it that you never told about your brother, Miss Dunkerley?'

She didn't answer, but two large tears tracked down her face. She looked appealingly at North, who looked back expressionlessly. She didn't look at Curleigh.

Derek waited. Then he said more gently, 'You saw him kill your mother, didn't you, Kate?'

She didn't answer, but Curleigh did.

'Yes,' he said simply, 'she did. But I convinced myself that the shock of it had blanked it out of her mind. And all those years I was afraid that if she saw me again, she'd remember and tell. What a fool. I've wasted years of our lives.'

'Oh Dunkie,' Kate said, 'all that time you knew where I was... and when you got famous, I thought you wouldn't want to know me...'

There was another silence. Kate and Curleigh looked at each other soppily, and the rest of us kind of tried to look the other way.

Then Derek sprang his big surprise.

'And are you prepared to tell us now, Mr Dunkerley, about your *other* connection with Len Gilmore?' he asked, in a tone I'd hardly ever heard him use. It was the voice he used questioning a really disgusting villain, when he couldn't hide his dislike.

Charles North started to speak, but Curleigh flapped a dismissive hand at him.

'Let it go, Charles,' he said wearily. 'You can't protect me from everything. Yes, OK, Gilmore got in touch with me years ago. As soon as Kate told him about her early years, I suppose. He threatened to dig up what happened about my mother's death and give it to the tabloids. He said he had enough influence with Kate to get her to tell the truth. He reckoned it would ruin me, and I thought he was right.'

'Oh no, Len would never–' Kate started to interrupt, but Curleigh went on, now avoiding her eye. All the emotional looks between them had dissolved. Now there was mistrust on her side and coldness on his.

'So what was his price for silence?' Derek prompted. 'You may as well tell us. We already know about your connection with some of his enterprises.'

I managed not to show my surprise at this stupendous bit of bluff. We knew no such thing, but it was a brilliant guess. It worked, too.

All the bounce had gone from the famous designer. His shoulders slumped, and his voice was flat.

'First it was help with his counterfeit perfumes and

cosmetics, and I could live with that,' he said in a monotone. 'It was easy, in my position, and very low risk. But then, when it came to money laundering, and I realised that he was forging currency as well as designer labels, I couldn't go on. And he'd started hinting about taking over another branch of the late Jack Roc's business, too.'

'Yes, we know your views on drugs, your campaign has been well publicised. That must have been the last straw for you. So you used Christine Smith to help you to have him killed,' Derek said. 'All that story about protecting your sister from the unhappiness he caused her was a cover-up, wasn't it? Duncan Dunkerley, I am arresting you on suspicion of commissioning the murder of Leonard Gilmore...'

Kate started screaming. She opened her handbag and started throwing the contents at Curleigh, one by one. It was pathetic. She pelted him with a lipstick, a comb, a credit card holder, a diary, a tiny powder compact, a little notebook, a pen, while we all stood about, paralysed with – what? – I don't know, embarrassment, amazement? And even when she rushed up to him, still screaming incoherently, none of us moved right away to pull her off him. Until we saw she'd plunged a nail file into his eye.

Derek got to her first, but he couldn't hold her. She was like a madwoman, kicking, biting, waving her little bloody nail file around. As I went to help him, I saw Curleigh fall to his knees, his hands over his damaged eye. Blood was pouring down his face.

It was difficult for me, still having one arm in plaster, to hold Kate down, she was chucking herself about so much. By the time Alfie came bursting in and flung himself bodily on top of her, she'd managed to get that sharp little weapon right through Derek's hand.

*

Superintendent Moon was beside himself, but not with rage this time. If it wasn't too corny, I'd say he was over the moon.

'All very well to say we've solved our case, and that old one besides,' he said, 'but how are we to proceed? I must say, Derek, I'm absolutely baffled. What are we going to charge everyone with? It's all so convoluted. True, we've unravelled the late Gilmore's little empire of crime, and a damned good job we've all done there. But we're going to have a few deep sessions with the CPS before we can decide exactly what crimes have been committed and who we can charge with what. I mean, there's that Slipworthy woman for a start…'

'That's true, sir,' said Derek, resting his bandaged hand on Mr Moon's desk, 'but we've got a good result all round, don't you think? After all, we've solved the Gilmore murder and the Winkelhorne killing, even if we don't know the position about the old Catherine Dunkerley case. And we've unravelled a complicated puzzle.'

'I still can't understand how Curleigh just gave up at the end and admitted everything,' Mr Moon said. 'Why do you think he did that? He's got a whole firm of top lawyers working for him. He's rich and famous and very popular because of all his charitable work…'

'But that's the whole point, sir,' Derek argued. 'However the case turned out, he knew he'd lose all the love and admiration that he gets from the public now. And when you look at the man's background, you can understand that was the most important part of his life, what he really lived for, the fame and the glory, do you see?'

'Oh yes, but it makes my head ache. People who need all that adulation always do. I'd rather think about something else.'

He opened his bottom drawer and took out the famous whisky bottle that I'd heard so much about from Derek. But only one glass.

'And now, Greta,' Mr Moon turned to me, 'have you decided whether you want to go for promotion yet?'

I looked anxiously at Derek.

I didn't know what to do. That's unlike me. If there's one thing I'm good at, it's making decisions, right or wrong.

After all, if you want to succeed in the Police Force – sorry, I mean Police Service – you've got to be ready to take quick action without spending ages pondering what to do next.

But this was different.

This was to do with feelings, not physical activity or the law.

I still didn't know where we were.

Did Derek feel even partly about me as much as I did about him?

Should I give up my hopes of him, and concentrate on my career ambitions again?

'Tell you what, Greta,' said the Super in his most jovial tones, 'it's a full moon tonight. Why don't you take Derek for a long walk and talk it over with him?'

THE END